# THE LAST MARINE

JE GURLEY

SEVERED PRESS
HOBART TASMANIA

# THE LAST MARINE



*WWW.SEVEREDPRESS.COM*



*ISBN: 978-1-925597-55-4*

# 1

Dax Wyldd leaned back in his seat, eyes closed, with his size-10 boots propped up on the control console in front of him. He wasn't asleep, although it would not have made much difference if he were. The nearest object with which *Fortune's Luck* could collide was 1.2 light years away, and the collision alarm would have warned him long before the ship neared the bright blue F-class star that was his destination. A soft blues ballad, heavy with alto saxophone riffs, played through the earbuds jammed tightly into his ears, barely audible in the silent ship's bridge. Occasionally, his right foot would twitch in time with the rhythm as proof he was awake.

From previous bitter experience, his crew had learned better than to disturb him when he was in his zone, his release from the monotony of deep space cargo runs. The blues calmed him, the more melancholy the better. His prized collection of 5,000 blues tunes covered a span of nearly three hundred years. His crew was in favor of anything that kept Dax calm. Therefore, the hand on his shoulder shaking him awake elicited a quick and expected response.

He swatted away the offending hand and growled, "Leave me the fuck alone," slightly louder than his normal speaking voice because of the music playing in his ears.

Andy Byrd, 26, co-pilot and chief communications officer, liked living on the edge. Jousting with Dax was like slipping his hand into an alligator's mouth and yanking it out before the snapped shut. He met Dax's gruff response with an equally brusque and strident, "Distress beacon."

Dax pushed back the baseball cap with the faded Atlanta Braves logo covering his sandy curls, opened one emerald green eye, and squinted at Andy in the dim light of control panel. "Lights at fifty percent," he called out, and the bridge overheads increased to half capacity. In the brighter light, Dax's gaze focused on Byrd's blue eyes with the intensity of a rifle shot, but the ire had vanished. "Commercial or military?"

"Automated military beacon. Why?"

Dax kicked the control panel with the heel of his boot. "Damn! I hate the military. They're always a pain in the ass. How far away?" To Dax, the only thing worse than a distress call from a Navy ship was one way off their course,

"It's only two hours away."

"Two hours? That's odd, but it's good, although with the military we could be stuck there for God knows how long. They're bastards for red tape. See if anybody else is responding to the beacon. Maybe we'll get lucky."

Andy did a double take. "Way the hell out here? Who's gonna be out here but C-class cargo ships like us? I don't even know why the military is this far out of the usual traffic lanes."

Dax sat up, clicked off his music, and sighed. "You're right. What are they doing out here in the middle of nowhere? Okay. We'll take a gander. Maybe it's abandoned, and we can claim salvage rights," he added.

Andy shook his head slowly, his blond locks sliding across his forehead. "That's my mercenary, Captain. If there's a buck in it …"

"Gotta make your creds anyway you can out here, kid. There's no free ride."

"So you've told me a hundred times."

"It's good advice, Andy. Heed it, and someday you'll be a forty-five-year-old captain with your own over-mortgaged rust bucket to fret over," he grinned at Andy, "instead of a twenty-something pain in the ass." He sat up in his seat. "Full illumination." He blinked as light flooded the bridge. He switched on the screen of his console. "What's the heading?"

Andy read off a series of coordinates. "About 5.5 million kilometers distant."

Dax punched in the coordinates and cocked his head to one side when he saw the location displayed on *Fortune's Luck's* flight path. "That's almost along our course." In the vastness of space, that seemed too close for coincidence.

Andy smiled. "I thought that might get your attention."

"Okay, I'm officially intrigued. Change our heading. Inform Syn to get the grasshopper ready. We'll fly over. There's too much protocol involved in docking with a military ship."

"Plia's already on it. Luigi's got a pot of coffee on if you're interested."

Dax grinned again. Andy was the only one of the ship's crew that called Luigi Romero by his Christian name instead of his nickname Romeo. "Good. They don't serve anything but that God-awful synthetic java on Navy ships. Tastes like used lube oil."

*Fortune's Luck* was an outdated, converted ore carrier well past its prime, but it was Dax's ship. Although barely profitable, he made certain to stock the pantry with real Earth coffee. He would tolerate no synthetic java or tasteless ersatz coffee on his ship. They might skimp on meat a few meals, but coffee was one of the essential building blocks of a happy crew. Coffee was not his only vice, but it was the only one for which he had no regrets.

He stood, stretched his arms, and yawned. "See if you can raise them on the com. I don't like going in blind." He left the bridge.

He met cargo specialist Tish Holder in the corridor. He enjoyed the way the petite dishwater-blonde filled out her jumpsuit in all the right places, but mostly he appreciated the fact that she was smart and soft where he was hard. She constantly worked on his people skills and coached him in the fine art of diplomacy, a necessary skill when dealing with unsavory clients with the tendency to pull a weapon when negotiations stalled, a skill that he sorely lacked. He reached out an arm to either side of the bulkhead to block her path. She stepped into his embrace, gave him a quick peck on the cheek, and then slipped beneath his arm and continued down the corridor.

"No time for hanky-panky, Dax. Plia needs a hand."

"Not even a quick panky?" he called out after her.

"Later," she promised, as she turned a corner and disappeared from sight.

He and Tish had promised each other not to become romantically involved, just a mutual relief of sexual tensions on the long voyages, but things had progressed well beyond that point. Normally, he didn't like attachments, but he was growing used to her. She was soft and cuddly at the proper times, a hard worker when he needed it, and shared more than a few of his sexual idiosyncrasies. They made a good team. Moreover, she put up with his crankiness.

Tish was ten years his junior. In his mind, that placed an undue amount of stress on his sexual performance. He considered himself in good physical condition and a great lover, at least he had had no complaints, but their vigorous sessions left him feeling young on the inside but older on the outside. He hoped she hadn't noticed his longer than normal showers after sex when he stood in the jet misters to massage away the aches and pains.

As he bounced down the corridor, he noticed the artificial gravity was off by a few points, closer to .75 G than the .8 G he usually maintained. He would have to speak to Nate about that. He also absentmindedly made a visual inspection, noting several non-functioning overhead lights, the storage locker doors slightly ajar, and the odor of overheating insulation coming from an electrical panel. He would enter them later on his daily repair log, which seemed to grow longer each trip, one of the problems with a ship long past its prime.

As he entered the wardroom that also served as ship's lounge, rec room, and mess hall, Luigi 'Romeo' Romero, chief cook, bottle washer, and assistant communications officer, met him with a steaming cup of coffee – black, no sugar – the way he liked it. Wearing his ubiquitous floppy white chef's hat and white apron, the tall, skinny cook reminded Dax of a mop, but Romero was a top-notch chef in spite of his youth. The enticing aroma of the spicy meatloaf he had cooked for lunch still lingered in the room, defying the air scrubbers. From the oven drifted the smell of fresh-baked bread mixing with the other subtle odors saturating the ship. He didn't know why the twenty-four-year-old galley virtuoso had chosen *Fortune's Luck* as home, but Dax was glad to have him. His own culinary masterpieces ranged from reheating canned soup to nuking frozen dinners.

"You think the Navy could spare a few fresh eggs, Captain?" Romeo asked.

Dax liked the way Romeo called him 'captain'. The others called him by his first name except when in port. He didn't mind, but hearing his rank every now and then made him feel good, like he had earned it. "Sheesh, Romeo! Did everyone know about the distress call before I did?"

"You were in your zone. We drew straws to tell you." He grinned at Dax. "Andy lost."

"Well, if they have some fresh eggs, I'll see that they're part of the fee I'll charge for services rendered."

"Good. I'd love to make a sausage and spinach quiche for breakfast. What about fresh rosemary? Some of those Navy ships have a hydroponics garden the size of our cargo bay."

Dax shooed Romeo back toward the galley. "Go! Go! Make a grocery list. I'll see what I can do."

"Thanks, Captain," he called out over his shoulder.

He finished his coffee in three quick gulps and headed for the cargo bay. Dax loved the cargo bay. For one, it was the profit center of the ship. Through it flowed the cargoes that kept them from becoming penniless ground-pounders. He took a deep whiff of the air, relishing the acrid smell of lube oil and the earthy tang of the dirt from whatever planet they last visited. It was as close as he wanted to get to most planets. They were always too hot, too cold, too wet, or too dirty. The gravity was too high, or the politicians were unbearable. He preferred station-to-station runs, but the *Luck* took whatever job presented itself. Old cargo vessels took the leavings of the new, sleek, corporate ships. *Fortune's Luck's* days were numbered. He just hoped they both went out together.

He eyed the cargo destined for the Research Station K124 on Loki. It was the usual shipment of barrels of lube oil, spare tires for the ATVs and vans, spare solar panels, lumber, foodstuffs, a couple of cases of liquor, and boxes carefully weight-allotted of personal items. He longed to open a few and see what stranded scientists thought of as essential personal items, but it was against his policy to break seals.

He found Tish and Plia Syn working on the grasshopper, a small, two-person, liquid-fuel space scooter. He noted that Tish and Plia were almost polar opposites. Where Tish was in her mid-thirties, petite, well proportioned, and blonde, Plia was tall, gaunt to the point of emaciation, and dark complexioned, with a skullcap of coal black hair and eyes to match. She had listed her age as thirty-eight when she joined the *Luck's* crew, but she did not look a day older than she did eight years ago. Tish was ebullient and confident. Plia was quiet, terse, and seemed to be perpetually brooding, as if life had dealt her a severe blow sometime in her past, but she was good at her job and didn't take any of his shit. He liked that.

Plia saw Dax enter. "She's fueled and ready to go."

"Good. Did you …?"

"Pistol's in the pocket beneath the seat, loaded, safety off."

He admired her efficiency, if not her brusqueness. He carried a Heckler and Koch .40 caliber semiautomatic on every trip because he liked to be prepared. Nate had designed the special pocket beneath the seat to report a false signal to a causal electronic weapons sweep. It would not pass a thorough visual inspection, but he found most security relied too heavily on their electronic toys, a security lapse he often found useful.

"Excellent. You just never know."

Tish frowned. "Expecting trouble, Dax?"

"Baby, you should know me by now. I always expect trouble. That way I'm seldom disappointed."

The intercom hissed as Andy announced, "No contact. Automatic distress beacon logs the ship as the *UNN Abraxas*, a 7,200-ton *Decatur*-class Navy frigate with a crew of thirty-five. She's dead in space. No other com traffic."

Dax was afraid of that. "It looks like it's up to us. Pop us out of Skip Space 2,000 clicks out. We'll move in real slow before we commit." He removed his cap and scratched his head.

"Bad feeling?" Tish asked, noting the look of concern on his face.

"Yeah, my head's itching like I got fleas. Something's not kosher. What the hell is a Navy frigate doing way the hell out here in the Deep Dark? There's nothing out here except Asgard and a couple of nearby nondescript red dwarfs. A Navy frigate in distress along our flight path and a somewhat secretive research base on Loki is too much coincidence for my comfort zone."

"We could keep going to Asgard, not stop."

He had considered and dismissed that option. "No, if they're just playing possum, we could never outrun them, and if they're really in distress and we don't answer their call, they could yank my permit. We'd wind up hauling garbage for some orbiting station. No, we'll just have to take our chances." He glanced at Plia. "Just in case, you might want to install that weapons pod we picked up at Calicos II in the airlock. If our dead ship is a pirate vessel with a stolen Navy beacon, half a dozen *Wasp Sting* missiles might be a good bargaining chip."

Her lips creased slightly, as close to a smile as she allowed herself. "Twenty minutes."

"Don't arm them unless we need them. If they scan us, I don't want to start a shooting match."

"Pirates? Out here?" Tish asked.

He shrugged. "Yeah, I admit it's highly unlikely, but so is a Navy frigate in distress."

The military surplus weapons pod and missiles had cost him his entire profit for six months runs, but he considered them worth the expenditure. Plia had constructed a fiberglass shell over the pod, disguising it as a hazardous waste locker with a bright yellow 'Full' sign painted on it. During infrequent port inspections, no one bothered checking it. There were occasional pirates plying the void, though usually not in the middle of nowhere. Not every cargo the *Luck* hauled was totally above board. Sometimes, clients preferred no witnesses to illegal deals and that went against his policy of self-survival.

Tish hugged herself and shuddered. "You're making me nervous, Dax."

"You know me, hon. Just cautious. If I really expected trouble, I'd reverse course back to Kinta Station."

She did not look reassured by his words.

He didn't bother checking the grasshopper. Plia knew her job, and she had never let him down. She was reliable to a fault. He had a good crew. As he returned to the bridge, he couldn't help himself from stopping to secure the open lockers. A little OCD was a good thing on a small ship, but he tried not to let his Obsessive Compulsive Disorder control him lest his crew think him a total nut job.

Like about two percent of the population stricken with OCD, he was aware of his idiosyncrasies, and tried not to allow them to rule his life. Little rituals, like laying out his toiletries in the order he would use them, making certain he cut his meat into an even number of pieces, or eating his meal one item at a time raised a few eyebrows, but elicited no comments. He could attribute neatly straightening the chairs in the wardroom before a meal or making certain the locker doors were secured properly to proper ship maintenance. He took his SSRIs every day. He didn't know if the Selective Serotonin Reuptake Inhibitors really worked, but they had become part of his daily ritual. At least he hadn't developed any nervous tics.

He noted the smoke odor was now gone. He didn't know if that was a good or a bad sign.

On the bridge, Andy was playing with the com and frowning. "Anything?" Dax asked.

"Just the beacon. Now, I can't raise the Loki station."

Dax glanced out the forward view port, a meter-and-a-half by two-meter window onto the universe. There was little to see. The faint band of the Milky Way covered the lower left-hand corner of the screen. Four stars scattered across the screen glowed with the spectrum shift of Skip Space. It was a stark vista, but one which Dax found soothing. The nearest, a bright blue sun, was Asgard, their destination. His head started itching again. He resisted the impulse to take off his cap and scratch. His lunch suddenly lay heavy in his stomach like a black hole trying to suck him in. "When did you last hear from them?"

"Day before yesterday during the routine contact."

"Not yesterday?"

"No, but missing a scheduled transmission isn't that unusual. They've done it before, especially during a dust storm."

Dax nodded. The dust storms that regularly swept across the planet played havoc with communications and made landing difficult. "No problems?"

"They didn't report anything, although Hickman was a little distracted about some new discovery."

Dax relaxed. "There you go. They're all down in the caverns drooling over old bones."

Loki, one of two habitable moons circling the gas giant Odin, had once been home to a thriving advanced civilization on par with Earth's Mid-Twentieth Century-Industrial Age. Two thousand years ago, the entire population inexplicably abandoned the surface and moved into an extensive network of inactive volcanic lava tubes running deep beneath the crust. A century later, they had vanished without a trace. Research Station K124, staffed by twelve archaeologists, climatologists, biologists, and few -ologists Dax had never heard of, took up residence in search of answers.

*Fortune's Luck* was the sole bidder for the contract to supply the station, for reasons Dax had later come to understand. The twice yearly, three-month round trip was tedious and boring, but it paid the bills, allowing him to seek out other more lucrative jobs.

Dax's simple explanation did not convince Andy. "They usually leave someone on the surface at all times."

"You can bet the *Abraxas* came from there. Maybe her captain can supply a few answers."

Andy wrinkled his eyes and frowned. "Uh, yeah, about that, Dax. I did some checking. The U.N. Navy logs show the *Abraxas* currently on station at Sirius B."

That lump in his stomach rolled over. "Are you sure?"

"The logs are current. Either this beacon isn't the *Abraxas* or someone's playing hot and loose with the official logs."

"Hmm. Make that distance 5,000 clicks when we come out of Skip. I want some wiggle room." He had been half-joking with Tish about pirates. Now, he wasn't so sure.

"Will do." Andy punched in the new coordinates on the console; then looked up at Dax. "Say, you don't think they found something down there, do you? Something secret?"

That thought plagued Dax's mind as well. The Navy certainly loved its secrets. "We'll find out in forty-five minutes."

# 2

Cargo Specialist Seaman Yeager Hines wore a silly grin as he rolled the two-wheel dolly from the aft cargo bay to the Deck 1 supply closet. Of all the supplies they had picked up in route, he thought this load the most important – four cases of toilet paper. He didn't mind recycled water or boring as hell Navy rations, but government-issue toilet paper was as bad as it came, a real ass scratcher, like 800-grit sandpaper. Four cases of civilian name-brand toilet paper was a special treat. He intended to make sure a few rolls reached the enlisted men's quarters before the officers snatched it up, as if their asses were any more precious to them than his was.

The dolly's wheels squeaked a tune so familiar he whistled along with it. He could have oiled the wheels, but he had gotten used to the irritating sound, and Petty Officer Anker, the midwatch supervisor, had not. Anything that set the pompous Norwegian's teeth on edge was worth cultivating.

The United Nations Navy frigate *Abraxas* had left station three weeks earlier than scheduled. The news to depart had been received with enthusiasm. Circling a white dwarf, while the science department made astronomical observations, was as boring as a mission could get. To the entire crews' consternation, instead of heading back to Earth for a long-awaited shore leave, they had long-Skipped across half the Lower Arm. If not for a quick rendezvous with a civilian cargo vessel to resupply, they would have been eating cold rations and ripping pages out of magazines for toilet paper by the time they made it back to Earth from Loki.

He didn't mind the long Skips in spite of the headaches and queasiness that ensued. He had joined the Navy to see the galaxy. He had seen a large chunk of it on this mission, whatever their mission was. So far, the captain had not informed the crew. As a lowly E3, he would be one of the last to know.

Just as he passed the machine shop, the shriek of shearing metal rumbled down the corridor. He stopped and glanced into the shop, but it was empty at two a.m., and the lights out. The sound repeated a few seconds later. He stared back down the corridor at the cargo bay, which he now knew had to be the source of the noise.

"Drunk-ass forklift driver skewered a cargo container," he grumbled aloud. "Damn that Linc. Guess who'll get to clean that mess up." He shook his head. "I hate midwatch."

When he heard a bloodcurdling scream, sounding as if torn from the throat of a banshee, followed by an earsplitting roar, his blood turned to ice. Another, shorter scream followed. It did not sound like an accident. Petty Officer Second Class Geir Anker and Cargo Specialist Third Class Linc Arvida were the only two crewmen in the bay when he left. What the hell were they doing to one another? He turned to check on them, when Anker lurched out the door backwards into the corridor. He turned and glanced in Hines' direction. The look on the burly Norwegian's face was one of terror and disbelief.

"Anker. What the bloody hell is going on? It sounds ..."

Hines stopped talking as a meter-long claw emerged from the open door, impaled Anker through the chest, and yanked him back inside the cargo bay. The sound of crates falling and cargo sliding across the deck drowned out any further screams. For thirty seconds, silence reigned. The pounding of his racing heart and his gasping open-mouthed breaths sounded eerily loud. He was too frightened to investigate. As he cowered there, eyes blinking in horror, the bulkhead around the cargo hatch bulged outward in a slow motion explosion. He held his breath, as the three-centimeter-thick steel split and peeled away from the frame with the sound of heavy cloth ripping. When a giant monster lunged into the corridor and faced his direction, Hines knew he should run, sound the alarm, or something, but his muscles refused to budge. His bewildered mind could not come to grips with the reality of the impossible creature standing in front of him filling almost the entire corridor.

Like some four-meter-tall, mutant, tailless spiny echidna, spiky, black shiny scales with upturned points covered the creature's body. It had no eyes, but the flaps of its nose billowed as if smelling him. The mouth, set in a short broad muzzle, opened in a roar, revealing rows of long, jagged teeth. His stomach roiled in revulsion, as he noticed shreds of uniform and pieces of human flesh belonging to Petty Officer Anker lodged between the teeth. The stench emanating from the creature reached his nostrils and his stomach rebelled. He bent over and puked on the deck, but his eyes never left the monstrosity.

As if vomiting had been a catharsis, the grisly sight sent a surge of adrenaline through his body and melted the ice in his muscles. He darted down the corridor and up the steps as fast as he could run. He heard the creature lumbering after him, crashing into walls, but he did not look back.

Others had heard the commotion as well. A squad of Marines, some wearing only their skivvies and a helmet, armed with laser rifles, shoved him against the wall as they brushed past him, racing down the steps. Torn between running away and watching the creature that had killed Anker and Arvida die, he stopped to see what happened next. The hiss of lasers firing punctuated the creature's ferocious roars as they grew louder and closer. Screaming and strident yells erupted from the corridor below. The din of the melee quickly reached a crescendo, and then went silent. When he heard the metal treads creaking under the weight of the creature climbing the steps, he took off.

Like most of the crew, he had been irate at the announcement of no shore leave when they reached Loki. Months cooped up in the ship on station at Sirius B were bad enough. After eight gut-wrenching days of long Skips across space, to walk on a planet's surface and breathe fresh air would have been a blessing, even on a barren dirtball like Loki. At least they had women. Instead, a shuttle departed the ship and returned in less than two hours, bringing aboard two large cargo containers. Now, he knew what was inside the containers.

*My God! There were two containers.* The thought of two of the creatures lent speed to his steps.

By the time he reached the midships crew's quarters, alarm klaxons were sounding throughout the ship. Marines, some in battle armor, and bleary-eyed sailors poured from doorways into the corridors in various states of undress and confusion, unsure if the ship was under attack, on fire, or holding an unscheduled drill. It was utter chaos until Chief Petty Officer Vanosh Klusky, wearing pajama bottoms, his uniform jacket showing his rank, and a cap, strode down the corridor yelling, "Make way! Make way!" He saw Hines and demanded, "What the hell is going on, Hines?"

Hines swallowed, took a deep breath, and in a rush replied, "A monster in the cargo bay."

Klusky opened his mouth to reprimand him, but saw something in Hines eyes that stopped him. "What the hell are you talking about, sailor? Monster, my ass." He leaned forward to smell Hine's breath. "You hitting the hooch?"

Hines understood Klusky's confusion. It all seemed unreal. "Petty Officer Anker is dead. So is a squad of Marines." He raised his arm and pointed down the corridor. As if cued by the motion, the creature emitted a screeching howl that echoed down the corridor, overpowering even the klaxon. Klusky's face paled, but he recovered quickly.

"Kill that thing," he snapped at a sailor, who shut off the alarm. Alarms in other parts of the ship still rang. He turned to face the crew, who stared at him like lost puppies. "Matthews, take two men; go to the arms locker and bring some weapons. The rest of you get dressed. Dog the hatches and stand by for further orders." He tapped Hines on the chest. "You, come with me to the bridge. We have to inform the watch crew."

Hines followed Klusky eagerly, anything to place distance between him and the creature. Halfway to the bridge, he felt a slight pressure in his temple and ringing in his ears as the ship dropped out of Skip Space. He didn't have time to ponder the reason. Moments later, the lights and artificial gravity failed. They floundered in total darkness for the short time it took the emergency lights to come on. The dim red lights spaced along the corridor revealed an eerie spectacle – Klusky pin wheeling end over end, and sailors clinging to whatever handhold they could find. Hines' heart crawled up his throat, as he pushed off the wall to grab Klusky. He intersected the CPO and carried him to the opposite wall. Without magnetic boots, they could not walk, but everyone knew how to swim in Zero-G. Together, they pushed off for the bridge.

Hines knew the unscheduled drop out of Skip Space and the power failure bore some relation to the creature's appearance on the ship. With a sickening feeling, he knew he would never see home again.

* * * *

Sergeant Charles Jackson Ivers came awake immediately when he heard the klaxon. He slipped on his one-piece jumpsuit and boots and stepped out into the corridor. Behind him, fellow Marines spilled from their bunks and gathered around him.

"What's a 'appening, sarge?" Private Duncan 'Dog' Nicholson asked in his clipped New Virtue brogue.

"Damned if I know, Dog. Grab your rifles and follow me."

He and six half-dressed Marines stormed down the corridor, shoving bystanders out of the way. He heard a gut-chilling roar in the distance and swore. He was only a lowly Marine sergeant, but he could connect the dots between the remains of two fossilized creatures they had picked up on Loki and the commotion near the cargo bay. He didn't know how and didn't really care why the two monsters, which everyone had thought dead, had revived and now ran amok on the *Abraxas*. That wasn't his department. His job was to stop them.

"Take up positions at the bottom of the stairs," he ordered.

When the creature came into view, the men shuffled nervously and glanced at each other in disbelief, but they didn't run. Ivers gave them credit for that, because the creature was a real monster, something from a DTs inspired nightmare or conjured up by smoking too much *Turish* blossom at the notorious *Thunderthighs Bar* on Hagman II. He resisted the impulse to pinch himself, thinking he had rather it be real than to believe his mind could create such a beast. It had looked harmless enough when they had picked it up on Loki, a shriveled-up, mummified relic from an archaeological dig. It was large and ugly, but presented no threat.

Hell, he had even touched its weird black armor plates. It didn't look so harmless now.

He waited until it was fifty meters away before ordering them to open fire. To his dismay, the lasers were useless. The black armor scales reflected the coherent light energy better than his battle armor. The few shots that struck the few areas of unprotected flesh only enraged the creature. It swiped at the bulkheads with one of its massive forelimbs. The three claws sliced through solid steel, exposing and ripping away electrical wiring and severing water lines. Water sprayed into the corridor like a water fountain.

"This isn't working," he said to his men, as he saw the futility of the lasers. "Dog, come with me to the armory. We need something bigger. You men continue firing but keep out of its way. Lead it toward the central core if you can. We need some elbow room."

The central core ran almost the entire length of the center of the frigate. The hollow space could be fitted with modular habitats for troop transport, landing craft, or science or medical modules. On this mission, it was empty. One section made a perfect basketball court and another contained a ten-meter by five-meter inflatable swimming pool. Ivers considered it the perfect spot to confront the creature.

He and Nicholson entered the empty wardroom and headed for the opposite door leading into the parallel corridor on starboard side of the ship. Just as he exited the wardroom, he heard a loud roar and screaming. He stopped and looked back. One of the men he had left in the corridor, or rather what was left of him, slid across the deck past the door, leaving a bloody trail. The head and most of the upper part of the torso were missing. The creature had moved much faster than he had thought it capable. His men had no time to run. The screaming stopped, and he knew his men were gone. He had ordered them to stay, and they had died.

"Wot is da thing?" Nicholson asked. His pasty face was a shade lighter at the carnage.

Ivers shook his head. "I don't know." He shunted aside his bitterness at the loss of his men. He had a job to do.

They took the stairs to Deck 2 two at a time and turned sternward to the aft weapons locker, but quickly ran into a mass exodus of sailors fleeing the aft section of the ship.

"There's some kind of monster in the engine room," one frightened engineer said as he raced by.

Almost as he spoke, the ship dropped out of Skip Space, and the artificial gravity and power both failed. He knew they would never reach the aft weapons locker. Their path took them past the engine room where the second creature lurked.

"Come on. We're going forward."

As they passed an airlock, he stopped. The creatures were hell bent on destroying the *Abraxas* and seemed capable of accomplishing that goal. "Get into a suit." Nicholson stared at him in disbelief. "Move it, Dog!" Ivers snapped. "Those things could rip the guts out of the ship and leave us sucking vacuum."

It was not easy donning his battle armor in Zero-G, but practice made the task less challenging. He felt safer with a little armor around him, even if was just half a centimeter of steel sponge inside a ceramic-metal alloy shell. It was more resistant to monsters than bare flesh. As soon as he closed the visor and sealed the helmet, he began receiving reports of the ship's com link. The chatter was frantic and confusing, as speakers talked over one another.

"We have it trapped in the Deck 2 engine room," someone reported. "We can't get to the engines or the generators to repair them."

"No, it's still on Deck 1 in 'C' Corridor near the environmental section," another argued.

Ivers cursed. The creatures acted as if they knew the most vulnerable areas of the ship. Knock out the Skip drive and power, disable the engines, and kill the atmosphere scrubbers – a dead ship. "Dog, go to the bridge. Monitor the viewers if they're still operational and keep me informed of the creature's location. I'm going to see if a shoulder-launched rocket can do any damage to that thing."

"Got ya, Sarge." Nicholson pushed off toward the bridge. Ivers clanked down the nearest stairwell in his battle armor. He spotted Lieutenant Lee Holders directing a group of sailors constructing a barricade across the corridor from steel cot frames pilfered from the bunkrooms and lengths of pipe from the machine shop. Ivers noticed only three of the men were armed.

"Holders, send men to fetch lasers from the Marine quarters. I'll be back with something heavier."

He was twenty meters from the forward cargo hold where the weapons locker was located when one of the creatures holed the ship. The rent in the hull was large; a rush of air propelled him backwards down the corridor. He activated his magnetic boots and settled onto the deck. Two sailors emerged from a room and began choking from lack of oxygen. He closed and sealed an airtight hatch, but atmosphere continued to bleed from the corridor. The creatures had punctured the hull in several spots, circumventing the airtight doors, perhaps even disabling the seals in the ventilation system that ran throughout the ship. He couldn't help the sailors. He had no oxygen except the pack attached to his suit. He watched them die.

"Smart bastards," he said. He wondered if the creatures were truly some kind of mindless beast or an intelligent creature. Of the two, he preferred a mindless beast.

He reached the weapons locker and retrieved a *Grom* MANPADS, a Man-Portable Air-Defense System. The handheld rocket launcher fired a 72mm rocket used to take out low-flying aircraft. He figured it would take out a creature as large as an aircraft. He loaded one rocket in the launcher, grabbed two more, and stuffed them through the utility belt of his suit. On his way to the central core, by the dim glow of the emergency lights, he saw one of the creatures bounding down the corridor in Zero-G toward him.

"Bastards can breathe vacuum," he said with grudging admiration. Whatever they were, they were no mere wild animal. He had never heard of a creature that could live in a vacuum. He clicked off the safety on the launcher and fired. With no gravity to affect its path, the rocket flew straight and true at the creature. Just before it hit, the creature wrenched a metal door from a room, dug it rear talons into the deck to brace itself, and held the door in front of it as a shield. The rocket struck the door dead center and exploded.

The blast did not move the creature, but it mangled the door. The creature casually flung the door away and launched itself down the corridor at him with a speed that belied its bulk. He loaded the launcher with a second rocket. This time, he waited until the creature was almost on top of him before firing. The rocket struck the creature in the head and exploded. The explosion slammed it into the wall. The concussive back blast sent Ivers flying backwards. If not for the battle armor, the collision with the deck would have knocked him unconscious.

He crawled to his knees and saw the monster was down but far from out. It immediately attacked and killed two men wearing respirators who floated into the corridor to investigate the explosion. It dispatched them quickly and focused its attention on Ivers, the bloody, dismembered corpses floating like a grotesque halo around its head.

Ivers backed into the forward cargo bay through the large open door and waited for the creature to enter. As soon as it was inside, it flew across the room at him. He bent his legs, demagnetized his boots, and pushed off. The creature could not change its forward momentum. Ivers let it pass him and fired again. The third rocket struck it just above the unprotected ear and blasted a fourteen-centimeter-deep hole in its head. Reddish-orange blood sprayed from the wound and splattered the wall. The creature bounced off the wall and flew back toward him, flailing its clawed legs. He could tell the wound was mortal, but it could still kill him before it died.

Ivers leaped into the weapons locker and sealed the door behind him. As he searched for another rocket, the creature continued to scratch at the door before going silent. He waited a few minutes to be safe and tried the door. It wouldn't budge. The creature's last act had been to use its body to seal him in the weapons locker with a limited air supply. He was more embarrassed than angry. He sat down to wait for a rescue he was not sure would come.

# 3

*Fortune's Luck* broke out of Skip Space in a brilliant rainbow burst of light but no sound. Like the sonic boom of a Mach 1 craft plowing through an atmosphere, the circle of bright light was the result of tachyons pushed ahead of the ship in Skip Space encountering gravity waves in real space-time. Dax breathed a sigh of relief each time the ship Skipped successfully. The idea of suddenly becoming a cloud of charged sub-atomic particles scattered through space did not appeal to him.

Technically, Skip Space was a mirror image of real space through which a ship equipped with black-hole technology could 'Skip' at speeds far greater than the limiting speed of light. *Fortune's Luck* could Skip five light years in ten days before re-entering real space to recharge her engines and calibrate her next Skip. A Navy vessel such as the Abraxas could cover the same distance in four days.

As usual, the Skip left Dax disoriented. His feet and hands felt too big for his body, and his tongue was numb. Each tick of his watch seemed like a full minute. The sensation would pass quickly. He disdained the drugs that softened the effects of Skips as often being as bad as the disorientation. He added the latest Skip to his mental list – 106 successful Skips. He would need no list for unsuccessful ones.

The beacon signal was loud, clear, and ominous over the com, and the radar indicated an object 5,000 kilometers ahead of them, right where the signal originated. Dax leaned over the back of the pilot's seat like a driving instructor showing a student the ropes.

He longed to be in the command seat, but he trusted Andy, and the kid needed the experience.

"Take us in nice and slow. Circle the ship once. Make sure they can read our name." He turned to Romeo, now manning the communications station. "Are we broadcasting our ID?"

"Yes, loud and clear."

"Good. Picking up anything?"

Romeo arched his eyebrows and shook his head. "Just the beacon. Should I try a laser?"

Flashing a coded laser message at the ship was a good idea as long as they did not interpret it as an attack. Even with no ship's com or power, someone with a handheld laser could return their signal.

"Do it."

Romeo grabbed a laser and stood beside the starboard viewport to flash a signal. Two minutes later, he gave up. "Nothing. Looks like no one is home. Want me to keep trying?"

Dax shook his head. "No."

As they approached visual range, the black outline of the ship was barely visible in the darkness of space. The ship was showing no running lights, but the outline matched that of a Navy frigate in *Jane's Fighting Ships* recognition book. At least it was not a pirate ship. Dax's hope of a salvage fee increased in proportion to his sixth sense of danger. His scalp crawled like a disturbed ant mound.

Andy completed his slow circumnavigation of the *Abraxas* and moved in closer. "Do you see that?"

Dax did, and the knot in his stomach clenched tighter. He leaned closer to the view screen and stared. The rear cargo hatch was missing, and a gash wide enough to drive the grasshopper through ran from the cargo bay deck to the deck above. A cloud of metal shards floated near the open hatch. More debris formed a halo around the vessel.

Andy's voice took on a new tenor. "What could do that to a ship?"

"Meteor, cargo hold explosion, pirates, Space Godzilla – I don't know. Take us in closer. Any radiation?" he asked Romeo.

"Nothing. I'm not getting any power readings at all. The ship is dead. Ambient temperature is 156 degrees Kelvin."

"To be that cold, she's been without power for some time, a couple of days at least. Okay, Andy, park us half a kilometer out, but keep the engines online. If you see me tearing ass back on the grasshopper, you come scoop us up."

"Who's going with you? Plia can take the com," he added, eager to go.

"I'll take Nate. We might need power for the computers. If no one's there, I want to see the ship's logs. If they abandoned ship, I want to know what happened. I want to know what could take out an armed frigate." He glanced at Andy, saw the disappointment in his face, and grinned. "I need you in command, kid, to pull my balls out of the fire if necessary." He smacked his palm down on the intercom button. "Plia, arm those missiles and be ready to fire on my command. Target the cargo hold and the engines." To Andy's unspoken inquiry, he pointed to the rent metal around the gaping open hatch. "That cargo hatch was blown outward, not inward, and that gash was peeled from the inside. Whatever happened over there originated in the cargo bay."

"Do you think …?" Andy began.

"I'm trying not to think right now. I'm going to the cargo bay. If I'm not back in an hour, you take this ship back to Kinta Station. She's yours, well, yours and the finance company."

"You be careful out there. This doesn't make any sense. A derelict Navy frigate that shouldn't be within twenty light years of here and a research station gone silent – it has a bad smell."

He patted Andy's blond head for luck. "You're learning, kid. I agree, but I want to see what could do that much damage to a Navy frigate."

Five minutes later, Nate and he narrowed the gap between the two ships in the grasshopper. He throttled back on the hydrazine engine halfway across and let it coast in, waiting until the last possible moment before impact to fire the thrusters, and came to a halt just inside the open cargo bay. With no artificial gravity, everything not properly secured floated above the deck, creating a jumbled, three-dimensional maze they would have to navigate to reach the main corridor. The untidy mess sent his OCD into a nosedive. He resisted the impulse to stow everything neatly in its proper place.

The full rack of excursion suits by the wall and the shuttle still in its docking cradle only deepened the mystery. No one had left the ship through the aft cargo bay.

He reached under the seat and removed the .40 caliber HK, making sure the safety was indeed off as Plia had informed him. He pointed to a comp console. "See if there's any power to that station."

He floated out of the grasshopper and clicked on his magnetic boots to secure them to the deck. He didn't know what frequency the Navy used for internal communications. He keyed his suit mic to broadcast on a wide range of frequencies. "This is Dax Wyldd, captain of the cargo vessel *Fortune's Luck* answering your emergency beacon. Is anyone listening?" He waited a moment before trying again. "Anyone, please respond to my broadcast. We have boarded your ship and are in the portside aft cargo bay." No one answered.

He walked around the bay examining the cargo, while Nate checked out the console. Most of the freight was what one would normally find on a Navy ship – foodstuffs, water, spare parts, and ammunition – nothing out of the ordinary or dangerous. Several mashed crates had spilled their contents to join the debris cloud filling the cargo bay. He brushed aside a large can of tomatoes that had frozen and burst, spilling its frozen contents like a splotch of blood into the air around it.

Because of the debris and clouds of frozen atmosphere, his helmet light penetrated only a few meters into the darkness. Still, what he saw dismayed him and brought his heart up in his throat. Frozen blood crusted one crate, and a severed leg protruded through a gap in the cargo netting as if frozen meat hung up in a meat locker. He had seen the aftermath of Zero-G accidents before. Severed and crushed limbs were common on cargo ships, but he had a gut feeling this was no accident.

"Heads up, Nate," he called out. "We've got bodies here. You getting this, Andy?"

Andy, who monitored their progress through their suit cameras, replied. “The quality’s lousy because of the shielding, but, yeah, I see it. What happened over there?”

“Unknown,” Dax replied. “We’re going deeper into the ship.”

The remains of two metal shipping bins in particular drew his attention. Both looked as if bombs had exploded inside them. The metal sides were shredded, and the tops wrenched from the heavy hinges. Oddly, both bore labels reading ‘Biological Specimens – Loki’. His scalp tingled. He reached up and tried to scratch his head but his helmet stopped him.

“This console’s dead,” Nate announced over his suit com. “No main power or auxiliary power in the cargo bay.”

“We’ll try the bridge.” He swiped his arm to indicate the mess around him. “I don’t get it. I see blood and body parts but no corpses.”

“They could have floated out the hatch.”

“Maybe, but I get the feeling they never made it that far.”

Andy chimed in. “A mutiny?” he suggested.

“In a mutiny, one side usually wins. I don’t think we’ll find any winners here, and the shuttle is still in the cradle. I see scorch marks on the bulkhead as if they were firing lasers at someone.” He thought of the two specimen crates. “Or something. Whatever happened here was no accident.”

It didn’t take long to find the first bodies. Fifty meters down the main corridor, they encountered a makeshift barricade of metal bunk frames, filing cabinets, and pieces of steel pipe hastily welded to the bulkhead. Something had plowed through the barricade with tremendous force, knocking aside the obstacles, and bending and twisting the pipes out of the way. A section of pipe pinned a CPO wearing pajama bottoms and his uniform jacket against the bulkhead by piercing him through his chest. His frozen eyes stared at the metal pipe in disbelief.

Nate examined the body and said, “The look on his face reminds me more of an expression of horror than of pain.”

Dax studied the frozen face. “Yeah, I guess being skewered by a water pipe would be horrible.”

Beyond, in a frozen cloud of human blood, floated enough torsos and severed limbs to Frankenstein-cobble together at least a dozen corpses. All were armed with laser rifles or heavy-caliber slug rifles. Whatever they had shot at had torn through them like a charging rhino through tall grass. After witnessing the extent of the carnage, he decided his .40 caliber pistol was too small for whatever had ripped up the ship. He clipped it to his suit and grabbed one of the laser rifles.

"Andy? You still there?"

"We're all watching, Dax. Tish is gripping my shoulder so hard I can't move it. What the … happened … there?"

"No clue yet." Andy's transmission hissed with static. "Can you boost your signal?"

"Negative. I'm at full gain. You're going too deep inside the ship. Too much shielding. Video is breaking up as well."

Dax didn't like the idea of losing contact with *Fortune's Luck*, but he didn't have time to set up relays and couldn't turn back. "Understood. We'll be off contact. We're continuing."

The bridge was located two decks above them just aft of the forward missile room. On Deck 2, the crew had constructed a second barricade at the top of the stairs. Like the first, it was in a shambles. Heavy metal cargo pods stacked atop each other would have provided an effective defense against an invading army, but they had not stopped whatever had attacked the ship. Something had shredded one pod into long strips of jagged metal and folded a second almost in half. Three dead sailors, torn apart by an incredible force, lay scattered over the debris, frozen to it by their blood. A trail of frozen blood ran down the corridor.

Dax felt the deck shudder under his feet. "Are you certain all the power is out?"

"Fairly certain. Romeo said he picked up nothing on the scanner. I felt it too. Maybe it was something large banging into a bulkhead."

Dax remembered the size of the smashed specimen crates in the cargo hold. "Yeah. That's what worries me."

With no power, the lift to the bridge was useless. Access was by a spiral staircase beside the lift. The metal stairs and handrails looked as if a team of jackhammers had assaulted them. Deep scratches marred the walls. Something had forced the five-centimeter-thick steel blast door at the top of the stairs inward and shattered the surrounding bulkhead, leaving dangerous jagged metal slivers. Dax carefully avoided them. A rip in his suit could prove fatal. Dax did not think the damage was from an explosion.

The bridge was at least four times as large as the bridge of the *Fortune's Luck.* Science, engineering, and navigation stations filled a horseshoe-shaped upper tier. Below it, four battle stations, communications, and ship's environmental systems stations formed a semicircle around a second tier with the captain's command chair sitting alone in the center of the bridge. The bridge was barely recognizable. Consoles were now so much metal confetti. One of the blast shields covering the shattered forward viewport bore gouge marks in the metal deeper than his fist. He spread his hand over the three equally spaced holes and grimaced at the apparent size of the hand that had created them.

The explosive decompression had blown much of the loose material out through the broken view port, but several mangled corpses floated in a cloud of frozen blood. The captain, identifiable only by the gold braid on his bloody uniform, lay pinned beneath a folded rail, a pistol in his hand where he had bravely fought to the last.

"I won't get any logs from this pile of junk," Nate said, slamming his gloved hand down on a smashed console.

"Look for a handheld pad or something."

As Nate rummaged through the debris scattered around the bridge, Dax felt a rhythmic tapping reverberate through the soles of his boots. He looked around but saw nothing moving. It was not as strong as the earlier thud.

"Do you feel that?" he asked Nate.

Nate stopped moving; then, after a few moments, glanced down at the deck. "It's coming from below, in the missile compartment. Do we investigate?"

As much as Dax wanted to turn tail and run, he needed answers. What he had seen so far had only generated more questions. He nodded.

They climbed down the forward stairwell to the deck below. Dax kept the laser rifle pointed forward, his finger on the trigger, although he realized it had done its previous owner little good. Their magnetic boots made no noise on the metal steps in the airless ship, but he could not help feeling they were nevertheless announcing their presence to whatever had caused all the damage. They passed more mangled corpses, more damage to the ship.

A crew of thirty-five – all dead. Even if some of them had died from decompression, what could kill thirty-five armed men? A decapitated body bumped into him. He jumped aside so quickly he slammed into the bulkhead.

"Jesus! Are there no whole corpses on this ship?"

Long, deep gouges along one corridor bulkhead penetrated into the rooms beyond, severing electrical conduits and water lines. Pools of ice covered one area of the floor, indicating the ship had gravity when the water lines were cut. Graceful icicle arches lancing across the corridor formed after the gravity generator failed.

"Whatever did this was pissed."

"You think some creature did all this?" Nate asked.

Math, except in determining profit/loss figures, had never been Dax's strong point, but he could add two and two and get four. The two smashed specimen crates and a destroyed Navy frigate added up to danger. "Do you think space-sick Navy swabbies rip people apart and punch holes in bulkheads?"

The forward missile compartment was sealed. He pressed his helmet against the metal trying to detect any sounds beyond it. "Nothing," he reported to Nate. Using brute force, they cranked the manual wheel to open it. It slid slowly into its recess, revealing a dark, cavernous space beyond. Rows of vertical and horizontal missile tubes lined the room like a forest. His mind quickly counted the sixteen tubes. Two elevators for delivering missiles from the armament locker below dominated most of the open space. There were no crewmen at their battle stations and no missiles in the tubes.

Dax noted the absence to Nate. "There was no outside threat, or they would have at least loaded the missile tubes."

The tapping began again. He walked around the compartment, finally locating the source near the portside hull below the deck.

"What's down there?" he asked.

"Should be the port forward cargo bay."

Dax listened to the tapping for a moment. “Is that Morse code?”

“Could be. The echo makes it difficult to read. I don’t remember much Morse code. It’s been over thirty years since I’ve used it.”

“I think I recognize the word ‘danger’, though it could be ‘anger’. It’s hard to jump into the middle of a sentence. Well, at least it’s human. I hope.” The irregular tapping meant someone was still alive. He needed answers. He couldn’t leave without knowing what had happened. “Let’s check it out.”

Two cargo bays located forward near the bow on the lowest deck were smaller than the main rear cargo bay, and when equipped with cradles for drop shuttles, used for rapid ground deployment of troops in Marine operations. The smashed-in, four-meter-wide cargo door at the end of the main corridor was the first indication that the ills that had befallen the *Abraxas* had reached the forward cargo bay.

He entered the dark space warily. When his suit lights illuminated the obscene creature floating at the edge of the room, he fired his laser without thinking. After three shots, he realized the creature wasn’t moving. Chagrined, he noticed the gaping wound in its head that his rifle had not produced.

“Somebody beat me to it.” He paused a moment to let his heart rate return to something near normal. “What the hell is that thing?”

Nate was too flustered to respond. Dax carefully circled the creature, noting the three curved talons on the forelimbs that matched the gouges in the steel bulkheads. The elongated, backward-jointed legs designed for rapid motion and leaping ended in claws almost as long as the talons. Jagged teeth the size of his hand filled the creature’s cavernous maw. It had no eyes, but the oversized ear holes surrounded by a series of concentric grooves and large, slit nostrils spoke of other heightened senses. Overlapping, spiky, shiny scales resembling obsidian armored plating covered most of the creature’s body, leaving only the lower part of the legs, the forearms, and parts of the head exposed. The flesh was thick and fibrous, like a tangle of mangrove tree roots.

As he drew close to a heavy door set into the bulkhead, the tapping resumed. He pointed the laser at the door partially blocked by the creature's dead bulk and got Nate's attention. He tapped the door with the butt of his rifle and received an immediate flurry of taps in response. His Morse code was rusty, but he recognized 'hurry' and a string of profanities that almost made him blush.

"Someone's alive in there." He glanced at the creature. "We've got to move this thing out of the way."

Using two grappling hooks, he attached chains to the carcass and secured them to a hand-cranked winch. It took all the muscle they could summon to budge the creature's considerable mass even in Zero-G, but as soon they moved it from the door, the door shot open. A dark-suited figure rushed from the door and launched across the room like an arrow from a bow. Dax trained his rifle on the figure, but the person seemed more intent on reaching a row of lockers along one wall than in accosting them. He turned, and through the clear visor, Dax saw it was a man. He discarded his air tank, let it float across the cargo bay, and quickly clipped in a fresh one.

Dax's suit com crackled. "Damn, that tastes good. I've been breathing fumes for ten minutes. I heard movement above and prayed it was human."

"Why didn't you answer my message?"

He hitched his thumb at the room from which he had emerged. "Weapons locker is titanium-vanadium steel; strong enough to keep this thing out, but it also blocks radio waves."

"What happened here?"

The man shook his head. "Later. We have to get off this ship."

Dax wasn't going to let some Marine buffalo him. He folded his arms over his chest but kept the laser rifle out front. "I need answers. Who the hell are you?"

The man looked at him undaunted by the laser. "Sergeant Charles Jackson Ivers, UNMC. And you are?"

"Captain Dax Wyldd of the *Fortune's Luck*."

Ivers nodded. "You're the captain of the cargo ship bound for Loki."

Dax's suspicion edged up a notch. "How did you know?"

"Later. We're in danger here."

Dax pointed to the dead creature. "From that?"

"No. There's another one trapped in the upper compartment of the engine room, but I doubt it will stay there much longer now that it knows you're here."

Dax's blood ran cold. He glanced around with apprehension. "Why didn't you say so?"

Ivers floated back into the weapons locker. He reemerged a moment later carrying a bulky-looking rifle in one hand, a bag slung over his shoulder, and a compact, low-yield nuclear warhead in his other hand.

Dax's attention fell on the warhead. Nuclear devices made him nervous. He pointed to it. "What are you going to do with that?"

"Vaporize this ship and its cargo."

"Not before I download the ship's logs. The Navy might have a few questions. I'd like to have answers for them."

Ivers tapped his helmet. "I downloaded the logs onto my suit comp, and I've got vid of everything that happened up until I locked myself in the weapons locker." The ship rang from a series of heavy blows. If the ship had not been in a vacuum, Dax was certain it would have sounded like the ship's death knell. He offered Ivers a quizzical look. "That's the other xenomorph breaking out of the engine compartment," Ivers said. "I think it's hungry. Want to meet it?"

"Fuck that! Let's go."

"I have to set the timer on this nuke. Ten minutes should be enough, don't you think?"

Dax didn't like the idea of relying on a Marine with a nuke. Ivers might feel like dying for the good of the service. Dax didn't, but he agreed with Ivers' thinking. If there was another of those creatures aboard ship, especially a live one, nuking it seemed a good, solid plan. "Bring it. I have a better idea."

Dax started up the steps to Deck 2. Ivers stopped him. "If the second xenomorph broke out of the engine room, it might be waiting up there. We can travel aft through the crew's quarters and the hydroponics garden."

Dax was for anything that kept them from meeting another one of the creatures face-to-face. "Lead the way, Sergeant."

He followed Ivers down a narrow passageway lined with machine shops, offices, and a small library. Seeing books, hand tools, nuts, and bolts floating in Zero-G was disconcerting enough, like walking through the bowels of a sunken ship, but when they reached the main open crew's quarters, things became bizarre indeed. Floating frozen bed linen illuminated by their lights looked like ghosts. Dax ducked under a horizontal mop and bucket filled with frozen mop water blocking the space between bunks as if he were doing the Limbo. He saw no bodies, no blood. Everyone had made it from his or her bunk before dying. *That's good. No one should die in bed but old people.*

Just as Romeo had said, the *Abraxas'* hydroponics garden was huge, half as large as the entire *Fortune's Luck.* Vertical and horizontal rows of tomatoes, beans, lettuce, squash, and carrots suspended in tanks that once held drip lines feeding the roots liquid nutrients were flash frozen, looking as fresh as they had a few days earlier when alive. One section of herbs sat along a bulkhead wall – basil, thyme, lemon grass, parsley, cilantro, and a few herbs he did not recognize. Dax considered snapping off a few herb stalks for Luigi, but he didn't have the time to loiter.

As they passed through the maze of plants in the frozen garden, Dax felt the deck shudder beneath his feet from a heavy sustained blow. The second xenomorph was making an appearance.

"That's damn close," he said.

He turned just as the bulkhead around the hatch to the hydroponics garden bulged outward. The metal split, and the hatch went flying across the room, shattered a row of plants, and crashed into a table. All three of their suits lights focused on the creature standing in the sundered hatch.

The dead creature had been fearsome; the live one was terrifying. It crouched on it rear legs with its foreclaws digging into the deck, staring sightlessly directly at them. Its huge bulk filled the space between deck and ceiling. It could not smell them in a vacuum, and they did not move, so it was unable to detect their vibrations, but it knew where they were nevertheless. Its head moved slightly in each of their directions, as if inspecting them, deciding who would die first. Dax suspected the creature possessed senses beyond the normal senses. He wondered if it could detect their heat signature. *If it can read my mind, it would be really pissed right now.* As soon as Ivers raised his ion disrupter, the creature charged.

It scattered tables and shoved aside hanging vegetable trays as it plowed down the center of the room. Ivers fired. The high-energy disrupter would have burned an unarmored human to a crisp and broiled alive one wearing battle armor. The xenomorph shrugged it off like a spitball shot at it through a straw. The black scales covering its body reflected the energy of the blast, thawing and immediately shriveling the plants around it. He knew Ivers would not have time to try for a shot at an unarmored part of its body. Its cavernous maw opened wide, revealing teeth that would have made a salvage yard car-shredding machine jealous. Dax was certain that if he could have heard the roar the creature released, it would have deafened him. He had a dizzying view down the creature's gullet, and it frightened him.

"How does it breathe vacuum?" he asked.

"Move it!" Ivers shouted.

Dax complied. Staying alive trumped answers on morphology. He shoved a stunned Nate to get him moving. He quickly realized running in magnetic boots was too slow. The creature was rapidly gaining on them.

"Shut down your boots," he told them. "Swim!"

As soon as he felt his boots release their magnetic grip on the deck, he bent his knees and shoved off as hard as he could. He grabbed the wall with both hands and pulled himself along like climbing a horizontal ladder. As he gained speed, he needed only slap at the wall to keep moving. He knew slamming into a solid bulkhead at such speeds, even in a suit, would probably break his neck, but haste was called for. He shot through the open airtight hatch and down the adjoining corridor just behind Nate. Ivers stopped long enough to seal the hatch behind them.

"That's not going to stop it," Dax said.

"It might slow it down."

The corridor made a series of right-angle turns around a gymnasium, a freshwater tank, and the $CO_2$ scrubbers in the ship's environment section. The massive creature would have a difficult time negotiating the tight turns. They emerged in the ship's cavernous central core. Exercise equipment, basketballs, and dead sailors floated like grotesque mobiles in the dark space. Large spherical globules of water from an exploded swimming pool looked as if they were devouring some of the bodies half-protruding from them. Dax became momentarily lost in the unfamiliar dark space. Ivers pointed toward the stern.

"That way," he said. "We don't have much time."

They were three-quarters of the way to the aft cargo bay when the creature burst into the central core. It did not hesitate. It came unerringly straight at them using its powerful legs to push off parallel to the deck, and then grab the deck with its foreclaws to set up for another hop.

"How does that fucker do that?" Dax asked aloud.

Ivers fired two blasts with the disrupter. His aim was true, but a globule of water floated into his line of fire. The water flashed into a cloud of super-heated steam, concealing the creature. The steam condensed to water vapor and froze into ice crystals. The creature exploded from the ice cloud and launched at them, hurtling like a catapult projectile. They ducked out of its way, but one of the rear legs brushed Dax as it flew by. The claws missed him by a hand's width, but the glancing impact disrupted his suit electronics as it sent him reeling across the room. He suffered a moment of panic before the system stabilized.

Nate, anchored to the deck, caught his hand and pulled him down beside him. He turned to look at the creature. It had used the opposite wall to rebound toward them. This time, it would not miss.

"Grab on to me!" Ivers yelled.

Ivers looked up to see the sergeant rushing at them holding onto an activated fire extinguisher, using the nozzle to control his flight. The one-and-a-half-meter tall extinguisher had wheels to move it around the ship, but it was now airborne, a carbon dioxide missile. Nate broke free of the deck, and the two of them grabbed Ivers' legs as he passed. Their added mass slowed Ivers' momentum, but they still traveled faster than they could have swum. The creature howled silently at their narrow escape. They reached a hatch just as the $CO_2$ ran out. Ivers dove for it and discarded the empty extinguisher. They disentangled and exited through the door. Ivers stopped long enough to dog it shut. They emerged in a short transverse corridor near the engine room. Ivers guided them to the aft cargo bay.

When they reached the cargo bay, Ivers stopped and set the nuke on the deck. "I'm setting the nuke for three minutes. We don't have much longer than that."

"Wait!" Dax shouted into his suit mic. "That's barely enough time to make it back to *Fortune's Luck* and Skip."

Ivers stared at him. "Vacuum doesn't stop it. If we don't destroy it now, it will cross over to your ship. Do you want the same thing happening to your crew that happened here or attack the next ship that investigates?"

Ivers was asking him to sacrifice himself for his crew and his ship. He liked to think he would do it if necessary, but he wasn't ready to die just yet. Ivers was military. He saw self-sacrifice as part of the job description. The thought of dying in a nuclear blast frightened Dax to death. He wanted to die in bed an old man.

"I have a better idea, one that won't end with us vaporized." Ivers hesitated. "Trust me, Sergeant."

For one brief moment, Dax thought Ivers was going to ignore him set the nuke for immediate detonation to take no chances. He didn't know if he could stop the determined Marine, but he would try. He would not allow the sergeant to kill him and Nate or endanger his ship if there was another way.

"Your plan had better work," Ivers warned and picked up the nuke.

Dax sighed in relief. He climbed into the cramped cockpit of the grasshopper. Ivers straddled the rear of the two-passenger conveyance cowboy-style, while holding the nuclear warhead tucked under one arm like a football. "Where's Nate?" Dax asked. He saw Nate at one of the consoles. "Come on, Nate!" he yelled.

"If I can use power from my suit, I can seal the inner hatch of the cargo bay. It should keep the creature penned up long enough to use the nuke."

"We don't have time. Get in and let's go."

"One more second."

The creature didn't give him one more second. It clawed through the bulkhead between the corridor and the cargo bay, widened the rip large enough to crawl through, and scattered floating cargo like balloons at a high school prom in its zeal to reach them. One large metal bin careened across the hold toward the grasshopper. Dax gunned the engine to move out of its way.

"Come on, Nate!" he yelled. He didn't want to wait around one millisecond longer than necessary and face a creature that could shrug off lasers and disruptors.

Nate couldn't reach them. The creature stood between him and the grasshopper, facing him, its rear claws digging into the metal deck. Ivers fired the disruptor from his hip, hitting the creature on the back of one leg. It whirled on them and roared silently into the vacuum. Nate used the opportunity to push off toward the outer hatch. Dax saw him and veered to intersect his path, while Ivers tried to line up another shot. Somehow, the creature detected Nate's motion. He made no sound or disturbed any air, since it was a vacuum. He did not collide with any cargo; nevertheless, the creature knew exactly where he was.

Nate, moving as if swimming in cold molasses, was less than five meters from the moving grasshopper when the creature leaped across the cargo bay and grabbed him by his leg. Nate screamed as the gigantic claws ripped through his suit and tore into the flesh of his thigh. Like a dog with a rag doll, the creature whipped Nate's body back and forth, and then released him. He flew across the cargo bay and smashed into a bulkhead. If the frenzied shaking had not snapped his spine, the high-speed impact with solid steel did. Blood floated from his ripped suit leg and the shattered visor of his crumpled helmet. He did not move.

"Nate!" Dax yelled, and released the controls of the grasshopper to go for him. He heard other voices from the *Luck* in his suit com, but he ignored them.

Ivers reached over his shoulder and slammed the throttle forward. The grasshopper shot out the hatch, while Ivers held him down in his seat.

"What are you doing?" Dax demanded, struggling to break free of the sergeant's steely grip.

"He's gone. Either we go with your plan, or I set off the nuke right now. It will take out both ships. You decide."

Dax linked to Nate's suit to check his vitals. Nate had no pulse or respiration. His body temperature was dropping rapidly. He knew Nate was dead, but leaving his body behind felt like a betrayal to their friendship. He had the rest of his crew to consider. "You bastard," he growled at Ivers and aimed the grasshopper at *Fortune's Luck.* He glanced back at the frigate and caught a glimpse of the creature in the aft cargo bay. It wandered through the space leisurely shoving debris around. It did not follow them.

Back aboard *Fortune's Luck*, Dax wasted no time explaining the situation to his crew. He ignored their plaintive looks. They had overheard the conversations on the com channel and had witnessed his death on Dax's suit camera, but had been spared the grisly details that would haunt him the rest of his life. His rage rose inside him like the aftermath of a bad bowl of Five-Alarm chili, burning his insides, and bringing hot, stinging tears to his eyes. He helped Ivers replace the warhead on one of the *Wasp Sting* missiles with the nuke. Plia had set the weapons pod to point out the open cargo hatch directly at the *Abraxas*.

The creature had seen *Fortune's Luck.* It used its powerful legs to launch from the *Abraxas* cargo bay aimed unerringly at them. It moved slower than the grasshopper, but it would reach them in minutes. He had to save his ship and crew.

Dax hit the intercom. "Take us out of here, Andy, half speed. I'll tell you when to Skip." The stricken frigate and the monster receded in the distance. When *Fortune's Luck* reached ten kilometers distance, Dax fired the missile and watched it race toward the doomed frigate following its laser guidance system. "Okay, Andy. Skip!" As the shimmer of folding space enveloped the ship, the frigate exploded in a dazzling flash of intense nuclear heat. The ring of superheated vapor reached toward *Fortune's Luck* like the last death grasp of the xenomorph, but she was no longer there.

# 4

"I'm ready for those answers now," Dax said to Ivers.

His heart still raced from their narrow escape from the doomed Navy frigate. He had never seen a nuclear weapon detonate from ten clicks and did not wish to repeat his experience. A few of the ship's systems were still acting up from the EMP from the blast, but he would deal with those later. By leaving Nate's body, Ivers had taken the decision from him, and that angered him, but his hot anger at Ivers was already becoming a numbing sense of loss. He was afraid if he did not maintain his ire at Ivers, he would have to dwell on his responsibility in Nate's death, and that frightened him more than the monster.

It was illogical, but he held Ivers at fault for the *Abraxas'* distress call that placed his ship and crew in danger. He needed somebody to blame and Ivers was handy. The U.N. Navy was not.

The entire crew squeezed into the small wardroom watching the Marine sergeant down half a pot of coffee and two plates of ham and scrambled liquid egg concentrate. Dax hadn't eaten in hours, but the smell of food nauseated him. He didn't know if he would ever be able to eat again. The crew was unnaturally subdued, visibly upset, and curious about Nate's death. Words had failed him when he had tried to explain. He prided himself on being a hard man, but losing Nate had hit too close to home. He had been the first to join the *Fortune's Luck* crew. He had been the solid core of the ship; the 'old man' at fifty-one the crew could bring their problems to, allowing Dax to maintain his carefully honed façade of aloofness. The others had not yet come to grips with Nate's death. The pain and heartbreak would set in soon.

Ivers finished his third biscuit and wiped his mouth with the back of his hand. He looked up at Romeo, who stood hovering over the starving sergeant, his pride as a cook reinforced by the sergeant's prodigious appetite.

"Thanks. I was stuck in that weapons locker for sixteen hours with no food or water and damn little air."

Dax wasn't interested in Ivers' hardships. "Did you kill that thing in the forward cargo hold?"

Ivers smiled. "It was a real monster all right, but a hand-held rocket launcher blew a hole in its head. It didn't die easy though. It tore up a lot of real estate and killed too many damn good men before it died. It trapped me in the locker."

He asked the question uppermost in his mind. "What are they?"

Ivers shrugged and pushed his clean plate away. Dax fought the impulse to line up the fork and knife Ivers had dropped haphazardly onto the plate. "Hell if I know. One of the scientists on Loki called it a xenomorph, but he also said it was dead, so what's his word worth."

"How did it get aboard your ship?" Dax asked. He couldn't understand how two large creatures had boarded a Navy frigate. They could only have arrived on a shuttle. What were they thinking?

"We brought it aboard. We loaded two of the creatures in shipping containers to return to Earth for study. They looked mummified at that time, about two-thirds the size they are now. They looked like damned fossils. Something brought them out of dormancy. They tore through the ship during the night watch like a shore leave party in a whorehouse. One made it to the engine room and brought us out of Skip Space before we sealed it inside. When the power went and the artificial gravity failed, things got really dicey." He held up a fork and pointed it at Dax. "I have a few choice words for Doctor Rathiri, the director of Station K124 on Loki."

Dax and Andy glanced at each other. Ivers noticed the silent exchange. "What?"

"We lost contact with Loki. Our last contact was two days ago. Maybe they have problems of their own."

Ivers' mien turned grim. "You still headed to Loki?"

"That's the plan. I've got a hold full of supplies for them."

"Good."

Dax stared at the sergeant. "Why are you so interested?"

His dark eyes caught Dax's and held them in his gaze. "They found four of those things."

Dax felt the hairs on the nape of his neck rising. "You think they're awake too."

Ivers nodded. "Seems likely. Whatever they are, a civilian research station isn't equipped to deal with them."

Dax was aghast at what he thought Ivers was suggesting. "You think we are?"

"You've got *Wasp Sting* missiles. I brought an ion disruptor. I imagine you have a few other lethal items stored somewhere onboard. Most independent cargo vessels do. There are a dozen people on Loki. Do you propose just leaving them there?"

"Hell yeah! I intend to drop their supplies at the front door and hightail it back to Kinta as fast as I can. Anyone still alive who wants a lift can join me. I'm not afraid to admit when I'm in over my head. I've already lost one man today." He cast a searing look at Ivers. "I won't lose anyone else."

"Then leave me your missiles," Ivers growled, "and I'll deal with them."

"Yeah, I saw how well the Navy did against those things. You think you can do any better?"

"I've got to try. I killed one of them."

"And got locked in a closet with no air for your trouble," Dax reminded him. "Why didn't you bring a rocket launcher with you?"

"Because, dammit, I ran out of rockets, and I didn't think you wanted to hang around long enough to find more."

The two men glared at each other across the table like two pit bulls sizing each other up. Ivers was a big man – slightly taller than Dax, broader in the shoulder, and more muscular. Dax wasn't afraid of a good brawl, and the sergeant's size didn't intimidate him. Finally, Dax nodded. "You can have my missiles in exchange for the *Abraxas* logs. What was she doing way out here instead of at Sirius B?"

"We received a message from UNNCC dispatching us to Loki ASAP to transport cargo. I thought it odd Central Command would bypass the usual procedures, but I'm just a sergeant, so what do I know. We were there two hours. That in itself was strange. We hadn't seen a port for twelve weeks. Even a research station at the ass-end of nowhere was a change of scenery, but we didn't have time to exchange pleasantries. We picked up the two crates and left. Twelve hours later, the first of those things woke up and busted free. We fought them off for a little over an hour." When he paused, his jaw twitched. He clenched it to stop the tremors. "You saw the results."

"I'm sorry about your buddies, I really am, but all that doesn't matter to me. I understand your need for revenge, but we're civilians. I won't place my crew in danger, at least not in more danger than we're used to dealing with. I've learned my bitter lesson."

Ivers face clouded and he half-rose from his seat. Dax tensed, ready to fight if necessary. "Revenge? You think I'm doing this out of some twisted desire for revenge." He eased back down into his seat. Dax relaxed. "Those creatures aren't native to Loki, something about their chemistry and their body morphology, the scientists said. If they didn't get there on their own, somebody brought them there. You think it's a coincidence the *Huresh* went underground and then disappeared without a trace? Think about it."

"That was two thousand years ago."

"I don't want to take the chance that whoever did in the *Huresh* are still out there somewhere. What if they target Earth? It's my job to find out what happened. Earth needs information."

"You can send a message to your command to inform them of the situation. Maybe they'll send a ship."

"I'll do that, but that could take weeks. The *Abraxas* was closest to the area. That's why the Navy assigned her to the mission. I can't wait. There could be survivors on Loki. Can you just leave them there with those things running loose?"

Dax pounded his fist on the table to emphasize his words. "It's not our job."

Tish placed her hand on his shoulder to calm him. He shrugged it off and stormed from the room. He didn't like anyone questioning his courage, least of all to his face. He was cautious and calculating, but not a coward. He didn't want to leave the personnel of K124 to their fates any more than Ivers did, but he had the safety of his crew to consider. They always came first. They depended on him to make the right calls. Risking all their lives against those creatures seemed like a bad call. He had already made one bad call, and it cost Nate his life. He wouldn't repeat his mistake, not for people he barely knew.

If the xenomorphs on Loki had roused at the same time as the ones on the *Abraxas*, they had been awake for over twenty-four hours. Even pushing *Fortune's Luck* as hard as he dared, they could not reach the station for two more days. The armed crew of the *Abraxas* hadn't lasted seventy-two minutes against the creatures. He held out no hope that unarmed civilians could last seventy-two hours. A rescue attempt was insanity, just what he would expect from the military.

Dax stood on the bridge thinking it would be a simple matter to reverse course. Ivers could do nothing about it. It would cost him his delivery fee, but he could find another job for the *Luck*, one that didn't involve four-meter-tall, man-eating monsters. He stared out the forward view port into the darkness of space and felt the darkness seeping inside, nibbling at his soul. The blue sun in the middle of the screen, Asgard, looked like a cold Siren beckoning him on to disaster. He could see tragedy looming in the *Luck's* future.

His hand hovered over the control console. It hand itched to reset the course. Then, he clenched his fist and dropped it to his side. He would deliver Ivers. Beyond that … he didn't know. He turned to leave. Tish stood at the hatch watching him.

"No one would blame you," she said, guessing what was on his mind, but he saw the doubt in her eyes.

"No one but me," he replied.

"Like you said, it's not our job. Let the Navy handle it."

He sighed. "I've never failed to make a delivery yet."

Her features softened and the corners of her lips lifted slightly in a half-smile. "I thought you protested too much."

"Don't get me wrong. This is strictly a business decision. A cargo ship can't afford to miss a delivery."

"Nate's death wasn't your fault. That thing –"

He cut her off. "The hell it's not. I took him over there. When I saw what condition the ship was in, I should have left right then, but all I saw were credits floating before my eyes for her salvage fee. I made it back. He didn't."

"You saved Ivers."

"It doesn't even out in my books. Nate was a friend. He was crew. Ivers is … Ivers is military."

She moved closer and laid her head against his chest. Her perfume wafted to his nostrils. The way it affected him, he wondered if it was pheromone based, or if danger got his hormones roiling. He wanted to take her right there against the flight console, but she was in a consoling mood of her own. The comfort she offered didn't include sex. Besides, it didn't seem right so soon after Nate's death.

"You've always seen us through," she said.

"It only takes once, baby, to break a winning streak."

Nate's death now had him obsessing about death. He felt an impending doom settling over him. The air on the bridge felt too thick to breathe. His worst fear was something happening to his crew. Now, it was no longer just a crazed obsession. It had started. He would do anything to prevent it. He would not let Ivers draw him into a dangerous situation. He wished he could just space the sergeant through the airlock, but he drew the line at murder, even of the military.

# 5

"I'm worried, Myles. They were supposed to be here long before now, and I can't raise them on the radio."

Cici Adar sat in front of the radio, staring out the window at the bleak landscape outside, hoping for just a whisper of an answer to her repeated calls to the main base. She twirled a lock of her long, auburn hair absentmindedly with two fingers as she spoke. She was worried. Ambrose Rathiri, the by-the-book project director of K124, or K, as the station personnel called it, ran a tight station. The supply shuttle was hours late to pick them up and drop off their replacements, and she had not heard from the station since their regularly scheduled contact yesterday. The ominous radio silence was uncharacteristic and a little disquieting.

"Maybe it's atmospherics. We had a big dust blow last night." He pointed out the window, where the air still swirled with reddish-ocher dust from the last vestiges of the nocturnal dust storm. "Or maybe it's trouble with the shuttle. I wouldn't worry too much about it if they're a few hours late."

The words of her companion, Myles Benson, did not reassure her. "Almost eight hours late," she corrected him.

"We have sufficient work to keep us occupied until they arrive."

Sometimes the easy-going climatologist's British imperturbability irritated her. He seemed to take nothing seriously unless it directly affected his field of study. "Aren't you even curious about the new find they reported?"

"Cici, I'm here to study weather patterns, nothing more. Whatever they find down in the Catacombs does not interest me."

"Well, it does me. I'm a xenobiologist. It intrigues me that in spite of an oxygen-rich environment, Loki has almost no flora or fauna. If the Lokians originated here, how? What happened to their world to change it into a nearly sterile dust ball? If they migrated here from somewhere else, from where did they come?" She pointed to her comp pad where she had been scribbling notes. "I've found nothing out here over the past two weeks except a few microorganisms, same as I found at the ruins. If they've uncovered something new, some previously sealed level, I need to be there."

"Sira Chang can handle it. She's competent enough."

Cici sighed. By his tone, Myles thought she was being jealous and petty. It was no secret that Sira had made moves on her. Cici found the biologist fun and good company, but her compass didn't swing that way. Maybe she was being petty, but she wanted to do her job. She had been away from Earth for nine months, and she had nothing to show for it but her mounting irritation. "Sira is a good biologist, but she has no xeno experience."

"They'll get here. In the meantime, I'll brew some tea."

"Tea!" Cici snapped. "Tea is your answer to everything – slice your hand on a sharp rock, have a cup of tea. Drop a culture dish and ruin two days work, have a cup of tea. Sprain your ankle, have a cup of tea. Lose contact with the main base, have a cup of goddamned tea!" She shouted the last word at him.

Myles remained nonplussed at her outburst. "I'm British. Tea is a panacea for all problems that fretting cannot solve." He cocked his head to one side and smiled at her in that way that annoyed her. "Tea?" he asked.

She swore under her breath, and then replied, "Yes, damn it. I'll take a cup of tea."

She hated giving in so easily, but Myles was right, even if he was a complete ass at times. Whatever the problem, she could nothing about it. K124B or 'KB', as most of the personnel referred to it, was 2,000 kilometers from K124. Driving there across the desert and the shattered terrain in the solar-powered rover would take three days, and it meant camping out at night where the temperatures could drop to -5 Celsius in a few hours, or a dust storm could blow in from nowhere and block the sun for days. The trip in the rover would coop her up with Myles even more than in the cramped quarters of the remote base.

She had been at KB for two weeks, and she missed the camaraderie of the others in the group. Myles, despite his or perhaps because of his perfect manners and lackadaisical attitude, got on her nerves. She was getting antsy and eager to leave. The delay annoyed her.

While he brewed a pot of *Willard's of Chelsea* tea, his favorite brand, she tried the com channel again, this time using the emergency frequency. Myles handed her a steaming cup of dark tea, and she almost dropped it when the speaker squealed.

"This in CG1905 *Fortune's Luck* to Loki Station K124. Over."

"It's the cargo supply ship." She grabbed the mic. "This is K124B. Come in *Fortune's Luck.*" Her heart raced with excitement. The arrival of the supply ship was always a big event, even more so now.

"You're wasting your time," Myles told her.

She shot him a shut-the-hell-up snarl. "Come in *Fortune's Luck*," she repeated.

"This is CG1905 *Fortune's Luck* to K124. Please respond."

"This is K124B. Hello? Hello?" She glanced at Myles. "What's wrong?" she shouted.

He set his tea on the table. "They can't hear you. We don't have enough power to send a signal off planet."

"The frigate *UNN Abraxas* was destroyed by your cargo. We are inbound to you. Our ETA is 36 hours. If you are receiving, please respond."

She tried again. "This is K124B at $112^{0}$24'15" latitude by $64^{0}$15'10" longitude. Our GPS frequency is …"

"I'll try again later, K124. *Fortune's Luck* out."

She slammed the mic against the table. "Damn! They didn't hear me." She stared at Myles, who, for the first time since she had known him, looked flustered. "A Navy ship destroyed? Why didn't they inform us a ship had arrived? My God! What did they find down there?"

Myles removed his glasses and rubbed his temple, as he shook his head. "I don't know. I just don't know. They must have had a reason." When he looked at her, some of his perfect aplomb had faded from his face. "I'll hook the extra solar cells for the rover to the radio and extend the antennae range with some heavy-gauge wire from our supplies. When the cargo ship gets close enough, we can try again."

"How long?"

He shrugged. "I can rig everything in a couple of hours, but it will be thirty-four or thirty-five hours before they can receive us." He saw her frown and added, "They'll have to be out of Skip Space to pick up our signal, but they will pass over us to reach the base. It should be enough."

"My God," she repeated. "What in God's name happened?" She had a horrible thought. "Are they all dead back at the base?"

"Let's not make things darker than they appear," he answered, but she noticed the haunted look in his eyes. "After I rig the extra antennae and solar batteries, we can try the base again. The ionization should have dissipated somewhat by then. We'll get through."

"Thanks," she said, more for his attempt to calm her than for his ingenuity with the radio. She felt a darkness growing deep in her soul that his words could not quell. She knew they were dead. Everyone she had lived and worked with for nine months, except Myles, was dead. They had unearthed something deadly deep down in the lava tubes, the Catacombs, as a few jokingly called the ruins. The joke didn't seem so humorous now.

* * * *

Gregor Pavlovich crouched beside a crumbled pressed-earth wall in the darkness, praying that he was invisible. The creatures were blind, but their sense of hearing and smell more than compensated for their lack of sight. He had spent the last two years at K studying the ruins of the vanished race who called themselves *Huresh*, but everyone at the station called Lokians. Little remained of their writing to explain what fate had befallen them, but the extensive ruins topside and the harsh conditions on the surface had led him to believe that a global catastrophe had driven the survivors underground to inhabit the vast network of lava tubes.

He now believed that assumption had been erroneous. When they had opened up Level 5 and discovered the mummified remains of four large, decidedly alien creatures, small pieces of the puzzle concerning the inhabitants' disappearance began to fit neatly in place.

No one could have believed that the creatures were not dead, were indeed merely hibernating. There was no doubt now. The same creatures that had murdered his colleagues and now hunted him had driven the *Huresh* to extinction – *Ravers*. At least that was the closest translation the linguists could derive from the few scraps of writing that remained. After having seen them in action, Ravers was an apt name for the creatures.

His flashlight grew dimmer as the batteries died. Without it, he would never find his way to the surface in the maze of ruined buildings and toppled walls. Though the creatures could not see the beam of light, he hesitated to use it lest it mark his position more than did his reeking body odor. He had heard nothing for several hours; otherwise, he would not have risked leaving the sanctuary. The tunnels were an oven. He felt as if the stifling heat had wrung every drop of moisture from his body. His brushed his hand across his cracked lips wishing he had a cup of Myles' wretched hot English tea, although even a sip of proper Southern sweet iced tea would taste like sweet nectar. He had cowered in the tunnels for almost two full days without rest, food, or water. If he did not make it to the radio to call for help before the Navy ship Skipped out of range, everyone on the ship would die. If he didn't find water soon, he would die.

His empty stomach growled. The sound did not carry far, but to him it sounded like a raging beast. He crouched lower behind the wall hoping the Ravers had not heard. He waited a full minute but heard nothing. Moving as carefully and as silently as possible, he reached the upper level of the ruins. He avoided looking at the twisted and shattered remains of his friends along the way, cut down by a nightmarish creature before they could fully comprehend what was happening. He tried to quell the terror rising in his chest, but it was like stuffing a cork into an erupting volcano. Each small sound loosened the cork ever more slightly.

He was not a strong man. As a chemist, he was more at home in his lab determining the composition of Lokian metals and native building materials. He was not suited for playing hide-and-seek with two-ton monsters from hell.

He fought a moment of panic when his flashlight flickered. He had sat in the dark as much as possible to conserve batteries, but it was failing. He recognized where he was, the main cavern near the entrance, the Atrium. A mound of fallen rock, rusted metal, and clouded glass lay beneath a hole in the cavern roof where a skylight had once illuminated the city. The gloom of night outside extended into the darkness of the cavern. Dust sifted downward from the last dust storm.

Less than twenty meters away, the open elevator they had installed to avoid the long, dangerous stone ramp the Lokians had installed from the surface entrance rose to the roof inside a steel girder framework. The elevator door was open, inviting. He knew that once he pushed the button, he was committed. The noise would echo throughout the city. If the creatures were close by, they could kill him before the doors closed. If they were on the surface, they would be waiting for him. He would be a snack on a revolving sushi bar conveyor.

He edged along a wall until he was less than five meters from the door; then, rushed across the intervening open space. His heart pounded so loudly he could not hear anything else. He hit the button and held his breath until the door closed. The elevator rose with a loud groan. He released his breath slowly. Through the steel mesh of the cage, he looked out over the cavernous space that marked the outermost edges of the Lokian city. Movement in the shadows caught his eye, but it was too far away to reach him.

Twenty meters up, the elevator shuddered, stopped for a moment, and then began climbing again. "Loose cable," he whispered. Ten meters more, and the elevator stopped. This time, it did not move again. The shudders became rhythmic, the sound of wrenching metal louder. A deafening roar above him almost shattered his eardrums. Something heavy landed on the elevator roof. It swung like a pendulum inside the open shaft. With a sound like ripping paper, three long gouges appeared on one side of the elevator cage. He lunged to the far side, as long claws pulled the rip wider. His heart froze, as he looked into the face of death incarnate.

The Raver's nasal flaps fluttered as it caught Gregor's scent. The mouth opened, revealing hundreds of 300-centimeter-long teeth. Thick saliva dripped from its lipless mouth and splashed onto the elevator's metal floor. The creature's overpowering breath reeked of rotten flesh.

The door of the elevator opened. Gregor stared out into space. He knew he was a dead man. His last decision would be how he met his death. He decided that plunging to his death would be preferable to sharing the ghastly fate of his colleagues. He lunged for the door.

He did not make it. The creature moved too quickly. Halfway out the door, a long claw skewered him through the back. He dangled outside the car, high above the ground, impaled on an ebony spike. He looked down at the claw protruding from his chest amid a fine spray of blood. He remembered insects he had pinned to display boards in a similar manner as an inquisitive teenager and regretted his actions. *At least*, he thought, *I consigned them to the kill jar beforehand.* The intense pain faded quickly, leaving only a dull ache and shortness of breath. He grew inexplicably cold. He almost enjoyed the absence of the ubiquitous heat. He barely heard the thunderous roar emerge from the Raver's throat, as the creature yanked him back inside the elevator car. He looked up at the rows of black teeth descending on him and closed his eyes. Death came quickly after that.

The creature, engineered to kill, instinctively knew no more of the enemy remained in the vicinity. It joined its brother and returned to the dark lower levels where it had spent two thousand years in hibernation. This time, it would not sleep. It would wait. It knew more of the enemy would soon come, and it could slake its blood thirst once again.

# 6

Dax pushed *Fortune's Luck's* worn engines as hard as he dared to extract every erg of energy. He did not think it proper to be late for his own funeral.

"That's it," he said aloud to the empty engine room. He pocketed a magnetic induction wrench and wiped his hands on his greasy coverall as if symbolically wiping them of the entire affair. "If I open the governor a millimeter more, the power coupling relays will fry, and we'll be stuck out here until someone finds us. I saved us a few hours. I hope it's enough to make a difference."

He usually didn't talk to himself, but Nate's absence made the engine room seem dark and empty. It was a sad day when even his own voice didn't cheer him. He patted the starboard engine housing as he had witnessed Nate do so many times in the past. The engine room bore traces of Nate everywhere from an extra coverall hanging from a hook by the door to a trade magazine on his desk with the page of an article folded over. The coffee mug with his name emblazoned on it still sat atop his desk, half-filled with long cold coffee. He could smell Nate's aftershave mixed with the odor of lube oil and ozone from the coils.

Nate did not share his OCD, but every tool was stored in its proper place, and he had labeled every cabinet and drawer with its contents. The engine room was always neat and tidy. The Skip Drives in the three nacelles were so clean a surgeon could perform an operation with no risk of contamination.

"She'll need some serious downtime to replace the relays when we get back to port. I'm sure you could have done a better job of it." He shook his head. "How could I let Ivers convince me that a lone Marine sergeant and a cargo ship's crew could accomplish what a Navy frigate couldn't? No matter how much he trains them, they won't be Marines."

Having made his decision to go to Loki, however reluctantly, Dax had allowed Sergeant Ivers to instruct his crew in the basics of weapons handling. If more of the creatures existed on Loki, they would need their new skills to survive. He, Nate, and Plia were the only members of the crew with any experience with weapons, and that was limited to occasional practice at the range or flashing a pistol when negotiations with black-market clients fell apart.

"We're just delivering Ivers, picking up any survivors, and lifting off that dirt ball. He can do the dirty work. We'll drop back down and pick him up when he's finished, if he's still alive."

Said aloud, his words rang hollow to him and sounded equally unconvincing. Was he making another big mistake? Just as he removed his cap to scratch that familiar itch in his scalp, the door to the engine room creaked open. *Needs some oil*, he thought, as he added it to his mental repair list. *I'll get to it later.* Tish stood there wearing shorts and a sweat-stained T-shirt, wiping her face with a towel. She did not look happy.

"Ivers is a real bastard," she announced, groaning.

Dax grinned at her discomfort while noting her hard nipples through the shirt's thin material. *Keep your mind on the job.* "Working you hard?"

She made a lion snarl face and swiped one hand at him with fingers curled like a lion's claw. "You don't want to piss me off now that I know how to fire a laser rifle."

"You were dangerous enough before, especially in the sack."

Her features softened. "I'm sorry I talked you into this," she said. Her voice held a note of contrition Dax had never heard from her before. Like him, her motto was '*Live life, take no prisoners, and never apologize*'. He wondered what had brought about this catharsis in her.

"You didn't talk me into anything. I still have some moral scruples rolling around in that big hollow spot most people call a heart. Not many, but a few."

She edged closer to him. Even the smell of her perspiration was enticing, but by the look on her face, Dax knew sex wasn't on her mind.

"What … what did it look like?" she asked. Her voice held equal amounts of anticipation and concern.

He knew what she meant. The creatures had been at the forefront of everyone's mind, especially his. The suit camera video never clearly showed the creature. For that, they should be grateful. "Like a demon from hell," he replied with conviction.

"You don't think anyone's still alive on Loki, do you?"

He didn't mind stretching the truth when the need arose, or when it suited his purpose, but he had never outright lied to her. He wouldn't start now. "No. I saw what it did to a ship full of trained, armed sailors and Marines. We can't raise Loki on the com." He shook his head. "It doesn't look good for them."

"What are they?"

He shuddered inwardly as an image of the dead creature flashed through his mind. He had given the creatures considerable thought. "Picture a monster from your worst nightmare and double its size. It had black scales like pointy armor plates and claws as sharp as diamond drill bits. Laser didn't seem to do much damage. It can breathe vacuum and survive in deep space cold. According to Ivers, it can hibernate for thousands of years. If I wanted to invent an organic killing machine, it would look like those creatures."

Her mouth opened and closed a couple of times in surprise. "You think they're artificial, that someone *made* them?"

He watched the color drain from her face and realized he had gone too far. Dangerous wild creatures were difficult enough to comprehend. Creatures deliberately manufactured by an alien race were beyond the pale. "I don't know what I think anymore. I'm just rambling to keep from thinking about them."

"And Nate," she added. "We all loved him, Dax. We'll all miss him."

Her words brought him no comfort and only reinforced his guilt. "But we didn't all kill him. I did."

Ivers walked in with an unlit cigar dangling from the corner of his mouth. He wore a pair of pants and T-shirt that Dax had loaned him while his clothing went through the laundry unit. The pants fit, but the shirt was tight in the chest and arms. Unlike Tish, he had not broken a sweat. He leaned against the bulkhead and crossed his arms over his chest. If the intimacy between Dax and Tish bothered him, he said nothing.

"Can you mount wheels on your missile pod for transport?"

"Sure. Actually, we have a remote-controlled tracked sledge for transporting heavy freight over rough terrain. I think Plia can break it out of storage and attach the pod without too much difficulty. I'll get her to add a seat. Does the weapons pod need to articulate?"

Ivers removed the cigar, pointed it at Dax, and grinned. "Now, that's what I'm talking about. Yeah, if I can aim the pod quickly, it would make things easier."

"Plia can have it ready in a couple of hours." He looked at Tish. "Can you help her?"

She sighed, nodded, and slipped away from him. "Shower first though. I stink."

"I've done all I can with the engines," he told Ivers. "This ship is older than me and twice as temperamental. You're really going after those things, aren't you?"

"Damn right I am. You saw what they're capable of. What if the fuckers breed? We search for survivors first, but I'm not leaving until they're all dead – real dead, not just hibernating."

"I won't take my crew down into the lava tubes. We check out the base; then we pull back to the ship. You and I both know that we won't find anyone alive in the tunnels, not if those things are running around loose."

Ivers raised an eyebrow and chewed on his cigar. "Suit yourself. You can leave if you feel you must. Just don't forget to send a message to a Navy outpost to come pick me up, or bury my body, whichever is appropriate," he added.

Dax couldn't disparage Ivers' courage, but he did doubt his wisdom. "Too bad you didn't bring another nuke."

"Yeah, I wasn't thinking far enough ahead of the game. I let that thing get to me."

Ivers' cavalier attitude outraged Dax. "Game?" he snapped. "You think this is a game? Did Nate die because of a stupid game?"

"All wars are a game, Captain Wyldd – strategy, attack, defense, move, countermove..." He stared pointedly at Dax. "Manipulation of forces. You play poker? The goal is to walk away from the table with all the chips."

"Even a good player can't win every hand. Luck plays a part in the deal of the cards, hence the name of my ship, *Fortune's Luck*."

"You make your own luck. It's not the single game that counts; it's the sum total. You win if you get up more times than they knock you down."

"My crew is good at their jobs, but they're not soldiers, or chess pieces, or poker cards. I have two women on my crew." He knew he was just making excuses with the latter. Tish was as tough as they came, and Plia was as hard as cold-rolled steel. She could probably take him down in a one-on-one match.

"I've seen some hard-ass women grunts in the Corp." Ivers pushed himself from the bulkhead and stood straight. "But I'm not building an army. I'll do all the dirty work. I just think it's important your people have a fighting chance."

Dax softened his stance and allowed a little to tension drain from his body. *Maybe if Nate had a fighting chance, he would still be alive.* "I'm responsible for them."

"Just get me down there and ferry any survivors off planet. That's all I ask."

He turned and left before Dax could form a reply. He didn't know what he would have said. He had placed their lives in danger on numerous occasions during shady black-market deals for a few under-the-table credits. Was what Ivers proposed any worse? Certainly, the stakes were higher, but dead was dead, whether for a noble cause or a purely mercenary one. Were the lives of strangers worth the lives of his crew?

He slammed his fist against the engine housing. "Some days it sucks to be me."

* * * *

*Fortune's Luck* emerged from Skip Space a safe 120,000 kilometers from Loki. Loki's smaller sister moon, Thor, a frozen snowball world, occluded most of Loki's face. The system's star, blue-white Asgard, shone through gas giant Odin's rings like the sun through Venetian blinds, casting a series of parallel shadows over both worlds. It was a spectacular sight; one Dax didn't have time to enjoy. As *Fortune's Luck* rounded Thor, Loki came fully into view. A raging dust storm swept southward across a third of the desert world's northern hemisphere. Dax was glad the storm had already passed through K124's location. He would not want to attempt a landing during such a maelstrom.

Andy sat beside him in the co-pilot's seat, but Dax handled the controls. Landing on Loki would be tricky with sudden wind shears and downbursts created by convections on the hot surface funneled down long, winding canyons, and broken by broad mesas. Ivers, chewing on another cigar, sat in one of the passenger seats staring out the forward view screen. Dax had not seen Ivers light any of his cigars in the two days he had been aboard the *Luck*. He noticed how tightly the Marine sergeant gripped the armrest. This was Ivers second visit to Loki in a week, and his inner turmoil marked his face with deep furrows and tightly stretched lips.

"Romeo, did you send another message to the Navy?"

"I sent the first right after we Skipped, a tachyon burst to the nearest relay beacon with all the info you gave me, including the sergeant's helmet cam vid." He glanced at Ivers. "That was some gnarly shit by the way. By the time it passes down the line of relay beacons, it should reach Kinta Station sometime today. Their transmitter is powerful enough to send a direct signal to U.N. Command. I'll send another now, but it will have to go through the same channels." He glanced at Ivers. "I wouldn't count on any help for at least a week."

Ivers grunted.

"Okay. Send out an update that we're landing at Station K124 to search for survivors."

"Add this priority code," Ivers said, "Delta Fox Charlie *Arrowhead,* Ivers, C.J., 1662541."

Dax cocked his head to one side. "What's that?"

"The call sign for Hostile Alien Contact. Maybe it will light a fire under their ass."

"Add it," he told Romeo.

The descent into Loki's atmosphere was worse than Dax remembered. The raging upper-level winds buffeted the ship like a leaf in a summer gale, slamming the craft from side to side or grabbing it by the nose and twisting it until the tail dropped. Dax fought the controls to keep the craft right side up, losing altitude as fast as he dared. The seat's restraining harness bit into his shoulder, as the craft bucked and heaved. He kept one eye on the scanners to avoid the worst microbursts. He longed to plug in his earbuds and listen to some blues to ease the tension, but he needed to keep an ear open as Andy called out wind vectors and altitudes. The five-minute descent seemed like thirty, as he worked his hands to reduce the cramps from gripping the controls.

Once they reached the lower atmosphere, the ride became smoother, but navigating around rising thermals still required a hands-on approach. He didn't trust the automatic pilot's computations as much as he did his instincts. It was like dodging trees in a forest at night while running full speed. Dust thrown up by the trailing edge of the storm pelted the view screen and the extended airfoils, sounding like hail.

"This is going to screw up my new paint job," he joked.

At 2,000 meters, he reduced power to slow the ship and followed a deep, winding canyon to the outpost. The control yoke picked up a slight vibration. He pushed the yoke forward slightly for a little added power. The vibration vanished.

"Anything from the station?" Dax asked Romeo.

"I'm picking up a faint ground signal between us and the station. It sounds like landing coordinates."

"That would be 'KB,' the outpost research station about 2,000 clicks from K124," Ivers said. "There are usually two scientists there on rotation."

"Yeah, I know," Dax said. "I've never been there, but I suppose we should set down there first and pick them up. Luigi, send them a message as soon as we're close enough for them to receive."

Ivers objected. “They can wait. We need to reach K124 ASAP.”

“I’m not leaving two people waiting in the middle of nowhere. They might have some useful intel, and I don’t like backtracking.”

“They wouldn’t know anything. We …”

Dax stopped him. “My ship, my rules.” He didn’t know if saving two lives could ever make up for wasting Nate’s, but Nate would insist he do it.

Ivers scowled at him but said nothing. Dax tried to suppress a smile at the sergeant’s restraint.

“I got through,” Romeo said, tapping his earphone. Then, he frowned. “They have a lot of questions.”

“Don’t waste time explaining. Inform them we’re dropping down to pick them up and to be ready; then, cut communications.”

Ahead, Dax spotted the small white dome of KB sitting on the edge of the two-kilometers-deep canyon they had been following, nestled into a small cleft in the reddish-brown bluff to block the frequent desert winds. Landing *Fortune’s Luck* would be tricky in a space barely wide enough to accommodate the station’s small shuttle, but he did not like the idea of landing on a more open mesa and hiking in, not with the possibility of more monsters.

“Use the thrusters to keep her tail pointed away from the rim of the canyon while I set her down,” he told Andy. “I don’t want her to slide over the edge.”

Ivers leaned forward in his seat intent on watching the landing. Dax wondered if the sergeant had any piloting experience, but then figured a good Marine sergeant would be a Jack-of-all trades. Dax took a deep breath and released it slowly as he powered down the engines. The ship settled easily onto the ledge and remained stationary. He turned to Ivers.

“I want you to come with me in case those things made it this far.”

“We might not have to go anywhere. Look.” Ivers pointed out the forward view screen to a man and a woman exiting the station. The woman raced toward the ship. The man followed at a more leisurely pace.

Romeo looked out the viewport and smiled. “She’s hot.”

“Keep it in your pants, Romeo,” Dax said.

Dax went to meet them at the airlock. There was no need to cycle through the lock, so he opened both the outer and inner doors. He sealed the outer door as soon as they were both inside. He noted the woman went to Ivers first, drawn by his uniform.

"What happened at K?" she asked. "We haven't had any word from them in two days."

Dax answered her question even though she had directed it at Ivers. "We don't know. They're not answering."

She ignored Dax. "You were on the *Abraxas*?" she asked of Ivers.

He nodded.

"Are they really …?"

"Dead? Yes, all of them."

She paled visibly and shook her head in disbelief. "I don't understand."

The man seemed to know Dax was the ship's captain. He offered his hand. Dax recognized him because of his glasses, an oddity in an age of easy eye corrective procedures, but couldn't recall his name. "I'm Myles Benson," the man prompted, "climatologist. This is Cici Adar, xenobiologist. Thank you for coming. As you might have guessed, we are understandably curious and somewhat apprehensive about what has happened to our friends."

Dax shook his hand. "Later. Grab a seat and strap in. We're lifting off in one minute."

"But you can't," Cici objected. "Our notes. Our equipment. You'll have to wait a few minutes while we retrieve them."

"We're not waiting for anything. Now, strap in."

"I refuse –"

Dax hit the panel, sealing the inner airlock door. "Take off will be rough. If I were you, I would find a seat." He nodded to her wrist comp. "I suggest you start downloading everything you can before we get out of range."

She glared at him but began frantically punching at her wrist comp. Dax ignored her, brushed past her, and turned to head to the bridge.

"Come on, Cici," Myles said, leading her to the wardroom. "We can pick up the equipment later."

He met Tish in the corridor, frowning at him. She had overheard the conversation. "That could have gone smoother," she said, following him to the bridge.

Dax didn't need a lecture from her on his lack of social skills. Every minute on the ground made him nervous. "I don't have time for hysterics."

Tish barked a short, harsh laugh of derision. "She wasn't hysterical; she was pissed. You do that to people, you know."

"It comes with the job. Go make sure she doesn't bounce around my ship and damage anything. Thirty seconds to lift off."

He strapped into his seat, hoping everyone else had settled in. Taking off would be riskier than landing. If he went straight up hard and fast, the cross winds rising from the canyon could slam the ship into the bluff. If he lifted off too slowly, the ship could slide over the edge of the cliff and flip over. Ivers slipped into the seat behind him.

"Hold onto your lunch, Sergeant," he warned. "Andy, be ready to retract the landing gear as soon as we clear the surface."

The safest way to lift off was the most dangerous, but he trusted his engines and his instincts. He powered up the vertical thrusters and slid the ship over the cliff. It dropped like a rock. The ground rushed up to meet them at a dizzying rate. The ship's artificial gravity couldn't compensate for the nosedive. The pressure pressed Dax back into his seat. He forced his arm forward and pushed the main engines to full throttle. The narrow airfoils bit into the air, turning the falling craft into an awkward glider. The nose rose reluctantly. He could almost hear Ivers' teeth grinding.

One-hundred-sixty meters from the ground, the ship leveled off and shot down the canyon, raising a trailing cloud of dust. The walls of the narrow canyon shot by much closer than Dax had anticipated. He glanced at Andy, who had his eyes closed, and grinned. He lifted the ship until it cleared the canyon rim before cutting the vertical thrusters. The maneuver burned a lot of fuel, but it was better than scraping *Fortune's Luck's* sides against the bluff or winding up a pile of smoking wreckage at the bottom of the canyon. Besides, he wanted to give Ivers a ride to remember.

"You're one crazy son of a bitch," Ivers said, but his voice held a note of respect.

"Sometimes you have to make gravity work for you." He glanced back over his shoulder. "I didn't hear any screaming from our passengers. I guess they found a seat."

Ivers unharnessed and left the bridge to speak with Cici Adar and Myles Benson. Dax was glad to let him inform the pair about the creatures unearthed at K124. They might believe a Marine sergeant, whereas they would probably just call him crazy.

"Still nothing from the station?" he asked Romeo, who still appeared a little queasy from the dramatic lift-off. Beads of sweat from his forehead rolled unchecked down his thin cheeks.

"Uh-uh. Not a thing, not even a homing beacon."

Dax frowned. That meant the station had no power. Evening had fallen at the station, which would complicate any rescue operation. The knot in the pit of his stomach balled tighter, reminding him of his doubt that anyone had survived. It had been seventy-two hours since the *UNN Abraxas* had left Loki, fifty-six since anyone had heard from the station. Given the ferocity of the creature that he had seen aboard the *Abraxas* and the amount of damage to the ship, the alien ruins down in the lava tubes would have become a slaughterhouse.

He understood Ivers' need to kill the creatures, though he considered it a foolhardy move. They could simply wait for a Navy ship to arrive within the week and nuke the entire planet if necessary. He didn't see what a single Marine could do but die horribly, a fate he personally strove to avoid.

Dax turned as Cici Adar burst onto the bridge. *What now*? He prepared for an argument.

"Captain, I apologize for my earlier rude behavior." Dax unclenched his jaw in surprise. "Sergeant Ivers explained the situation to me."

He wondered what Ivers had told her to produce such a dramatic change in her demeanor. He relaxed. "No problem. I just didn't have time for conversation."

"The sergeant's description of the creatures defies logic. They cannot be native to this world."

"Wherever they came from, Doctor Adar, they've been hibernating down in those tunnels a long time. Why did it take so long to find them?"

"Cici, please," she offered. "There are too many doctors at K124." She continued, "It's like a maze down there. Lava tubes run in every direction both vertically and horizontally. It looks as if the *Huresh* deliberately sealed certain tunnels as they abandoned them. The peculiar thing is that they abandoned them from the surface downward, as if ..."

"As if they were trying to keep something out. It looks like they failed."

"Doctor Rathiri was overseeing the excavation of a new level when I left, Level 5. The *Huresh* were a technologically advanced society. At the peak of their civilization, they had over twenty cities scattered across the world; not many, I grant you, but Loki is, after all, a moon and has limited natural resources." To Dax, she sounded as if she were apologizing for the *Huresh's* failure to survive. "They made use of advanced metal alloys and solar energy. Then, something drove them underground. We had believed the cause was some kind of global catastrophe, but now ... Their sub-surface dwellings became more primitive the deeper we went, but they constructed many spaces with metal rooms set into the native rock. We thought they might serve a religious purpose, but with these creatures ... I suspect now that they were sanctuaries. My colleagues could be there."

"What kind of weapons did the station personnel have?"

Cici looked at him aghast. Seizing upon his use of the past tense, she chided, "Did? Don't you mean does? We have no weapons. We are a scientific expedition. There are no living creatures on this world. We did not think we would have need of weapons. We considered our biggest threat someone becoming mentally unbalanced due to the isolation getting their hands on a weapon."

Dax shook his head. He couldn't understand people who thought not having weapons somehow kept them safer, as if knives or rocks wouldn't serve nicely as killing implements in a pinch. He had never shot anyone, but he damned well had rather kill someone shooting at him than die over a misguided principle.

"Did the station have vehicles, I mean besides the shuttle? I remember seeing a couple of ATVs last time I was there. In fact, spare tires are part of the cargo I'm delivering."

"There are two tracked vans for extended outings and four smaller ATVs." Her eyes lit up with hope. "Do you think they might have escaped?" She slumped her shoulders and looked crestfallen. "No, the vans have radios. They could have contacted us even if they did not have the range to contact your ship."

"No use speculating yourself into a tizzy. We'll be there in half an hour and see for ourselves."

She reached out, touched his shoulder, and grinned. "Captain, I don't think I have ever been in a tizzy, but I am worried about my friends."

He reminded himself that although he barely knew them from his irregular visits lasting two days at most, she had lived among them for almost a year. To him, they were just faces he could scarcely recall. To her, they were friends and colleagues.

"If they're alive, we'll bring them home."

"If?" she repeated.

He took a good look at her for the first time. Slim with large breasts, long auburn hair, and green eyes, she would have been attractive anywhere. On a small outpost twenty light years from Earth, she would have been Queen of the Ball. It was too bad she hadn't transferred to Loki on the *Luck*. Five weeks aboard ship would have been time to get to know her better, but the personnel preferred ships with a little more luxury than the *Luck* could provide.

"We can hope," he said. That was as much commitment he was willing to make on their survival.

He was still giving her the once-over when Tish appeared at the bridge door. She stopped when she saw Cici's hand resting on Dax's shoulder. Her face clouded briefly, but she quickly shrugged it off. Dax had never seen her jealous and hoped the incident didn't cause a rift between them. Cici was an extraordinarily good-looking woman, but he shied away from intellectuals. He preferred women who could handle the rigors of life in a cargo ship, like Tish, and Tish was far from a slouch in the brains department. Since they had become sexual partners, he had followed a 'look-but-don't-touch' policy with other women that seemed acceptable to her, or at least she had not overtly dissuaded him. Even after two years, he still had trouble reading her.

"Are you really going to allow the sergeant to go down into the tunnels alone?" Cici asked.

"I don't think I can stop him. Those military types don't put much store in civilian advice. Besides, we would only get in the way of his monster hunt."

Cici backed away a step and stared at Dax. "I just told you my friends could be hiding in one of the sealed rooms down there. We have to find them."

"Look, that thing ripped through a frigate's cargo hatch. If one attacks my ship, we're stuck here. If your people aren't where we can get to them quickly, we can't wait. The longer we're on the surface, the more danger we're in."

"Coward!" she flung at him.

Her calling him a coward stung, but not enough to change his mind. "I may be, but I won't face those creatures with a useless laser rifle, not for people who are dead already."

"You don't know that," she snapped.

Dax could see it was time for the harsh truth. "Face the facts. The moment those two creatures came out of hibernation, your friends were dead."

"You don't know that they did come out of hibernation. We don't know what awakened the two creatures on the *Abraxas*."

"True, but we've had no contact with the station for three days," he pointed out. "I don't believe in coincidences."

"They have no power. It could be a problem with the solar array."

"They have a backup generator. They also have a shuttle. No, there's only one reason for going dark; they're dead."

Cici sobbed and ran from the bridge.

Tish had watched the exchange. She shook her head. "You were pretty hard on her, Dax."

"She needs to face reality."

"You know, sometimes you can be a real bastard."

"It comes with the captain's chair. My ship, my crew, my client – that's the proper pecking order; the one that keeps us in business. Everything else is a distant fourth. Without *Fortune's Luck*, we're ground-pounders. In this case, that would make us monster chow." He didn't know why he bothered explaining. He usually didn't. They were crew and followed orders. He accepted their input on matters, but the final decision had always been his. Maybe it was because Cici had called him a coward, and Tish looked as though she believed her.

"Look, I'm not completely heartless; I agreed to attempt a rescue, but I am practical. You witnessed an entire U.N. Navy frigate and its slaughtered crew vaporized because of two of those creatures. I needn't remind you that Nate was on that ship as well. We know the research personnel down there found at least two more. What if there are dozens? Four of the things didn't drive the Lokians underground. They could be prowling the surface like a pack of stray dogs. Ivers is a grunt – point him at the enemy and stand back, but he's in way over his head. He's all GI Joe Gung Ho for revenge, acting on instinct, not rational thought. I won't let him take us down with him. We drop down, do a quick search of the station, and wait for the Navy to arrive. Let them do the dirty work."

She shook her head. "I used to respect you. I thought you were hard because you thought it brought you respect – the tough cargo captain image. Now ..."

Her barb stung. To retaliate, he steeled his voice and said, "We can talk about hardness after we gather up the pieces of bodies down there and stow them in cold storage. In the meantime, do your job and help Plia get the transport ready for Ivers."

He turned away from her and studied the controls. She hesitated before leaving the bridge. He hated putting her in her place, but he didn't have time for arguments. He glanced at Andy. "What?" Andy shook his head and glanced away. *Great! I've alienated my entire crew. What more can go wrong?*

"I got a brief contact on a shortwave band," Romeo announced. "I think it's a hand-held radio set on an emergency frequency. That takes less power than a voice transmission."

Was he wrong about survivors? "Where did it originate? Please tell me the station."

Romeo quickly checked coordinates against a satellite image map of the base. "From inside one of the ventilator shafts, maybe three levels down in the lava tube network."

*Give me a frigging break!* "You're sure?"

"Yes. It's too weak to be a surface signal."

Dax slapped the control stick. The ship shuddered as the gyros struggled to keep her level. He had no choice now. Someone was alive, or had been recently enough that the radio's batteries weren't dead. They would have to go in and see. "Can we reach them through the ventilator shaft?"

"Too narrow. It's barely over a meter wide with 90-degree turns. It's a miracle the signal made it out at all."

"Yeah, a real miracle," Dax replied. *One that's going to kill us all.*

# 7

Station K124 was a collection of three formerly white but now faded, wind-scoured, prefabricated domes and several outbuildings set among the weathered ruins of an ancient *Huresh* city, possibly the last inhabited city before the population moved underground. The three outbuildings were in a neat row, as were two of the domes. The third dome sat askew because of a crumbling wall. Every time Dax saw it, he wanted to bulldoze the wall and align the dome with the others. He didn't think the archaeologists would go along with that.

The city sat at the convergence of what had once been two mighty continent-spanning rivers, but were now wide dry canyons. The ruins extended for kilometers into the desert before the encroaching sand swallowed them. Estimates had placed the city's population at 200,000, while the estimated population for the underground dwellings was less than 25,000. What had happened to them in the meantime? Considering what he had learned over the last few days, Dax preferred not to think about it.

The first thing he noticed was the small shuttle on the concrete landing pad adjacent to the building that served as a motor pool. The station's personnel had not left that way. Though it was night, he saw no lights, no signs of life. The station looked as deserted as the city they had come to study. The landing pad for supply ships and larger shuttles was a cleared area two kilometers from the buildings. A square of blinking landing lights usually outlined the pad. It was as dark as the surrounding countryside. Dax ignored the larger landing pad and positioned the ship over the smaller landing pad adjacent to the motor pool. Walking two kilometers in the dark with the possibility of the xenomorphs lurking about seemed too risky.

Avoiding the station's com antenna, assortment of weather instrument masts, and two flagpoles bearing the weathered, sandblasted U.N. flag and the faded National Geographical Society standard, he eased the ship as close to the shuttle as he dared. The engines kicked up a cloud of dust that obscured everything around them. Cutting the engines, he waited for the dust to settle. He hoped to see someone exit one of the buildings, attracted by the noise, some sign that survivors were present, but no one came to greet them.

At his request, the crew and passengers gathered in the wardroom. Cici and Myles were eager to check on their friends, but Dax insisted they wait before he unsealed the hatch. He didn't want anyone running around conducting a haphazard search or getting lost. He had developed a plan of action and intended to see that they followed it.

"We'll inspect each building. In and out fast." He slapped the back of one hand into the palm of his other hand to emphasize his words. "Search for survivors. If you find any, bring them back here. No side trips, no souvenirs, no boxes of notes. Don't worry about bodies. We don't have time for burials." He let that last sink in before continuing.

"It looks as if someone might be alive on Level 3." Before anyone could speak, he said, "We go there after we search the buildings. We go in through the old entrance using the ATVs for mobility."

"The elevator is faster than the ATVs," Cici suggested.

"It also holds only four people. We don't split up underground. We all go armed and we stay together."

Cici was indignant at his directive. "I refuse to carry a weapon," she said. "It's against my –"

Dax didn't allow her to finish. "I don't care. No weapon, no need for you to go with us. You can wait on the ship." He glared at her until she sat back in silence.

"I'll remain with you until you effect a successful rescue," Ivers said. "Then, I'm going hunting."

"With my missiles," Dax reminded him. "I'll send the Navy a bill later. Ivers, you and I will check that the shuttle is operational. When we complete our part of this mission, I'm heading for orbit. If you make it out alive, you can use the shuttle. Give me a signal, and I'll pick you up. Otherwise, in twelve hours, I'm breaking orbit and Skipping to Kinta Station."

"Fair enough." Ivers' tone said just the opposite.

"Yeah, I think so."

Dax was glad the hard look Ivers shot at him wasn't bullets. He was surprised Ivers didn't take a swing at him. He couldn't blame him if he did. Dax rode the Marine sergeant because he was mad, and Ivers was a handy target on which he could vent his frustration. Ivers understood the situation, grasped that he stood little chance of success alone. Ivers needed help, but Dax didn't like the dismal odds. If Cici or Myles wanted to hang around, that was their privilege, though he doubted either would be of much use to Ivers. He wouldn't risk any more of his crew's lives. Killing a couple of xenomorph monsters wasn't high on his to-do list.

He handed out weapons in the cargo bay. Most were high-velocity .338 caliber rifles pilfered from a shipment bound for a hunting reserve world. Three were laser rifles, including the one he had taken from the *Abraxas,* illegal in civilian hands, but Dax didn't think anyone would object. Ivers had his ion disruptor, a high-energy pulse laser. Dax did not forget his .40 caliber pistol. After double-checking to see that everyone was properly armed, he opened the outer hatch. Hot, dusty air billowed in carrying with it a bitter, coppery taste that reminded him of rust. *Or blood.*

Except for the low moan of the wind, the night was eerily silent. Beyond the range of the ship's exterior floodlights, the buildings stood in shadows. The spaces between buildings were darker pools of night hiding anything he could imagine. He paused at the open door, licking his suddenly dry lips, wondering if it was too late to back out. He resisted the urge to scratch his head in front of his crew so as not to betray his trepidation.

"Okay. Andy, Tish, and Romeo – you take the main building. Stay together. Each team has a walkie-talkie. Use it if you find anyone or anything. Plia, you take Myles and Cici and check out the two other domes. The sergeant and I will check the outbuildings, the ATVs, and the shuttle. We all meet in front of the main building in twenty minutes. Fire three shots if you run into serious trouble." He looked at Tish and smiled. "Try not to shoot anyone." She flashed a quick grin that could not disguise her unease.

If he were a praying man, he would have said a quick prayer for them. They were walking into possible danger, and he had placed them there. The team at K124 meant nothing to him personally, but they were clients, and he owed them the same degree of loyalty he extended to other clients. The extent of that loyalty was yet to be determined. He had found two survivors already. That was more than he expected. There existed the probability of at least one more. He had to attempt to rescue them.

He set his walkie-talkie set to the station's frequency but heard only static. *Okay, the hard way it is then.* He felt as if he were walking into a lion's den smelling like blood-rare roast beef. He watched the other teams walk across the landing pad to their respective buildings before joining Ivers. The first building they came to was a small supply shed. Dax almost shot a shovel that fell across his foot as he opened the door. He glared at Ivers' grin.

"Don't you say a word," he warned.

The next building contained crates of artifacts labeled for destinations on Earth, his return trip freight. He would not be taking it. The motor pool's double sliding doors were open and rattled in the gusts of wind. Ivers stood in the open doorway shining his light inside.

"Clear," he said after a few moments and continued deeper into the building. Dax followed him. The last time he had been inside, the motor pool was a refuge from the inescapable heat. All the buildings were air-conditioned. Without power, the building had reverted to outside nighttime ambient temperature, which was only slightly less oppressive the heat of the day. He wiped sweat from his brow with the back of his hand.

The air smelled of dust, battery acid, and sawdust, the latter from a desk someone was constructing from used wooden pallets. Dax admired the workmanship. The builder cut and joined short pieces of wood for a blend of wood grains and textures that gave the desk a professional look. For a scientist, the builder had an artist's heart.

The space contained a long workbench along one wall, drums of fuel and oil in a barrel rack, and a hoist for maintenance. Two solar-powered, tracked vans sat at a charging station on one side of the building, and four ATVs aligned in a neat row covered the opposite wall. He checked the ATVs, and found three of them powered up and ready to go.

"I'll check the shuttle," he said to Ivers, as Ivers continued to prowl around the rear of the motor pool. Finally, satisfied, Ivers followed him to the shuttle and stood guard where he could watch Dax as he ran a pre-fight check. A few minutes later, Dax stepped out of the shuttle grinning. "Someone knows their stuff. The shuttle is in excellent shape." He looked at Ivers. "I set the com to *Fortune's Luck's* frequency."

Ivers nodded.

Dax's walkie-talkie crackled. "Dax, this is Andy."

"Come in, Andy."

"It looks as if one of the creatures reached the surface. The main building's rear door and half the wall are missing. The interior is a shambles. The com room looks as if a tornado hit it. Now we know why they couldn't respond to our message. We found splotches of blood but no bodies."

He expected as much. They would find no one alive on the surface. The xenomorphs had revived. That put a new, deadlier spin on things. "Okay, everyone to the rendezvous. Now!"

By the time they reached the main building, both of the other teams had already gathered out front. Andy's face was grim. "Whatever happened here happened fast."

"Same in the living quarters and the labs," Plia added. "No packing. A couple of the computers were powered up, but the batteries had died."

"They could have left a message," Cici said. "We should search the buildings again."

"No time," Dax reminded her. "They didn't have time for notes. If it wasn't for the signal we picked up, I'd pull out of here now." Cici scowled at him. Even Tish looked disappointed. "As it is, I think it's a fool's errand, but we'll go down there anyway to check out the signal." He directed his next comment to Cici. "We're not going exploring. We're not going to stand around yelling out people's names. In and out. Simple, clean, and fast. Andy drives one ATV, Plia and I will take the other two. Ivers will control the tracked sledge with his surprise package. We go in together with the spotlights covering as much of the perimeter as they can. Barring no unwelcomed company, we go straight to Level Three, make our rescue, and leave. Am I clear?"

He watched their faces. A few heads nodded but others looked reluctant to agree. He decided to lay the cards on the table so there would be no doubt.

"I saw what these things can do. Ivers fought and killed one, but he was damn lucky. Thirty-four sailors and Marines died, ripped to pieces. Nate, too. Alone, you will not survive. Even as a group, I don't like the odds, but we're committed. Don't be a hero and don't be a damned fool." He looked at Cici. "They call these caverns the Catacombs, don't they?" She nodded. "Nice. Let's hope it doesn't become a grave for us. Okay, let's move out. Ivers, you go first. Once inside, you're in charge until we separate." He enjoyed the look of surprise on Ivers' face. As much as he disliked and distrusted the military, Ivers was a pro. He was used to situations such as they were about to face. It would have been petty to allow his feelings to misuse their best asset.

The opening to the network of underground buildings was through an eons-old collapsed ceiling of one of the lava tubes. The *Huresh* had leveled and compacted the rubble to create a ramp, but centuries of weather had reduced it to its original form of loose rock, easily dislodged and prone to slides. The ramp was the reason the station had built the elevator. The dangerous slope required them to proceed cautiously. At times, negotiating the shifting loose rock was like surfing. The vehicles slewed dangerously sideways or bulldozed piles of rock before them, creating mini avalanches. The slope ended at the first defensive barricade, a concrete wall with a steel door set in the middle. This was Dax's first venture into the lava tubes. What he saw dismayed him. The door in the wall was missing, had been missing when the first team had arrived. The second barrier just beyond it was stronger, a solid steel wall with a thick gate, but it, too, had not stood up to the forces spent against it. Dax wondered how the archaeology team could have summarily dismissed the destruction to natural causes.

The third wall, five meters thick and constructed of heavy stones, remained uncompleted. Equipment used in its construction lay scattered about the site, long since rusted away to piles of scrap metal. It looked as if something had interrupted the *Huresh* construction workers mid-shift. Dax thought he knew what. Beyond, lay the grand cavern, dubbed the Atrium by the personnel of K124, containing the out-of-place modern elevator.

"That doesn't look good," Andy said.

Dax looked up where he pointed. About thirty meters above the ground, the elevator cage leaned at an odd angle, with parts of the surrounding steel structure twisted and mangled. The elevator door was open. He heard Cici's gasp from the ATV next to him.

"I don't think the last person out made it," he commented to Myles, who rode beside him. If he had harbored any doubts as to the fate of the station crew, the mangled elevator dispelled them. Hydraulic flood still dripped from a broken hose. "This happened recently."

"It doesn't mean they're all dead," Myles said, "though I have to wonder which of my friends was in the elevator at the time."

His voice was subdued, but Dax detected the underlying tension in it. The climatologist's trigger finger repeatedly rubbed the trigger guard of his rifle. His British resolve was nearing its breaking point. Dax wondered what he would do when it snapped. He glanced over at Cici. Her face was drawn and pale, visibly upset by the fact that someone had died at the elevator, someone she knew, but she did not fall apart. She looked determined, as though she had steeled herself for battle. She was as stubborn as he was. His respect for her went up a notch.

Few of the ancient buildings survived intact. Age, wind erosion, and earth tremors had reduced most to piles of rubble. Dax wondered how many of them had fallen to the xenomorphs. Narrow paths slicing through the debris indicated where archaeological digs had taken place. The Atrium was a city of multiple streets and blocks of buildings in a haphazard maze-like configuration, but they did not need a map. The tracks of the

*Abraxas'* transport vehicle were highly visible in the dirt and easy to follow.

When the ATV caravan entered the first of the lava tubes, the still air held the heat and pressed it against their bodies like a barber's hot towel. The hot, dry air immediately dried out his nasal passages and sucked the moisture from his eyeballs. Breathing became a challenge. He wished he had thought to bring along a canteen or even a thermos of Romeo's coffee. The air was musty with a subtle undercurrent of human occupancy – colognes, shampoos, and perspiration. The predominant odor was less subtle, the stench of decaying flesh, and the musky reek of animals, in this case, the creatures.

In the tunnels, the sprawled city became a long row of buildings lining each side of a single street. Many had collapsed. Most bore some signs of damage, more than could be attributed to the passage of time. A collapse in the lava tube wall drew Dax's attention.

"The *Huresh* did that," Cici explained. "We've opened several such cave-ins and found machine-carved adits with additional abandoned buildings." Her voice broke. "We had wondered why they later collapsed the walls."

"It was either an attempt to protect themselves ..."

"Or to bury the dead," she finished for him. "We found no preserved bodies, just a few bones from which we could derive DNA samples. The *Huresh* were remarkably humanoid. We could have been cousins. Of course, two thousand years is a long time for a body to survive exposure to the elements."

He did not suggest to her that the lack of bodies was due to the xenomorphs' appetites. Her grief was profound enough. He was certain that, given time, the creatures on the *Abraxas* would have devoured the dismembered corpses of the crew. A perfect killing machine fed on the corpses of its victims. Loki looked more and more like a world under siege by an unknown enemy that had resorted to the ultimate weapon, a deadly creature deriving its sustenance from the bodies of its enemy.

Using the readings from the GPS satellite in geo-stationary orbit above the station, they followed the winding lava tubes to Level 3. The route was not direct, requiring kilometers of travel for every hundred meters of depth. Because of the uneven ground and mounds of debris, the ATVs averaged less than thirty kilometers per hour, half their top speed. Dax's hopes for a quick search and rescue faded with every turn of the tunnels. His GPS reader indicated the ventilator shaft was still half a kilometer ahead.

The deeper they drove into the tunnels, the more his scalp itched. The uneven walls and tumbled-down buildings played havoc with his sense of order, setting him on edge. He eyed each shadow with suspicion and peered around every bend of the tunnel ready to spin the ATV and run for it if necessary. If not for his promise to Cici to reach Level 3, he would have turned around and left. He did not renege on promises. They were like oral contracts, the lifeblood of a merchant.

"A dig site tent is just around the next bend," Cici informed him. "It's the last place they were working when Myles and I left for the remote station. Director Rathiri had not yet decided on establishing a new dig on the lowest level, Level 5. That must be where they found the xenomorphs."

Cici spoke as if she expected to find her friends waiting at the dig site. Dax knew better. So did she, when the lights of the ATVs fell upon the destroyed remains of the tent and smashed equipment. Ivers called a halt. They saw no bodies, but they did see blood, lots of blood, leaving a disgusting stench in the air. Dark splotches of dried blood stained the dirty-white material of the tent. Congealed blood lay in puddles in the packed earth. Bloody marks in the sand indicated where the creatures had dragged away bodies.

Cici gasped and looked away. Anger burned in her brown eyes. "Oh my God."

"It was a slaughter," Myles said, his words almost a hiss.

Ivers stared at the destruction as if remembering the carnage on his ship; then, gunned the engine of the sledge and moved on, glancing neither left or right as he passed the site. Dax followed him.

The tunnel turned and twisted up and down. Twice, they passed concrete walls constructed across the tunnel, both smashed into rubble. The buildings looked as if blown apart from the inside.

Ivers pulled up beside him. “When I came down here with the cargo transfer team, I saw this and wondered why no one had suggested the *Huresh* were hiding from an enemy rather than fleeing a natural catastrophe. Surely, history is filled with enough fallen civilizations to suggest most end from outside forces. This has all the earmarks of a battlefield.”

Dax agreed. “A civilization doomed by natural catastrophe but fighting until the end sounds more romantic than another conquered people. No one wants to believe there really are monsters out there, civilized or of the bestial variety. I sure as hell didn’t.”

Half a kilometer farther along the tunnel, a dark metal door inset into a wall of hard rock stood out amid the decaying stone buildings. Although plain and unadorned, a prodigious amount of effort had gone into its construction. Three meters high by two meters in width, the door rested in an equally solid metal frame with fingers of metal inset into the surrounding rock to bolster it further. The door to the sanctuary was ominously ajar.

“The signal came from right around here,” Romeo said. He looked up and pointed to a dark, rectangular cavity in the tunnel’s ceiling. “That must be the ventilator shaft that allowed the signal to get through.”

“Everyone stay together,” Dax advised, as he stopped the ATV and got out.

He and Ivers entered the room first, their weapons aimed into the room. The ATV’s headlights revealed a four-hundred-square-meter room with walls of the same dark gray metal as the door. It had no other doors or windows. The room was empty.

“Damn it!” Dax yelled. “Whoever was here is gone.” He thought of the elevator in the Atrium. Whoever had contacted them had grown tired of waiting. “We came for nothing.”

Ivers pointed to a message scratched into the metal wall with a steel trenching tool. “Trapped here for over fifty-two hours,” he read. “No food or water. I haven’t heard the Ravers in hours. I must try for the surface to warn the *Abraxas*. If anyone manages to reach this room, stay here. I’ll get help. If I don’t return, it won’t matter anyway. Gregor.”

"Gregor Pavlovich," Cici explained. She stood in the open doorway staring at the message. Her face revealed her disappointment in finding the room empty. She knew the chances of finding anyone alive were now dismal. "He is, was, our chemist. He must have tried to use the elevator. Poor Greg, if only he had waited a few more hours."

"Ravers," Dax repeated. "The name fit the creatures well." He glanced at Ivers, whose face remained unreadable. "Time to leave."

Cici was aghast at his suggestion. "We can't leave. We have to go deeper. Someone might still be alive."

"They're dead," Dax growled at her. "Everyone is dead. No one reached the surface alive." He turned to Ivers. "You're a fool if you go down there. If the Ravers don't kill you, you'll probably bring the roof down on your head with the missiles. Hey! That's not a bad idea. Why don't we seal the cavern, trap those things in here?"

"One, we don't know they're still in here. Two, they can dig their way out with those tremendous claws. I can't leave until I know they're dead."

"Well, we're pulling out. This is no longer a rescue mission, and with no bodies, we're not a burial detail. If you're smart, you'll come with us."

"Thanks for the offer, but I still have a job to do."

"Ivers, you're a stubborn bastard. What are you trying to prove?"

Ivers clasped the ion disruptor to his chest. "Prove? I'm not trying to prove anything. I'm trying to do what the Corp trained me to do – nothing more, nothing less."

Ivers' obstinacy irritated Dax. He was stubborn, but Ivers was intractable, a pig-headed Marine. "Oh, come off it! You're suffering from survivor's guilt. Everyone died on the *Abraxas* except you. If you want to join them, just place the barrel of that disruptor to your temple and pull the trigger. It'll be a whole lot quicker and less messy than one of those creatures ripping you apart, and it will serve the same purpose."

Ivers sighed. "Take your people and go. Leave this to me."

"I intend to." Dax returned to the ATV and cranked it. "You're a fool, Ivers. Everybody, let's go," he called out to the others, most of whom stood around in confusion. He looked at Tish. She refused to meet his gaze. He didn't care what they thought of him. He had done all he had promised. As far as he was concerned, it was over. "I'm not kidding. I'm leaving."

She lifted her head and nodded. "I know you're not. I'll come with you, but I think it stinks."

As she slunk toward the ATV, Myles spoke up. "We can't leave. We have to help the sergeant. We must go to the lower levels and check for survivors. There's another sanctuary room on Level 4." His eyes pleaded with Dax, but Dax ignored him. "They're my friends!" he shouted.

Plia was already in her ATV revving the motor. Romeo had not left the vehicle. He sat in the rear seat with his rifle over his knees ready to return to the ship. Tish climbed in beside Dax but did not look at him. She leaned against the door, as if placing as much distance as possible between them. He didn't care. She would come around to his side eventually. Her instinct was to nurture and to comfort. His was survival.

Cici stood beside Myles. Her rigid posture declared her defiance. The line had been drawn, sides taken. He sighed at their foolishness. It would have been better if there were mangled bodies lying around for them to see. That might have brought home the harsh reality of the situation. She had not seen the video from the *Abraxas*.

"We'll leave the other vehicle for you in case you change your mind," he said.

Andy climbed out of his ATV and sat down beside Plia.

Cici glared at Dax. "I won't run away without knowing whether my friends are dead or alive."

Dax didn't know whether to admire her courage or curse her for her stupidity. "They're dead. When you see this creature, you'll wish you had run away, like me, but it will be too late by then. You'll die too."

"Don't you even care?" she shot at him.

"I care about my crew. I intend to keep them alive. This isn't our fight."

"Then go!" she shouted at him. "And damn you!"

Dax chose not to respond. Nothing he could say would change her opinion of him, and he had long ago given up caring what people thought about him. He cranked the ATV, but the loud roar he heard was not the motor revving. It was one of the creatures roaring from back toward the entrance to the lava tube complex. He quickly killed the motor and motioned for the others to do the same, but he knew it was too late. The creatures had surely heard them. A series of barking chirps preceded another roar, followed by more answering chirps from farther away. The creatures were calling to one another. The Ravers were in no hurry. The creatures knew where they were. Foolishly, they had allowed the Ravers to trap them in the lava tubes. *I allowed them to trap us,* he thought, correcting himself. *I was a fool for coming down here.*

"You won't have to hunt them after all," he told Ivers. "They're hunting us."

"Am I crazy," Andy asked, "or were they talking to each other?"

"Just announcing their positions like a pack of wolves," Ivers said.

Dax wasn't as certain that's all it was. "I think there was a lot more information in those chirps than 'Here I am'."

"You think they're intelligent?" Ivers asked.

"God, let's hope not," Cici said.

"We can hide in the sanctuary," Tish suggested.

"They'll just wait us out and starve us. Damn!" he yelled, hammering the steering wheel with his fist. "I was stupid to come down here. Now, we'll have to fight them, both of them, or all of them if there are more than two."

"They can come at us from two directions here," Ivers pointed out. "We need to find a spot more advantageous to us where we can concentrate our field of fire."

"There's a short cul-de-sac we opened up not far from here," Cici said. "The entrance is barely three meters wide."

Ivers nodded. "It will have to do. Lead the way."

They loaded into the ATVs with Myles driving the third one, and rode deeper into the labyrinth of tunnels, not the direction Dax had intended, but it now seemed their only choice for survival. He knew the deeper they traveled into the tunnels, the farther they would have to fight their way back to the surface, but they weren't fighting yet. They were running. He didn't see the Ravers in the thick darkness beyond the lights, but he knew they were nearby, watching. He could feel them, like a change in the air before a bad storm. His scalp itched so badly his head ached.

Just as Cici had described it, the entrance to the cul-de-sac was barely wide enough to admit two vehicles abreast. It was not a natural lava tube, but rather an adit carved from the native rock by the Lokians. As soon as they were inside, Ivers turned the tracked vehicle with the missile pod around and pointed it at the entrance. Then he killed the headlights.

"Turn off all the headlights. Point the floods at the walls. We don't want too many shadows to throw off our aim. I suggest everyone take cover in the buildings on either side," he said. "We'll set up a crossfire."

Dax noted the buildings were little more than piles of collapsed stone, rusted steel, and crumbled concrete. They would offer little protection against the Ravers. He directed them to follow Ivers' suggestions about the lights, though to him the indirect lighting of the cul-de-sac made it eerie. He split the group into teams, pairing good shots with those less experienced. "Tish, you come with me. Plia, take Andy with you. Romeo, you pair up with Cici and Myles and watch Ivers' back."

True to his nickname, the *Luck's* chef walked over to Dax and said quietly so that only Dax heard him, "I'd rather watch Cici's back." His face bore a wolfish grin.

"She's a bit old for you, Romeo," Dax replied, "but you have good taste."

Romeo inserted himself between Cici and Myles, giving her the once over while she wasn't looking. Dax admired Romeo's tenacity. He played the hound dog even when faced with man-eating monsters.

Ivers chose his own position on top of a narrow ledge thirty meters from the entrance. This provided an unobstructed view of the entrance and part of the lava tube beyond. He sat with the ion disrupter beside him and the remote control for the missile pod in his hand. He reminded Dax of a big game hunter waiting for his quarry. They all waited. After half an hour, Dax began to think the creature had forgotten about them.

"What do you think?" he asked Tish.

"About what?"

"That chirping and roaring – are they talking?"

"I don't know. They're communicating certainly. I don't know if it's anything more than that." She looked at Dax. "They can't be intelligent, can they? I mean, they're animals."

The idea clearly frightened her. It scared him too. Giant hungry monsters were bad enough. Smart monsters were a bit over the top. "Maybe I'm just thinking too hard. You know it hurts my brain." He grinned at her. She smiled back, but it faded quickly.

He saw Ivers tense. "Get ready," he said.

The Raver shot through the entrance in a blur of motion, silently, brushing the side of the wall, and sending rocks scattering ahead of it. Tish's sharply indrawn breath betrayed her fright. He squeezed her hand to reassure her. Ivers was ready for it. The missile pod moved slightly. The Raver turned toward it and snarled. Ivers fired. The missile shot straight at the creature's head. Its reflexes were too quick. Using its powerful rear legs, it leaped to one side, crashing into and through the side of a building. The missile shot past it and exploded outside in the tunnel.

Ivers had anticipated the creature's reaction. He had seen how quickly it could move on the *Abraxas*. The missile pod tracked the creature's movements. A second missile, fired milliseconds later, caught the creature midstride. It exploded just behind the Raver's enormous head. The black armor absorbed most of the explosion, but pieces of shrapnel peppered the unprotected portion of its left forelimb. It roared in pain and fell onto its side, as the injured limb gave way beneath its weight. It rolled across the ground, smashing walls and bringing down buildings in a cloud of dust.

"Now!" Ivers shouted.

Dax fired his laser. Everyone else followed suit with whatever weapon they had. The whine of bullets and the buzz of laser fire filled the cul-de-sac. None of the fire did any serious damage, but it kept the creature swatting at bullets until Ivers could line it up in the sights of the disrupter. The high-energy beam sliced into its neck, sending a shower of blood over the ground. Even injured, it did not give up on the hunt. It dug its claws into the dirt and pushed with its rear legs, while simultaneously dragging its body forward with its one good forelimb. With a determination bred into its body by its creators, it crawled across the ground toward them.

As it clambered over a low wall, it reared its head, revealing a black scale below its jaw broken off by the explosion. Dax took a deep breath, aimed, and fired three quick shots into the exposed flesh. The laser passed through its tough, fibrous hide, continued through the mouth and tongue, and into the brain. It screamed once and fell dead. To make certain it was truly dead, Ivers continued to bathe its body with the disruptor until its flesh ignited, filling the tunnel with the sickening stench of seared flesh.

Dax's legs turned to rubber. He leaned back against a wall with his laser held down by his side, the barrel dragging in the dirt. His breath came in rapid gulps. He had held his breath since firing at the monster. His hands hook so badly, the laser rattled. He thought he had been frightened before, but watching the creature clambering over the wall toward him topped all previous episodes.

"Yes!" Andy yelled, pumping his fist in the air.

Dax felt a moment of shame at his fear compared to Andy's exultation, but the young co-pilot had not been aboard the *Abraxas*. He had not seen firsthand of what the creature was capable.

"Don't celebrate too quickly," Ivers warned. "Its brother is out there somewhere. It will be a little more leery now and not so easy to kill."

"Maybe we can escape now," Tish said.

She sounded so hopeful Dax hated to burst her balloon. "At thirty kilometers per hour, we could never outrun it. We're safer here."

"How much safer?" she asked. She glanced at the dead Raver.

Dax followed her gaze. Somehow, it looked even more frightening dead. The reflected lighting accentuated its worst features – the long, black teeth and the sharp claws. He couldn't argue her point. Even dying, the creature had crawled to less than ten meters from them – too close for comfort. They had expended half their ammunition, nearly depleted the power packs of the lasers, and had only three *Wasp Sting* missiles remaining, but the creature was dead. *One down and how many to go*?

"I suggest everyone make his or herself comfortable," Ivers said. "I don't think the last Raver will be in any hurry."

*No, it knows we're not going anywhere*. He noticed Ivers said 'last Raver' as if he didn't believe it. Neither did Dax. Four of the creatures couldn't destroy an entire civilization. This was his worst-case scenario, trapped in the underground labyrinth with an unknown number of Ravers. *No, in a worst case, we would already be corpses*. It was the reason he had refused to enter the labyrinth of tunnels. He wished he had stuck to his guns.

Dax chose a spot facing the entrance, sat down, and leaned his back against a wall to wait. *When I screw up, I don't do it by half measures*.

# 8

Dax's stomach rumbled, reminding him he hadn't eaten in hours. He had expected to be long gone before now. Make a quick search for survivors, and then back into space – quick, easy, and relatively safe. Instead, they sat around in an ancient rubble pile of concrete, stones, and rusted steel that had once been a city but was now grave markers for a vanished race. The chances of their joining the late Lokians, the *Huresh,* were good. No one had said the latter aloud, but it was what everyone was thinking.

The archaeologists had found no statues or engravings of the *Huresh*, but their buildings with their rectangular, human-sized doors and the methods of construction denoted a bipedal species very similar to humans. Traces of *Huresh* DNA indicated many similarities with humans, even in the same number of chromosomes. As Cici had stated, the two races could have been cousins. Dax wondered if they felt what he was now feeling, as they huddled against the Raver onslaught – a sense of hopelessness.

The dead Raver lay just a few meters away as a vivid reminder of their peril. He had studied it until his eyes hurt, but he still didn't understand it. It was an ancient killing machine, almost perfect in its organic simplicity, created by an unknown race and unleashed upon the hapless *Huresh* twenty centuries earlier. It had done its job and had slept away the intervening centuries. During that time, its creators had not returned for it. That intrigued him. Were they that afraid of the weapon that they had created, or had they become victims of their own creation, like Victor Frankenstein and his monster?

Something had awakened them from their deep hibernation, and they had resumed their former occupation as killers. If there were only four of the creatures as Ivers had stated, only one remained. If, as seemed more likely, its creators had unleashed many of the creatures, it was anyone's guess how many remained. Dax always preferred to err on the side of caution. His vote went to more than one remaining monster. That made their choice easier. In a headlong rush to the surface, they might make it, though he doubted they could lift off before the creature damaged the ship. If more existed and trapped the humans between them, they would die quickly and in a most grisly manner.

Cici sat on one of the walls, tossing stones one at a time at the dead Raver. Because of the heat, she had loosened several buttons on her shirt, revealing the curvature of her breasts. She had Romeo's undivided attention. For lack of anything more productive to do, Dax stared at them, too. He had decided they were not quite as large as Tish's, but worthy of ogling nonetheless. If not for the heat and Tish's presence, he might have hit on her. If she was aware of the effect of so much bare skin on the men around her, she did not show it. *Too many academic types,* he thought.

She abruptly grabbed a handful of stones, jumped up, and threw them all at the creature. "Grr! Now I know why Gregor risked running," she said. "This waiting is driving me crazy."

Her sudden eruption worried Dax. In their current situation, impulsiveness could get them killed. "We've only been here three hours," he reminded her. "He was down here for two days."

"He didn't have weapons." She held up the .338 caliber rifle she carried.

Dax snickered at the change in her attitude about guns. "That thing wouldn't hurt the creature if you shoved it up its ass and pulled the trigger, assuming it has an ass."

She scowled at him with pursed lips. "Then why did you insist I bring it?"

"I felt better with everyone armed. Besides, it's a great little noisemaker."

He glanced at Ivers, who had stopped pacing after pounding the same footsteps for the better part of an hour. "The captain is right, I'm afraid. The ion disruptor is effective against it, but with a laser, you have to hit a vital spot. Out there, we would be helpless. We have the missiles, but they can point in only one direction at a time. For any chance of survival, we must make it come to us."

"Then why is it waiting?" she whined.

"Perhaps it isn't hungry enough yet," Dax said.

"I don't understand …" She went silent and her face paled as the implication of his statement struck home. "Oh, I …" She shook her head, buried her face in her hands, and began sobbing.

Tish shot an icy glare at him. "Dax, sometimes I think you don't give a shit about anyone." She walked over and placed her arm around Cici to comfort her.

He shrugged. "Sorry if the truth hurts. Maybe it's best to understand why we've found no bodies. For me, it's an added incentive for survival."

He had been harsher with the biologist than necessary, but the waiting was getting to him as well. The heat was stifling, and the Raver smelled even worse dead than it did alive. Worst of all, he didn't have his blues tunes to ease the strain. He was angry with himself for giving in to the humanitarian urge to search for survivors. His first instinct had been to drop Ivers off and leave. First instincts were usually the best.

"If there were more than one, wouldn't they have attacked by now?" Andy asked.

The youngest member of his crew was holding up well under the circumstances. In fact, his entire crew was coping with their circumstances better than he was. He was a man of action. He hadn't always been a sedate cargo ship captain. He had begun his career working on an independent trading ship as assistant cargo officer. By the time he was Andy's age, he had been in his fair share of scrapes with local overlords, militias, and the U.N. Navy. Only when he had assumed the responsibility of his own ship and crew had he settled down. His former life was trying to superimpose itself over his present life. If it had been just him and Ivers, he would prefer to go down fighting. The trouble was he had made a promise to his crew. He would not risk their lives unnecessarily.

Ivers answered. “One or more, it doesn’t matter. It’s a hunter, a predator. It can smell fear. Fear makes prey weaker. When the scent of our fear reaches a certain level, it will attack. Waiting increases our fear.”

“And then what?”

“We live or we die.”

“That’s just great,” Cici said. She was already in tears from Dax’s comments. “I suppose you’ll die happy knowing you’ve killed two of them.”

“Technically, two kills and one assist,” Dax countered, but both Cici and Ivers ignored him.

“It’s what I do, Doctor Adar,” Ivers answered. “I’m a Marine. We don’t like throwing our lives away, but if necessary, we will die for the Corp. My primary goal is to get someone out alive to warn the Navy about these creatures. After that, well it doesn’t much matter if I die here or on some dirtball world fighting some tin pot dictator with higher ambitions. Dead is dead.”

“I have been considering our present predicament.”

Dax looked over at Plia. The taciturn cargo specialist had been quiet for quite some time, as was usual for her. Gone was her ubiquitous sour expression, replaced now by a pensive one. “Find any solutions?” he asked.

“Perhaps. If we go back into the lava tube and there is more than one Raver remaining, we face attack from either direction. Our chances of survival would be abysmal.”

Dax was disappointed. “You considered this a long time, have you, Plia? Tell me something I don’t know.”

She scowled at him but continued, “We could increase the odds in our favor by using one or two of the missiles to bring the roof down deeper in the tube. Then, we would not have to watch our backs. If the Raver is between the surface and us, we could face it with a missile and our weapons. The odds increase slightly in our favor.”

“A bold plan, but what if there are more than one of the creatures between the surface and us?” Dax pointed out.

"In that case, we would all likely die." Her delivery bore no trace of humor. To her, it was simply a given to consider.

"Are you crazy?" Cici burst out. She seemed incredulous that Plia had suggested such an idea. "That's not a plan; that's a death wish. Besides, we have to check the lower levels for survivors."

Ivers' concern was more practical. "Would a single missile collapse the roof? Using two missiles places us at a serious disadvantage if we're attacked."

"Perhaps it would, if we chose the proper spot. I once visited South Africa on Earth. The rock here is very similar to Kimberlite, a loose aggregate found in lava pipes in South African diamond mines. It should fracture easily. Two missiles would do a better job, though."

Dax looked at Plia in a new light. In the eight years he had known her, he had not known she had visited Earth. She never spoke of it. In truth, he knew very little about her. She did her job well, she presented an exceptionally strong poker face in the weekly card games, and she never complained. That was all he had bothered to learn about her. *Maybe I should make a better effort to know my crew,* he thought. *If we get out of this.*

Ivers objected. "No. Using two missiles is too risky."

Cici shook her head in dismay. "I can't believe you two are even discussing this. We came here to rescue my friends. Now you want to cause a cave-in and kill all of us."

To Dax's surprise, Tish was in favor of it. "Waiting here feels wrong. Maybe taking the initiative will catch it by surprise. Besides, dying that way might be preferable to the Ravers."

"No one's dying," Dax snapped. "I promise."

"You can't keep that promise, Dax," she replied.

"I … I …" He turned away. She was right. He wasn't in control of the situation, the Ravers were. "I can try," he said, but his words fell flat to his ears. Tish looked unconvinced.

"That's not a bad idea," Plia said. "What we need is bait to draw the Raver to the right spot. Crushing it beneath tons of rock would be better than trying to trap it."

"Are you volunteering?" he asked Plia.

His sarcasm was lost on her. She wrinkled her nose. "No, my desire to escape does not include volunteering as bait."

"I'll do it," Andy said. He stood rocking on the balls of his feet, as if pumped up on adrenalin.

Dax envied him his youth, but not his stupidity. "Whoa, now," he said. "No one is going to act as bait. We'll figure something out."

"I'm faster than any of you." To Dax, he sounded like a high school kid boasting to his friends. "I can draw the Raver to the right spot and get away before the roof collapses."

"You're not faster than a Raver. That's suicidal. I won't let you do it."

"You can't stop me," Andy retorted. He took a few steps toward Dax.

Dax accepted the challenge and met him halfway, glowering at him. Jabbing a finger in Andy's face, he said, "The hell I can't. I'll reduce you in rank to assistant cook. You can fly a sauté pan with Romeo. I'll, I'll fire your ass."

"Then I quit!"

"Boys! Boys!" Tish yelled. "Stop your testosterone prancing." She stared at Andy until he averted his gaze. "Andy, in his own blundering way, Dax is trying to say he doesn't want you to risk your life."

The tenor of Andy's voice dropped at Tish's admonition, but his blood still ran hot from the argument. His eyes flashed, but he was more sullen than hostile, as he said, "We have to do something."

"It's my job," Ivers burst out. "I'll do it."

Everyone turned to stare at Ivers. His face was grim. "I'm the professional soldier here." He walked over to Dax, handed him the ion disruptor, and held out his hand. Stunned, Dax gave him his laser rifle. "I'll move fifty meters down the tube and make some noise with this." He held up the laser and looked at Plia. "When the Raver investigates, you fire a missile at the roof above us. If this works, and the roof comes down, you head for the surface. You've done your job."

"That's suicidal," Dax told him. Ivers' blithe willingness to die bothered Dax. It also touched upon his guilt for not volunteering, but he tried to shunt that inconvenience aside.

"Worse, it leaves us one gun shy when we leave. Let's concentrate on all of us getting out of this alive."

"Do you have a better idea?" Ivers challenged.

Dax clenched his jaw to fight back a sharp comment. "I'm working on it."

The sergeant's eyes were squinted as he stared at Dax. "Sometimes things come at a cost. Sometimes that cost is a sacrifice."

Dax chopped his hand through the air. "No blood sacrifices. We're not Aztecs or Mayans. We figure something out."

Myles raised his hand as if in a meeting; then, when they ignored him, spoke up. "I think I have an idea." Both men glared at him. He looked uncomfortable being the center of attention. He removed his glasses and tapped the earpiece against his lower lip as he spoke. "The plan as proposed will not work. We passed a junction on Level 2, a secondary tunnel."

"So?" Dax said.

"It comes out on Level 4. Even if we trap the Raver deeper in the tunnel here, it could simply circle around and come up behind us again."

"So what's your plan?" Dax asked.

Myles blinked several times. "We could go deeper into the tunnels. The creature would likely follow us. We utilize the bypass tunnel on Level 4 leading back to Level 2. At some point before it reaches Level 2, we seal the cavern behind us and run like the dickens for the surface. The Raver would have a much longer distance to traverse, giving us a fighting chance to beat it."

The idea of going even deeper into the lava tubes struck Dax as almost as suicidal as Ivers' plan. "If we can't seal the tunnel, what then? We'll have twice as far to go with one of those things snapping at our heels. Or what if there are more than one?" He shot a withering look at Myles. "I think you just want to search for your friends." He shook his head. "I'm against it."

"I may have something to even the odds." Ivers reached into the bag he had been carrying since leaving the *Abraxas*. Dax hadn't asked what was in it. He had assumed it was extra power cells for the disruptor or some personal item Ivers couldn't part with. He pulled out two small square boxes unfamiliar to Dax, each the size of a tissue dispenser.

"What are those?" Dax asked.

"Proximity thermal mines."

"Prox ..." Dax backed up three steps, stunned. His nostrils flared. "Thermal mines. You've been carrying proximity thermal mines around on my ship. Are you insane? A single mine could turn *Fortune's Luck* into a cloud of molten metal droplets."

"They're harmless until activated."

"How do you intend to activate them? Do you have a remote detonator?"

"No."

Dax shook his head. "This gets better and better. Expanding the scope of my first question, how do you intend to activate them manually without frying your ass or all our asses?"

"They have a fifteen-second delay between manual activation and when the sensors go online. Of course, in an enclosed environment ..."

"Yeah," Dax chimed in. "Exactly. They detonate when they sense anything within range, like a cavern wall, or a person."

"Or a Raver. Bang – no more Raver. It should bring down the roof as well from the intense heat they produce."

Dax glanced at Plia for confirmation. She nodded, but he still wasn't convinced. It sounded simple, which made the top of his head itch. Simple plans could easily blow up in your face. In this case, literally. "Why not just head straight for the surface and blow the tunnels behind us?"

"There may be more than one Raver. If so, they can come at us from two sides. At the junction on Level 2," He glanced in Myles' direction, "they could attack from three sides. The odds would be against us."

Dax hated the plan, but it made better sense than his or Plia's. There was a chance that the creatures would not immediately attack if they moved deeper into the network of tunnels rather than try to escape. The more distance they placed between themselves and the creatures, the safer he would feel. He thought it ironic that in order to save his crew from danger, he would have to take them deeper into it.

"I think you kept quiet about the mines because you planned something like this all along – seal the tunnel so we could escape, while you became a posthumous hero by killing the Raver."

Ivers said nothing, but Dax thought it revealing that he did not deny the accusation. He shook his head. *Military types*. "Jesus Christ Almighty! If the choice is waiting here until the Raver attacks us, or going deeper into the ground in the slim hope that we can seal the tunnel behind us, I chose waiting. I'd rather miss a few meals than become one. In fact …"

Myles cleared his throat. "Uh, I'm afraid that might not be possible."

Dax shot the climatologist a glowering look, annoyed at the interruption of his rant. "Why the hell not?" he shouted.

"I took weather readings before you picked us up at KB. The air pressure has been dropping rapidly for six hours. Another storm is approaching the area from the north, an *etesian* wind."

Both Dax and Ivers stared at Myles. "What is an etesian wind?" Dax asked.

"It is a more or less annual occurrence; however, this storm seems to be expanding particularly rapidly."

"So?" Dax said. "We get a little dusty. No big deal."

"I'm afraid you don't understand. Let me show you." He pulled out his pocket comp. "Here's the current satellite image."

Dax and Ivers looked at the small image on the screen. Dax's stomach tightened when he saw the enormous reddish-brown cloud bearing down on the station from the north. It covered five-thousand square kilometers from just below the northern pole and obscured all topographical details. Even the infrared scanners on the satellite could not penetrate the thick cloud of dust.

"Are you sure about this?" Dax asked

Myles looked as if offended by Dax's doubt. He put his glasses back on. "I am a climatologist," he replied.

"*Fortune's Luck* could never fly in that," he said. He looked at Myles. "How long?"

"The leading edge should be here very soon, perhaps two hours. In four, we won't be able to breathe outside without respirators, which, I might point out, we don't have. Even these tunnels will become dangerously uncomfortable with choking dust."

Dax shook his head. He hated choices that all sucked. "So it's stay here and choke until the monsters come for us, make a run for it and take our chances in a blinding dust storm, or seal ourselves inside the metal room and wait it out, in which case we still have the Ravers to deal with later. How long will the storm last?"

Myles removed his glasses again and scratched his temple with the earpiece. He grimaced and said, "Five days at least."

Dax's heart skipped a beat. "Five days! In five days, that creature could dig its way through a solid metal wall. It won't much matter. We'll die of thirst before then. We don't have much choice. It's either leave now or never. The question is which way – up or down?"

He disliked having decisions thrust upon him. Luckily, it wasn't his to make. He had told Ivers he was in charge. In this instance, he would not go back on his word. His decisions had proved too costly. It was time to let someone else carry the burden. He turned to Ivers. "What do you say, Sergeant. Your call."

Ivers scratched at his jaw for a few seconds wearing a somber expression, then said, "Down. Let's load up and go."

The pit of Dax's stomach rumbled. He didn't know if it was from hunger or from fear. His vote went to fear. It was all he could do to keep his knees from knocking. He would have chosen running for the surface. He didn't like planets, and he liked being underground least of all, but he had abrogated his right to decide in favor of Ivers. He knew the danger, and he wasn't happy about it. At least the decision was out of his hands. He wouldn't get his hands any bloodier than they already were.

"Move it," he snapped to the others. He handed Ivers the ion disruptor and reclaimed his laser rifle, then climbed into the ATV and laid the rifle over his lap. Tish took the seat beside him, looking almost as frightened as he was. Ivers crawled into the seat on the missile sledge. Plia drove with Romeo. Andy took Cici and Myles. He took a deep breath, strapped himself into the driver's seat, and cranked the vehicle. He checked to see that the others were ready and shot out the entrance of the cul-de-sac at full throttle, leaving a plume of dirt in his wake. He jerked the wheel to the right and led the convoy deeper into the lava tube network.

*Monsters, deep dark twisting tunnels, a blinding dust storm – this is not going to end well.*

# 9

Cici had never been as frightened in her entire life. She had developed a debilitating fever from alien insect bites in a dismal swamp on Ferrell's World and almost died from a high fever and dysentery. She had fallen into an ice crevice on the southern polar cap of Paton searching for lichen and waited two days for rescue. She had barely escaped trampling during a stampede of elephant-sized Shogun lizards on Kozumi III, but those paled in comparison to the dread she now felt. Two days of agonizing over the fate of her fellow scientists while waiting on the cargo ship, discovering a dark and silent station, and then the blood and the fight with the Raver – she expected to die at any moment. In spite of her fear, it never dawned on her to abandon the search for her friends until she was certain they were dead.

The headlights of the three ATVs and the sledge rolling over the uneven ground cast eerie moving silhouettes, reminding her of a Japanese *Bunraku* shadow puppet theater using the smooth walls of the lava tube as a paper scrim. While she had been down into the Catacombs on several occasions, it had never been so dark and foreboding. Lights strung along the ceiling had offered a streetlight atmosphere, and she had always come with a sense of discovery, not one of dread. With no power, the surrounding darkness was absolute, absorbing the edges of the headlights and floodlights as if devouring it.

She glanced over at Dax in the next ATV. His face was grim. He was intent on driving and did not look her direction. She had caught him staring at her breasts earlier and buttoned up her shirt to her neck. She was perspiring up a storm, but she didn't want him ogling her. He confused her. She had never met a man like him in academia circles. He was self-centered, mulish, misogynistic, and a borderline coward; yet, he was not afraid to take charge. In spite of his obvious shortcomings, she found herself attracted to him in a purely physical way.

After months of living with men more interested in their careers than in the opposite sex, or men like Myles, who was too polite and well bred to make at pass at her, Dax was a breath of fresh air. Attractive, ruggedly handsome, and self-confident to the point of egotistical, he nevertheless exuded a kind of manly charm and sexual essence of an obviously alpha male. She understood Tish's attraction to him and did not want to come between them. Still …

Butting heads with the captain of *Fortune's Luck,* who refused to search the deeper tunnels, and Sergeant Ivers, who was more determined to kill the Ravers than search for her friends, had torn her up inside. Deep down, she knew they were dead, but she could not accept that two-thousand-year-old monsters had snuffed out their lives. It seemed too surreal to be true. People died from accidents, disease, old age, and, rarely, killed by others, but to die in such a horrible manner … it sickened her.

She mourned for Gregor Pavlovich. She suspected the others were dead as well, but he was the only one of whom she was certain from his message left in the sanctuary. Her determination to search further arose more from her unwillingness to accept their deaths than from hope of finding them alive.

The ATV in which she rode took a wild swerve to avoid a pile of debris. She held on with both hands, as the rusty rebar thrusting like a dead plant from the concrete rubble shot by centimeters from her elbow. She glanced at Myles. He sat immobile, upright in his seat with a dazed expression, rocking with the motion of the vehicle, but paying scant attention to their surroundings. She worried for him. Intent on remaining unfazed by events to retain his air of British poise, she was afraid the next horror they faced would break him. She had thought him the strong one. Now, she felt compelled to offer him comfort.

"Myles." When he did not respond, she repeated his name louder. "Myles." He blinked several times and turned to look at her. "Are you all right?"

He opened his mouth to say something, but then shut it. After a few seconds, he said, "I feel cold, Cici."

"Cold?" It was 35 degrees Celsius inside the tunnels, a blustery summer day in Tucson, Arizona, her hometown. She perspired heavily. The dust thrown up by the vehicles stuck to her skin like dry rub spices on a pork shoulder. Beads of sweat poured down his face as well. "I don't understand. It's as hot as Hades down here."

"Inside. I'm cold inside, Cici. I feel …" He shook his head. "We're going to die down here."

The tone of his voice and the finality with which he pronounced their doom alarmed her, as if he were calling down doom upon them. She shivered in spite of the heat. "We'll make it, Myles. Just hold on. Captain Wyldd and Sergeant Ivers have a plan. You helped craft it, remember?"

He did not reply. Instead, he stared at her unblinking for several seconds before turning away and resuming his posture of indifference.

His fear and pronouncement of death reminded her of her naïve boasting to Dax about the rifle she held in her hands, after they had killed the Raver, the first weapon she had ever touched, thinking it would protect them. Knowing how little protection their weapons offered, she now had second doubts about her conviction to find her friends. That was not their main goal. Escaping was, but going deeper into the tunnels served her purpose. If any of her colleagues remained alive, they would be there.

She looked back up the tunnel. There, at the edge of darkness, something moved. She tensed. A Raver was stalking them. She glanced down at her hands and saw them trembling.

*Oh, God. Myles is right. We're going to die.*

# 10

Dax didn't have to turn to know the Raver was following them. He could almost feel its hot breath on the back of his neck. The top of his head burned from itching. He didn't know how close it was until Tish glanced back. Her eyes grew wide, and her face went ashen. Her fingernails dug into his leg.

"Go faster," she urged.

He maneuvered the ATV through an obstacle course of ruins and piles of rubble at breakneck speeds. He pushed the ATV to its top speed of 55 kph. Any little mistake would send them crashing into a solid rock wall or spill them on a tight turn, either of which could kill them. If the crash didn't kill them, the Raver would. The other vehicles kept right behind him, preferring the dangers of speed to what was pursuing them.

The creature took the easiest course, pushing straight through piles of debris or hurtling over them like a track star. It closed on them much faster than Dax liked. He pushed the vehicle for every kph he could, but the station had chosen the ATVs for their durability, not their speed.

The tracked sledge lagged behind the group. The overheated gearbox rattled like a dice cup at a casino craps table. Smoke billowed from the gasping engine. Dax knew the overburdened sledge would never make it. Its manufacturers had not designed it for high speeds, and it had almost ten-year's wear on the engine. Even Nate could not perform miracles. At a bend in the tunnel heading down to Level 4, Ivers called him on the walkie-talkie.

"We'll never outrun it. I have an idea."

Dax dropped back beside the right side of the sledge. Without warning, Ivers raised his disruptor and fired a blast at a rock wall leaning precariously over the roadway supported by a makeshift framework of two-by-fours and planks installed by the K124 team. A neatly lettered placard read 'L4 1652'. He assumed it was a grid marker for their records. They would not have approved of Ivers' actions. The wooden two-by-fours splintered from the heat. Dax watched the wall falling, gunned the motor, and veered left to avoid it, slamming into the sledge. He hit the brakes to allow the sledge to pass. It shot by with Ivers staring at him in shock.

Dax immediately gunned the engine. Large rocks bounced off the vehicle, knocking it sideways into the buildings lining the left side of the tunnel. He jerked his arm inside the vehicle to avoid losing it, as the ATV brushed the wall. Dust and shards of rock peppered Dax's face. A piece of fiberglass fender skirt ripped from the left front wheel well bounced off the roll bar. The wall collapsed directly behind them, almost engulfing both the rear end of the ATV.

"You almost killed us," Dax yelled into the walkie-talkie.

"I didn't see you drop back. I didn't have time to explain."

With a loud crash, dislodged stones fell from the makeshift blockade the fallen wall had created. The Raver hammered at it from the other side.

"It won't hold long," Ivers warned. He eased back on the sledge's throttle, but the labored engine continued to sputter.

As they neared the tunnel leading back to Level 2, Dax noticed another steel door like the one on Level 3. As they drew closer, he saw the door was slightly open. Then, the door began swinging open wider. *Raver*. Dax spun the ATV to a skidding halt and pointed to the door. Ivers aimed the missile pod at it. Running wouldn't save them. The Raver could catch them before they made it thirty meters. They had no choice but to face it.

"If it gets out of there, it'll be all over us," he told Ivers.

When he saw a shadow in the doorway, he took a deep breath and squeezed the trigger on his laser rifle. Ivers yelled, "Wait!" He started to curse the sergeant; then, he saw what Ivers had seen first – a human. The man staggered from the sanctuary room toward them.

"Help me!" he yelled.

Tish helped the man into the back of the ATV. Through the filthy, sweat-stained clothes and dirty face, Dax recognized Dr. Ambrose Rathiri, the station's director. He looked like he had been through hell.

"Thank God you came," he croaked. "I've been trapped three days." Then he recognized Ivers on the sledge. "You were on the *Abraxas*. You transported the ..." His face paled. "It woke up."

"Both of them. They killed everyone on the ship but me."

A muted gasp escaped his lips. He finally recognized Dax. "Captain Wyldd. Thank you for rescuing me."

"We didn't know anyone was left alive down here. We're drawing the Raver to us to try to seal it in."

"Draw ... drawing the Ravers to you. That is insane."

Something in the director's voice made the hairs on Dax's arm rise. "How many Ravers are there, Director Rathiri?"

Rathiri shook his head. "I don't know. I don't know. Fifteen. Sixteen. More. Stefani reported six or seven of the creatures left the cavern and headed east toward the remote station three days ago. I, I lost my radio somewhere. We have to warn them."

"They're here with us, Director. Jesus Christ! More than a dozen. We're not getting out of here."

"We can hide in the sanctuary." He swiped the back of his hand across his mouth. His lips were parched and swollen. "Do you have any water or any food? I haven't ..." He began coughing.

"We didn't bring anything. We didn't think we would be staying. It doesn't matter anyway. A dust storm is coming shortly. In a couple of hours, the dust will be too thick to see or breathe. It will last five days. We won't."

"Oh, My Lord."

The other two ATVs came back to investigate. Cici leaped out and rushed to Rathiri. "Dr. Rathiri, you're alive."

"Just barely," he replied, patting Cici on the back. "You're safe."

"What about the others?" she asked.

"Gregor left the lower level ahead of us to check on an experiment he was running. We were all down here except Stefani Wimbley who had station duty." He shook his head. "I don't know. I haven't heard … You see, I lost my radio. I had it, but in all the running and hiding, I, I dropped it somewhere. It is good to see you, oh, and Myles, too. So good." He wiped his mouth. "Do you have any water?"

Dax saw the lost look in Rathiri's eyes and cringed. The director had witnessed horrors that would have driven lesser men insane and endured days inside a metal box slowly roasting in the heat. It was a wonder he could still function.

"What about the others?" Cici asked again.

Rathiri's face twisted into a mask of horror. His lips trembled. His voice went up an octave. "It was horrible." He shuddered, but then seemed to pull himself together. "We didn't know what was happening until it was too late. We packed two specimens for the Navy, although I filed a former protest with the U.N. They should not have jurisdiction over a civilian enterprise."

Cici placed her hand on his arm. "Go on, Ambrose," she said gently. "What about Sira and Estelle?"

He blinked a couple of times. "I'm sorry. I was ranting, wasn't I? The other two specimens we placed in a sealed examination tent. During the night, when most of us were excavating the new site, they, they just woke up and began slaughtering everyone – Sira Chang, such a lovely girl, Estelle Mavins, Bob Rosenthal, Lee Bivens, and Matsui Hokomida. Matsui shoved me out of the way of one of the creatures. He died in my place." He closed his eyes and shuddered again. "Rand Evans and I raced for the nearest sanctuary. Evans didn't make it, poor lad."

"Neither did Gregor."

"Oh, that's too bad." He slumped forward. Cici caught him before he fell. "I'm sorry. I'm so very tired. I heard the vehicles and came out to warn you about the Ravers on the lower level."

A large rock fell from the barricade Ivers had made with a loud thud, raising a cloud of dust.

"We have to go," Ivers said. "Dr. Adar, get in the vehicle, now." He pulled one of the mines from his bag. "I hate to use this now, but I have no choice."

Seeing what Ivers was about to do, Dax made a momentous decision, one he hoped he lived to regret. "Give that to me," he said. "The sledge is too slow." He turned to Tish. "Get out."

Her mouth opened as she stared at him. "I want to –"

He didn't give her time to argue. "Go!" To Ivers, he said, "Take Tish with you. Get everyone out of here. Take the *Luck* … take the *Luck* and get off the planet."

He didn't wait for Ivers to reply. He snatched the mine from his hand and drove toward the fallen wall. No matter what he thought of the sergeant, everyone stood a better chance of surviving with him in control. He was a better shot than any of them were, and he had the ion disruptor. He had already proven he could fire the missiles as well as Plia, if not better. One way or another, Dax was determined to keep his promise to his crew.

He had been wrong about searching deeper in the lava tubes. If the others had listened to him, Director Rathiri would have died alone and in the dark. No one should die in that manner. His decision to use the mine was an act of atonement, to make penance for killing Nate and almost killing Rathiri. He hoped it wasn't an act of suicide.

As he approached, smaller rocks tumbled from the pile. One of the Raver's claws protruded through a gap between larger rocks. In another few moments, it would break through and be on them. It stuck its maw up to the hole and chirped. This time, the series of calls sounded to Dax like someone conveying a lot of information. The chirps were of different durations and scaled up and down the frequency spectrum. He heard a few repeated patterns and knew they were not random calls.

He didn't have time to think about what he was doing. He hit the activation switch, threw the mine at the pile of rocks, and drove away as quickly as he could, dodging piles of rubble at a perilous speed. Fifteen seconds later, the lava tube lit up like the inside of a tanning booth bed, throwing dancing shadows across the walls and floor. A wave of heat, funneled by the narrow lava tube, washed over him two hundred meters down the tunnel, singeing his hair, and blistering the exposed flesh on the back of his neck and hands. His ears felt as if they were melting from the heat.

The thermal mine produced little noise when it exploded, a muted pop like a giant's knuckles cracking, but as the heat increased, the sound of rocks chipping from the ceiling and walls sounded like popping corn. Less than twenty seconds after detonating, a fifty-meter-long section of the roof at the center of the conflagration crumbled and collapsed. A cloud of hot dust pushed down the tunnel and enveloped him. He breathed in a lungful of scorching air and almost choked. During his coughing spasm, the ATV struck something in his path. It canted onto its left side, balanced on two tires for several seconds, before rolling over onto its left side and sliding to a stop. He hit the release for the harness and rolled out of the driver's seat, spitting out a mouthful of dirt. He lay there for a couple of minutes racked by a coughing fit. When it subsided, he tried to stand but couldn't. The roll bar had pinned his left foot between it and a large rock. He dug at the dirt with his bare hands, but it was too hard. The effort brought on another bout of coughing.

At the sound of a footstep, he reached for his laser rifle just out of reach. He pulled his .40 caliber pistol from his holster and peered into the darkness, half blinded by the dust. The crash had broken the floodlights and only one of the headlights still worked. Ivers called out from the darkness, "Don't shoot. It's me."

Relieved, Dax lowered the pistol. "What the hell are you doing here? You should be with the others. Why do you think I took the mine? Who's driving the sledge?"

"Plia's on the sledge. Andy and Romeo are driving ATVs. I came back to help you." He raised his hands in the air waist high. "If you're okay, I can just go back."

"Damn you. Help me roll this bastard over and let's get the hell out of here."

"What were you going to do with that pistol?"

Dax grinned. "I don't know. It just felt better than laying there with a rock in my hand."

Ivers lifted the edge of the ATV just enough for Dax to pull his foot out. He stood without pain. "Just bruised, I think," he said to Ivers' questioning glance. They rocked the ATV until it tipped back over onto its tires.

"Rathiri said most of the Ravers were still down on Level 5 digging out their fellow monsters, if this explosion doesn't bring them running. The crazy bastard walked down there yesterday to check on them. I imagine that's where the bodies went, to feed the newly awakened Ravers. It might be a good idea to keep them bottled up down there."

Dax knew where Ivers' story was headed, and he didn't like it. "Rathiri's half mad from dehydration and shock. He's probably delirious."

"Still, if he's right …."

Dax shook his head. "Man, you really do want to die don't you?"

Ivers locked Dax with his intense gaze. Dax found himself unable to look away. "Would you die for your crew?"

The question did not take Dax by surprise. He had been asking himself the same thing since they had landed on Loki. He thought about taciturn Plia, young, full of vim and vigor Andy, blithe, spirited Romeo, soft, delicious Tish, and dedicated Nate, for whom he had been too late. It was for them that he had taken Ivers' place with the mine and Ivers knew it. Now, he expected even more from him.

"Yes, I would," he answered. "I'm their captain."

"I thought you would when you went back to face the Raver. This is a chance to save them all, or at least even the odds for them. We don't know how many creatures are between us and the surface, but we do know more are down there." He pointed down the tunnel. Dax followed his pointing finger and imagined he could see the creatures digging out their hibernating kin. "What do you say, Captain?"

Dax sighed and picked up the walkie-talkie where he had dropped it. He keyed the mic. "Plia, get them out of here. Don't wait for us. Hit orbit as fast as you can. If we make it, we'll take the station's shuttle."

Plia didn't answer. Tish did. "Dax, don't do this, please. I need you."

The tears in her voice broke his heart. He knew he could not let her sway him. It would be far too easy. "I've got to, babe. I promised to keep you safe."

"No, Dax. Not this way."

"Listen, in the safe in my cabin there's a document. The combination is my birthday. It … it divides the *Luck* among you all equally, in case … in case I die. Andy will be the *Luck's* new captain, but all of you listen to Plia." He clicked the mic off and back on. "Oh, hell, forget that. I'll be back. I'll meet you in orbit in twenty minutes."

He clicked off the walkie-talkie. He couldn't take anymore, or he would start blubbering. "Let's do this before I change my mind."

Ivers nodded. "Now, you're a captain."

Now that he had made up his mind, the fear receded. "How do we do it?"

"We leave the ATV here, go in slow and quiet, and reconnoiter on foot. If they're down there, we blow the ceiling on top of them."

"It won't work. They'll know we're coming."

"The explosion?"

Dax shook his head. "No, they are communicating with each other. I'm betting they know how many of us there are and what color underwear you're wearing."

"You're serious," Ivers replied.

"These aren't some dumb beasts. If an alien race created them, why is the idea they made them smart enough to cooperate such a difficult concept?"

Ivers' face turned grim. "If that's true, they're even more dangerous than I thought. We have to destroy them."

"I'll settle for sealing them in long enough for us to get our asses out of here."

"Okay, then we go in hard and fast. We drive in like berserkers, toss the mine, and run like hell before they know what's happening."

It sounded like a recipe for disaster, but he had no better idea to offer. "Sounds like a real plan."

"How much charge left in your laser?"

Dax checked the power gauge and frowned. "About a quarter."

"Hmm. Five or six shots. The disruptor is about the same."

Dax pulled out his .40 caliber pistol. "I've got this."

Ivers grinned and pulled out an army knife with a fifteen-centimeter blade.

Dax climbed into the ATV, laid the laser in front of him so that the barrel pointed out the broken front windscreen, and strapped in. The harness bit into his tender, blistered flesh, but he didn't think he would have to worry about the pain for very long. Ivers laid his disruptor across his lap and set the remaining thermal mine between the seats where either of them could reach it. To his surprise, in spite of the rough treatment, the ATV cranked on the first try. Feeling like a man in a hurry to reach the gallows, he pressed the accelerator to the floor and took off.

With only one headlight, the lower ruins, which had received little attention from the K124 crew, looked like piles of rocks strewn randomly across the floor of the lava tube. They appeared suddenly like ghosts at the edge the light, racing at the ATV. He swerved to dodge the jutting bones of walls and natural solidified lava ledges the *Huresh* had left in place. He raced up a sloping fallen roof and hit air on the other side. The ATV came down hard and bounced precariously for a moment but remained upright. The shocks were taking a beating and the steering column had picked up a lot of slack. He hoped the vehicle held together long enough to escape.

By the time the *Huresh* had retreated to the lowest level, they no longer had the resources they had lavished on their earlier buildings. There was no roadway or any standing buildings. It was a war zone. The Ravers had demolished the last refuge of the *Huresh* in their zeal to kill its occupants, or perhaps the defenders had caused the destruction in the efforts to defeat the Ravers. Then, having completed their mission, the Ravers dug crypts for themselves, and slept away the intervening centuries.

A faint glow down the tunnel confused Dax until he rounded a bend and saw battery-powered LED work lights strung along the tunnel's ceiling left by the archaeology team. Gathered in front of one tunnel wall, five Ravers scraped at the hard-packed earth with their enormous clawed feet. Three semi-conscious Ravers lay on the ground, freshly excavated from their graves. As Ivers had reported, they were smaller than the live creatures and looked like shriveled fossils. A sixth Raver fed them bits of flesh with its mouth. Dax saw the mound of rotting corpses from which the flesh had come at almost the same time the stench hit him. He retched and almost threw up. Here was the missing crew of K124, reduced to bits of flesh for monsters to feed upon.

His fear of dying vanished, as an overwhelming desire to kill as many of the creatures as possible raged inside him like an erupting volcano. Just as the Ravers turned as one to face them, he slid the ATV to a stop. A cloud of dust swept past them and partially obscured the Ravers. The two adversaries, human and Raver, stared at one another for a few heartbeats; then, both he and Ivers opened fire at the same time. His laser did little physical damage, but he poured his hatred into every shot. Ivers' carefully aimed shots from his disruptor brought panic to the creatures. They milled about trying to decide whether to attack or defend the immobile Ravers, roaring their confusion. One fell kicking at the ground with wounds to its leg. A second ran headfirst into a wall and knocked itself out when Dax shot it in the snout.

As the bloodlust waned in Dax's veins, he turned the ATV around. The Ravers' confusion ended at the same time. After much chirping and grunting among the group, all but two resumed the freeing of their companions. The two chosen launched themselves at the fleeing ATV with a fury that explained the fate of the *Huresh*. They charged through the rubble heedless of any injuries, leaving a cloud of dust and a cascade of strewn stones.

Dax gunned the engine, but staying ahead of them was not easy. If not for the head start, it would have been impossible. The creatures' long strides ate up the intervening distance at an alarming rate. He pushed the ATV to its limits, driving like a madman, weaving through the rubble with no thought to the consequences of losing the race. The pair of Ravers crept inexorably closer. Ivers turned in his seat to fire at them, but Dax's weaving and the creatures' leaping and dodging made a hit impossible.

He swerved to avoid a mound of rocks and clipped the side of a building. The ATV went into a spin. As he fought the wheel to right the vehicle, a Raver rushed headlong at them from the darkness ahead of them. Dax's hands were full with the steering wheel.

"Ivers!" he shouted.

Ivers, who had been firing at the Ravers behind them, whirled in his seat, saw the Raver rushing toward them, and fired the disruptor. The energy bolt seared the hood of the vehicle and struck the creature dead center of the forehead, stunning it. It splayed its legs in a comical ballet effort to maintain its balance, stumbled, and hit the ground face first. Dax had no time to swerve. The ATV struck the creature's head, bounced into the air, and landed nose first on the two front tires. It continued forward twenty meters standing on its nose before slowly tipping over onto its roof and sliding through the rubble. The impact ejected Ivers. He soared through the air for three meters before slamming hard into the ground and sliding on his back. Dax held on and stayed with the vehicle as it rolled.

When it stopped, he scrambled out. The Raver they had hit trembled on the ground, its legs kicking out wildly in spasms. Dax didn't know if it was dying or merely stunned. He dismissed it to focus on the pair of Ravers racing up the tunnel toward them. On foot, Dax knew their chances of surviving were slim. His gaze fell upon a small, four-wheeled multipurpose tractor parked next to a dump trailer. The tractor had a front-end loader rock bucket attached with which the archaeologists had removed overburden and rubble. He leaped into the driver's cage, cranked it, and turned it toward the advancing Ravers. With the bucket raised Raver-head high, he met the leading creature head on, while Ivers stood his ground firing the disruptor. Tractor and Raver met. The impact shoved the tractor backwards with its wheels spinning. The Raver had underestimated the tractor's threat. The teeth on the bucket sliced into the Raver's neck. Blood gushed from the wound as it pawed at its neck in confusion.

As it stumbled around bleeding its life away, he sparred with the second creature. Seeing an object almost as large as it was and witnessing what it had done to its brethren, the second Raver hesitated in pressing the attack, instead, moving around, seeking a better angle. He forced the creature backwards into a pile of rubble. It stumbled and fell over backwards. Seizing the opportunity, Dax backed up and used the tractor to push the dump trailer sideways across the tunnel; then, used the tractor to seal the small gap between the trailer and the wall, partially blocking the tunnel and penning the Ravers on the far side.

"Come on!" he yelled to Ivers. He knew the heavy machinery would not impede them for long. "Do it!"

Ivers nodded and triggered the mine, but he did not toss it away immediately. Dax stared at him as the lights on the device began blinking rapidly. He began running up the tunnel. Finally, just as he thought Ivers was going to sacrifice both their lives, he took a running start and lobbed the mine over-handed beyond the tractor then joined Dax in a hasty retreat. Eight seconds later, the mine detonated.

Dax had thought the heat from the first mine had been scorching. This time, he felt as if he were surfing the corona of a supernova in a Speedo. Although he faced the opposite direction, the bright flash almost blinded him in its intensity. He blinked back tears and dodged barely discernible objects in his path. He took refuge behind a broken wall, but the intense heat spilled over and around the wall, turning exposed stone blistering hot. The heat baked his body through his heavy shirt and melted his hair around the edges of his cap. His already blistered skin felt as though it was peeling away from his bones. He tried to suppress a scream, but it erupted from his savaged throat feeling like a ball of fire. His clothing smoldered. A cloud of hot dust and air descended on them like a vengeful god, engulfing them. This time, he kept his mouth closed to avoid inhaling the hot dust and smoke.

Ivers fared no better. He lay on the ground a few meters away, his clothes smoking from chips of hot rock blasted out by the explosion. Dax crawled over to swipe them away, but the pain in his hands forced him to stop and curl up in a fetal position. He didn't know how long they remained laying there. He assumed they had succeeded or the Ravers would have eaten them. He tried to turn his head to look at the damage they had caused, but his blistered neck refused to allow it. Finally, the screaming pain receded to a dull constant hurt in the places that were not entirely numb from overtaxed nerve endings. He could barely feel his swollen hands.

The heat and dust dissipated but the steady rumble increased. The floor of the tunnel trembled. The stone wall behind which he had sought shelter disintegrated into a loose pile of rock. Chips of rock flaked from the roof of the tunnel and fell around them. With the sound of two bowling balls colliding, the roof cracked. Dax glanced at Ivers, who had the same look of fear in his eyes. The blast had weakened the entire lower-level tunnel. They were about to be buried alive.

They leaped from ground, ignored their pain, and raced up the tunnel. Larger chunks of rock from the roof followed them. Ivers switched on the flashlight attached to the ion disruptor to light their path. The crack outpaced them. Dax watched the spider web of fractures in the roof spread and widen. He held his arms over his head to ward off the cascade of rocks and dirt.

As if squeezing a tube of toothpaste, the collapsing lower end of the tunnel moved toward them, forcing dust and hot air over them. Dax knew they could never outrun it. He could barely see. He ran with his hand touching the side of the lava tube to maintain a straight course. When his hands touched metal, he stopped – the sanctuary where they had found Rathiri.

"Here!" he called to Ivers.

Ivers charged out of the dust darkness, almost colliding with him. They found the open door and tried to pull it closed it behind them. It wouldn't budge. Dax kicked at the rocks, blocking the door until the massive door began swinging shut. Rocks pounded on the door as it closed as if the devil were seeking entry. Once inside, he collapsed on the ground coughing from the dust and the strain. Ivers collapsed with his back against the door. The air in the sanctuary was dusty but not as bad the air outside. He saw Ivers wrinkle his nose at a foul odor and play his light around the room. It settled on a pile of human excrement in the corner.

"Rathiri," he said. "Thanks, Director."

The rumbling continued for several minutes more before slowly subsiding. Ivers tried the door with no luck. Dax climbed to his feet and leaned into the door. Together, they managed to open it just wide enough to wiggle through the narrow opening. To Dax's dismay, the falling rock had blocked the tunnel leading to Level 2. Since he had already collapsed the roof of the tunnel to Level 3, they were going nowhere.

"We are thoroughly and intimately fucked," he said.

Ivers stared at the tons of fallen rock. "Well, we did what we set out to do. We either killed or trapped the Ravers on Level 5."

Dax glared at him. "I didn't set out to suffocate or to bake. Hell, I thought the first explosion would kill me. When it didn't, I allowed myself to hope. Now, my crew has my ship, and I have you for company until the air turns foul. Like I said, we are fucked."

"We could try digging our way out," Ivers suggested.

Dax looked at his bleeding, blistered hands. "I can't feel my fingers. I don't think I can dig."

Ivers sat down and leaned against the metal door. "We'll rest up awhile." He pulled a small container from his belt and opened it clumsily with his burned fingers. "Here."

"What is it?"

"A mini first aid kit. It contains a tube of burn ointment with antibiotics, a few pain pills, and shot of Boost for energy."

"I'll share the burn ointment with you and split the pain pills, but I don't need more energy."

Ivers handed him the ointment and two pain pills. "We'll need it later when we dig ourselves out."

Dax rubbed the emollient on his hands and dabbed a little on his face. At first, it stung, but then the burning abated to a dull gnawing pain he could live with. He was glad he couldn't see the extent of the damage by the dim light cast by the flashlight.

"You are an optimistic one, aren't you?" he said.

"We ain't dead yet."

Swallowing the two pills dry with his savaged throat proved impossible. He let them dissolve in his mouth and wished he hadn't. The bitter taste was worse than the pain.

He heard a rustling sound. "What are you doing?"

"Getting some sleep."

Dax was flabbergasted. "You can sleep now?"

"I can sleep anywhere, anytime. You should too. We have a busy day ahead of us."

Dax lay back on the ground and groaned when a rock rubbed against his burned neck. "Yeah, and we don't have any coffee."

He wouldn't bet the family jewels on the odds of their digging their way out. At least Tish and the others made it. That was his primary goal. His survival was a hoped-for secondary concern. He didn't think he could sleep, but the relief that Tish would survive eased his troubled mind. He slept in spite of his aches and pains.

# 11

As Cici and the others reached the Atrium, the distant rumble of the collapsing ceiling reverberated through the tunnel. In a panic, Cici grabbed the walkie-talkie. “Dax, are you okay?” she yelled. She got no response. Tish looked at her with an agonized expression marring her face. “It’s the rocks,” Cici told her. “They’re blocking the signal. I’m sure they made it.”

A tear leaked down Tish’s cheek. She swiped her hand across her face to brush it away and shook her head. “No, I don’t think so. He knew he was going to die. He did it to save us.”

Cici grabbed Tish by the shoulders and shook her. “Don’t give up hope. If they killed the Ravers or sealed them in, they’ll find a way out.”

Tish turned away, but Cici could see her shoulders shake as she sobbed. She felt sorry for Tish. It was obvious she cared deeply for Dax. It surprised her that she did too. She grieved for him. He was a strange man with a strange moral code, but in his own way, he was trustworthy and honorable. He blustered and roared, but he was more thunder than lightning.

The sledge slowed.

“Are you waiting for them?” she asked Plia. In spite of her assurances to Tish, she didn’t think Dax or Sergeant Ivers had survived the cave-in. They faced their own danger.

Plia moved the spotlight attached to the seat Nate had welded to the end of the sledge until it outlined a Raver standing on top of a wall less than a hundred meters away, scarcely visible through the dust blowing in from the storm outside. Though they could barely see it, Cici was certain it sensed them as plainly, as if it had eyes. It immediately darted out of the light. Then, Plia swung the light to reveal a second creature on the opposite side fifty meters away. It, too, ducked for cover. Cici's heart sank.

"That's why," Plia replied. Her voice was bitter.

She resumed driving with one hand and tracked the missile pod between the two creatures with the other. If both Ravers attacked at the same time, she would be able to fire at only one of them. Romeo and Andy had the two laser rifles. Romeo positioned the ATV he drove in front of the sledge to cover both directions ahead of them. Cici looked down at the .338 in her hand and remembered what Dax had said about its lack of effectiveness against the Ravers. She made sure the safety was off. At least she could make noise, as he suggested.

A brief blur of motion along the right side of the sledge drew her attention to a low row of buildings. "Over there," she said.

As if summoned by her words, one of the Ravers appeared on top of a wall. It followed their progress with its head. Its hind claws gripped the rock wall so tightly the rock began to crumble beneath it. She heard the missile pod track toward the creature. She needed to make sure the Raver didn't disappear again so Plia had a clear shot.

She hopped down from the sledge and took two steps away from it toward the creature. "Hey! Over here you ugly bastard," she yelled, waving her rifle.

She tried not to dwell on the fact she was using herself as bait. She trusted Plia's abilities. She fired a shot at it to get its attention. The bullet struck the wall beside the Raver. It amazed her that she got that close to it. The Raver lifted its head, chirped a series of fluid notes; then, growled and leaped from the wall. It plowed through the rubble like a bulldozer aimed directly at her as if accepting her challenge.

"Anytime you're ready, Plia."

Plia stopped the sledge and tracked the Raver's approach with the missile pod. She waited until the Raver was less than thirty meters away before firing. At the hiss of the missile firing, the creature veered to its left, but it was too late. It lost its footing on the loose rock and skidded toward them. The missile struck it in the shoulder joint. The creature squealed in pain, as shrapnel sliced through its left forearm, cleanly amputating it. Shards of black scales flew from its chest. Shrapnel from the missile peppered the sledge. One small piece whizzed past Cici's head and bounced off the sledge's side.

Romeo swung his vehicle around and drove toward the Raver firing his laser, pumping bursts of energy into the Raver's open wound. The Raver remained on its feet and continued advancing toward the sledge in spite of its injuries. Cici aimed her rifle and fired again. She didn't even know if she hit it.

"The rest of you watch the other side," Plia warned.

The Raver, suffering from heavy blood loss, finally stopped moving. It tottered for a moment, and fell over onto its side. Its chest heaved out its last dying breath. Romeo spun the ATV around and headed back to the sledge. They had no time to rest. The Ravers were smarter than anyone had thought. While they focused their attention on the Raver attacking them, a second creature sneaked in silently from behind them.

Cici heard Tish's strangled, "Andy! Don't." She turned and saw the brash young co-pilot leap out of the ATV, yelling, "Over here!"

The second Raver approached the sledge through the haze of dust at the edge of the light. Plia turned the missile pod toward it, but it tracked too slowly. Only Andy was in any position to shoot it. She knew it was a bad move on his part. He was either too cocksure of himself or felt the responsibility fell on his shoulders to protect them in Dax's absence. It was a one-sided battle. The creature was too fast for Andy's laser. It bobbed and weaved through the debris, using it as a shield instead of forcing its way through it, a change of tactics that caught Andy by surprise. It disappeared from sight for a moment; then, suddenly burst into view only five meters away. The Raver leaped high into the air, covering the intervening space in one bound.

Andy saw it coming but too late. He backpedaled toward the ATV, but couldn't move quickly enough. He screamed just as the creature landed on top of him, driving a claw through his chest, and crushing him beneath a ton of flesh and bone. Andy's high-pitched scream cut off abruptly.

Romeo stopped his ATV beside the sledge, leaped out, and using the edge of the sledge to rest his laser, fired. The Raver ignored the others and immediately focused its rage on him, as if aware only the laser he held presented any danger to it. Romeo fired once more and had the presence of mind to drop and roll beneath the sledge as the Raver rushed at him, pushing his slim body as far beneath the undercarriage as he could manage. The Raver slammed into the side of the sledge with enough force to lift it onto one set of treads. Tish held on to the base of the missile pod to keep from falling off, while Cici scrambled out of the way, fearing it would topple over on top of her.

Romeo fired twice more at the creature's feet, forcing it to drop the sledge back down onto the ground. As the Raver backed up, it banged into the ATV in which Myles sat. It whirled on the vehicle. Myles froze. He didn't raise his rifle or make any effort to defend himself. He stared at the monster as if in disbelief it was real. The Raver noticed him and emitted a loud screech. Its massive jaws snapped shut over the hapless climatologist's head, lifting him from the vehicle before decapitating him. Blood spewed from his neck as he fell to the ground, twitching in his death throes. Cici screamed and fired her rifle as quickly as she could pull back the bolt to chamber a round, but in her anger and haste, her shots went wild.

"Damn you!" she yelled and went after the Raver using her rifle as a club. She landed one blow on the creature's head before it swatted her away with a flick of one of its rear legs. She slammed against the edge of the sledge and hit the ground hard, knocking the air from her lungs. She felt as if a speeding semi truck had sideswiped her. Dazed by the blow, she struggled to draw a breath and waited to die.

Romeo saved her. At close range, the laser was more effective. He fired from beneath the edge of the sledge. The bolt of energy struck the Raver just in front of its ear hole, one of the few spots of its body not protected by armor. The flesh around the ear smoked and burned. The Raver screamed in agony, leaped over the sledge, and disappeared back into the shadows. Plia threw herself off the sledge to avoid the creature's sweeping claws. To Cici's dismay, an answering call erupted from nearby.

Plia clambered back aboard the sledge and hit the button to fire the last missile at the fleeing Raver. Nothing happened.

"Damn!" she swore. She tried again, but still it did not fire. She looked down at a tangle of wires ripped out by the Raver's claws. "No time to repair that. Let's go!"

Romeo crawled from beneath the sledge and leaped into the ATV with Rathiri in the back. Cici took the driver's seat of Andy's ATV with Tish in the passenger seat. Neither of them looked at the wet blood staining the seat and floorboard. Cici slammed it into gear and shot forward. Plia dropped from the sledge into the passenger seat of Romeo's moving vehicle.

Outside in the open, the storm had intensified. The wind whipped the dust into a raging frenzy. The sharp sand particles bit into Cici's exposed flesh like a rasp drawn across her tender skin. Through the swirling dust, she saw *Fortune's Luck* and felt a small glimmer of hope. Then, she noticed the long gash in the hull near the engine room, and her heart sank. The Ravers had gotten there first. She didn't know if the ship could fly, but at least it offered the protection of a steel hull between them and the Ravers.

Tish hit the remote control to open the cargo hatch. The first ATV bearing Plia, Romeo, and Rathiri shot through the door and spun to a stop. Cici steered her ATV toward the door, as Tish started the hatch cycling closed. She swerved to avoid the other ATV, hit the brakes, and slid to a halt just centimeters from a bulkhead. With the hatch sealed, she should have heard silence. Instead, he heard an ominous whistling from the engine room compartment, as the wind whipped in through the rent hull.

Plia leaped from her ATV and barked, "Tish, prep her for flight. I'll check the engines."

Tish stood and stared at her, still stunned by the deaths of Myles and Andy and Dax's decision to leave them. Her lips trembled on the verge of tears.

"Now's not the time to grieve," Plia snapped. "Doctor Adar! Secure the ATVs. Romeo, take the co-pilot's seat." She looked Doctor Rathiri. She noticed his haggard and confused face. Her voice became gentler. "Please find a seat and strap in."

"Yes, yes, I will," he replied.

Plia raced to the engine room. Cici worked frantically to lash the ATVs securely to the deck using straps and tie downs. Rathiri ambled around the cargo bay lost. Cici worried the ordeal had been too much for him. He looked ten years older than when she had last seen him ten days earlier. She was helping Rathiri to the wardroom when Plia emerged from the engine room. Her expression was grim. Cici's stomach sank.

"Just as I feared, the Raver attack was not random. The rip in the hull severed the controls to the Skip Drive. Without Nate, I don't know if I have the skill to get it back online. The rip passed through two compartments behind a section of hull impossible to reach from the inside. Given time, I could repair the hull from the outside, but the creatures will not be that accommodating."

"So, what does all that mean?" Cici asked, fearing she knew the answer.

"It means we're not going into orbit. I'm not sure we can even lift off. If I missed something, some damage behind a bulkhead, we might explode instead."

"So, we're stuck here?"

"For now until I can run an engine analysis on the computer."

All the tension and fear that had been keeping Cici going instantly evaporated, replaced by a lethargy that sapped her will and numbed her legs. She leaned against the wall to keep from falling. "They can get to us, can't they?"

Plia nodded. "Eventually, yes."

Cici saw the blank expression on Director Rathiri's face. She sighed and pushed from the wall. "I had better make Ambrose comfortable."

Plia headed for the bridge. "I'll inform the others of the situation, and then see what I can do about the engines."

Cici took Rathiri by the hand. "Come with me, Director."

"Yes, yes, Doctor Adar. I will. Thank you. There is something about the creatures I must tell you, perhaps Captain Wyldd as well." He frowned. "It was important, but I seem to have let it slip my mind. It's about the *Huresh* and the Ravers –"

"Later, Director. You need rest. You'll be fine."

He sagged into her arms. "Yes, yes. So tired."

Cici's grief threatened to overwhelm her. Facing the creatures, she had not had time to dwell on Myles' death. Now, it didn't seem real. She kept expecting him to walk into the wardroom and ask her if she wanted a cup of tea. All she could think of was the times she had berated him for his conviction that tea was a panacea for all ills. That his death was her fault cut her to the quick. In her naiveté, she had refused to consider the dangers in attempting to rescue her missing colleagues. She had refused to listen to Dax, thinking him a simple coward. Even when faced with the carnage at the station, she still held out hope for the others. Her insistence on going into the Catacombs had killed her friend, as well as one of *Fortune's Luck's* crew, maybe Dax and Ivers as well.

She sat Rathiri in a flight seat in the wardroom and harnessed him in. "I'll get you something to drink, Director."

He smiled through parched lips. "Oh, that would be nice, Doctor Adar. I am so very thirsty. Perhaps some tea?"

She almost burst into tears at the mention of tea. "Yes, Director. Some tea would be nice."

As she went into the galley and searched through the cabinets for tea, she felt a tear roll down her cheek. She brushed it away, but more followed. Finally, she could not hold them back. She sat on the deck, leaned her back against the cabinets, and wept for Myles, for her friends, and for herself. She did not think she would be leaving Loki. The Ravers would see to that

# 12

Dax awoke to the sound of hammering. When he moved to get up, the aches of his bruised muscles and battered flesh hit him first; then, as the blistered skin cracked with movement, those pains ripped through him like a buzz saw. He almost decided to remain where he was, but he noticed Ivers standing in a pool of light from his flashlight, attempting to pry a large boulder from the daunting pile of rocks blocking the tunnel with the butt of the disruptor. He sighed. He couldn't allow Ivers to hoard all the glory of getting them out.

"Move over, John Henry. Let a real coal miner take over." He eyed the small cavity Ivers' efforts had produced. "At this rate, we'll be here until we're old and gray."

"I just started," Ivers replied. "Go back and get your beauty rest."

"No, I insist, unless, of course, this is still a military operation."

"You don't like the Navy, do you?"

"I have no good reason to. I worked the Tanis Sector on a cargo ship when I was younger. Because of the U.N. blockade, we had to deal with some unsavory types. The Navy didn't bother to distinguish blockade-runners from free traders. I lost some friends in an unarmed freighter when the Navy didn't bother boarding our ship. They just stood off and lobbed missiles at us. Six us of managed to reach escape pods. Eight didn't."

"I lost friends at Tanis too. The blockade-runners, as you call them, had a nasty habit of blowing their Skip Drives and taking out a Navy vessel with them when cornered, especially if they had just transferred a cargo of weapons for the secessionists."

Dax glared at him. He hadn't known about the suicide ships and wasn't sure he believed Ivers. "We delivered food and medical supplies – no weapons. I know because I was the cargo handler."

"I'm sorry for your friends, but you helped turn what would have been a short siege into an eight-month campaign. Thousands died in a useless fight for no good reason. None of the planets in Tanis Sector was self-sufficient. They could not have survived without outside help. It was never about independence from Earth. The whole thing was an attempt by the Ducati clan on Bene Prime and the Wingate family of Archimedes to take control of the Vanadium mines on Tanis III and set their own prices."

"People were starving."

"Not the miner barons. They raided two planets for their personal storehouses with no thought to the people they left without food. In the end, they retained the mines under U.N. treaty and got a hefty price increase for their ore. They didn't even bother to petition the U.N. for relief for the beleaguered worlds they used as pawns. A couple of religious groups did what they could, but hundreds more died before the relief effort reached the outlying provinces."

"That was never in the news."

"No, I guess not. The U.N. wasn't proud of caving in, but the new fleet they were building needed the vanadium."

Dax lifted a large rock from the pile and tossed it aside. "Why didn't the U.N. Human Rights Council do something?"

"The Wingate family controls six of the largest news organizations on Earth. The press heralded them as poor rebels fighting for a noble cause and the big bad Navy as the aggressor." He looked at Dax. "Sound familiar?"

Dax winced. "I didn't know."

"Few did. The Navy didn't want to open old wounds, and the U.N. Secretary General was happy to let things die down."

"Were you at Tanis?"

He paused. "I was on the ship that blew up the *Tigress*, your freighter."

Dax glared at him and balled his fists. Ivers noticed Dax's reaction. "I wasn't a sergeant then. I was just a corporal. I didn't like what we did, but no one asked my opinion. Too many sailors had died for anyone to care about a blockade runner."

Dax unclenched his fists. It was no use fighting old battles. "Let's dig our way out of here. I'm getting hungry."

"I've been thinking about that."

"And?"

He tossed a rock away in disgust. "I figure it will take about a month to move enough rocks to get out. There may be another way."

"I'm interested."

He pointed to the ventilator shaft above the sanctuary door.

"We can barely fit inside, and it twists and turns before it reaches the surface. We'd never make it."

"No, not to the surface, but they must connect with each other. All we need to do is find one that takes us around the cave-in."

Ivers plan made sense except for one detail. "How do we reach the opening?"

Ivers pointed his flashlight at the door. "See those markings? At first, I thought they were some kind of decoration. Looking closer, I saw they are notches deep enough for a human foot." He grinned. "They're a ladder to the opening."

Dax eyed the notches with suspicion. It was precarious climb under any circumstances. With blistered and numb hands, it would be an ordeal, as would be negotiating the ventilation shaft itself. In the end, what choice did he have?

"Let's get going."

Ivers led the way. Climbing up the shallow indentations proved more difficult than Dax anticipated. The *Huresh* surely had smaller feet to fit into the small notches. His size-ten boots barely fit, and he slipped often, leaving him hanging by one blistered hand. The going become tougher once they reached the opening. The shaft, carved from the native rock, went straight up for ten meters. Romeo had slightly underestimated the ventilator shaft's size, but it still measured less than one-and-a-half meters wide. The interior was not smooth, providing traction for his feet, as he wiggled up the shaft behind Ivers. He pushed his laser rifle ahead of him, balancing it on the top of his head. He used muscles he had not exercised for years. By the time they reached the first horizontal junction, his calf muscles and shoulders burned from the exertion.

Folding at the waist and sliding along on his belly, he made the 90-degree turn into the horizontal shaft. The tight, enclosed space played tricks with his mind, closing in on him. He closed his eyes and concentrated on crawling along like a worm. The air was scorching hot and dry. Two thousand years of dust had accumulated in the shaft. It was difficult to draw a deep breath, but he realized his mind was trying to force him to stop the punishment he inflicted on his body.

The shaft seemed to continue for a dozen kilometers, but he knew it could not have been more than one before they came upon a second opening above the roof of one of the ruins. The shaft above the opening made a tight bend before continuing on its horizontal course. They could go no farther. It was a five-meter drop to the roof below. Because of the narrow confines, they could not turn around to drop feet first. Ivers slid headfirst into the opening and fell. Dax watched him hit the roof amid a cloud of dust. He groaned, cursed loudly, and rolled out of the way for Dax to follow.

Dax took a deep breath and repeated Ivers' graceless maneuver. He tried to use his hands and legs to cushion his fall, but he landed on his back hard enough to knock the breath from him. As he lay there hurting and gasping for air, the roof sagged beneath him. With a loud crack, the supporting beam snapped, dropping the roof and its two occupants onto the floor below.

Ivers pulled himself from the rubble. "That's one way off the roof," he quipped.

Dax pushed a pile of rocks from him. "Where are we?"

Ivers checked his watch. "GPS says we're in the bypass tunnel to Level 2."

"If the fall didn't break your watch," he groaned. "I think I broke my back."

"You'd better hope not. I'm not carrying you."

Dax pulled his laser rifle from beneath him, the source of the sharp pain in his back. Clenching his teeth against the pain, he pushed himself from the floor, brushed off the chunks of masonry, and sat up. His muscles ached and his hands were raw and bleeding, but he could move.

They climbed down from the third-floor room through a former stairwell half-filled with debris. In the lava tube, Ivers shone his light across the floor until the beam picked out three sets of tracks – the sledge and two ATVs.

"They made it this far anyway," he said.

Dax hoped they made it all the way out.

They walked. Dax felt more movement in the air and more dust. The storm Myles had predicted had hit the city. As they neared the Atrium, another odor mixed with the flinty smell of dust. Ivers noticed it too.

"Cordite," he said. "Your Plia used a missile."

That meant Ravers. Dax checked his rifle and switched off the safety. When Ivers' light illuminated the sledge, he felt sick at his stomach.

"I don't see the ATVs," Ivers said.

That fact gave him slight hope, until they drew nearer the sledge. The smell of blood was strong, as was the foul stench of the dead Raver lying on its side.

"She got one of them," he said.

Ivers had spotted something else. He pointed to the two bodies in the dirt. One was headless; the other crushed into the ground. His heart pounded with dread, fearing that one of them was Tish. He felt a moment of relief when he recognized Andy by his flight suit; then, immediately regretted taking comfort that one had been spared at the cost of another. He imagined Andy playing the hero and held himself to blame. The young co-pilot had constantly sought Dax's approval, but he had been too hard-nosed to give it.

He approached the headless corpse slowly, not wanting to look. He steeled himself. The body was male and too tall for Tish. That left Myles or Romeo. The clothing was too drenched in blood and dust to tell if it was a flight suit or casual clothing. He decided the corpse was not thin enough for Romeo. Dax returned and knelt by Andy's body. A large hole bored through his chest where a Raver had clawed him before crushing him with its enormous weight. He looked around but didn't see any more bodies.

"There's a missile left in the pod," Ivers said. "I wonder why she left it." He crawled up on the sledge. "Oh, I see."

Dax brushed his hand across Andy's hair in a last goodbye gesture and joined Ivers. A nest of shredded fiber optic wiring protruded from a severed cable. Ivers fingered the wires.

"Oh, I see." He began tracing wires with his finger.

"What are you doing?" Dax demanded. "We need to go."

"Why walk when we can ride?"

"Plia wouldn't have left it if she could repair it."

"Maybe she didn't have time." He looked around. "If you haven't noticed, we're being watched."

If they were in danger, Dax wondered why his scalp didn't itch. Then he realized the flesh on his head was so burned it was numb. He heard a rock bounce down a wall to his left and peered into the darkness.

"Maybe you had better hurry with those missiles."

"Just a minute." He opened an access panel in the floor of the sledge. "Now, if Plia is the woman I think she is … Aha! A fiber splice kit."

He took a multi-use tool and stripped several of the wires. He worked deftly and quickly but with the knowledge that cutting off too much wire might leave him short. He set the lock assembly on the deck of the sledge, placed a fiber lock splicer in the press, and inserted a matching stripped wire in either end. He pressed the lever, connecting the fiber optic cables. He repeated the process with two more cables. Dax willed him to hurry. The sound of a Raver grew louder as it came closer. The floodlights snapped on. "One more wire," he said. The missile pod illuminated. "There. That should do it."

Dax almost kissed Ivers in appreciation. "Right. Let's move." Dax took the makeshift seat and grabbed the remote control.

"We might need this," Ivers said, tossing Andy's laser rifle onto the sledge. He hopped up and aimed his disruptor toward the noise. "Okay, hit it!"

Dax cranked the sledge and gunned the engine. Just as they took off, a Raver raced at them from the darkness. Ivers fired two shots at it, driving it back into the rubble. A second Raver joined it. Both popped out from behind a building behind them. Ivers turned the missile pod upward. "I hope this works," he said, as he pressed the switch.

"You're aiming too high," Dax yelled, but it was too late.

Their last missile streaked down the tunnel and struck the roof sixty meters behind them. The explosion rocked the cavern. Long, jagged fissures opened in the roof. Pieces showered down, pelting the sledge with fist-sized rocks. A low ominous rumble in the distance grew louder. The floor began to bounce beneath the treads. Ruined buildings collapsed around them. Finally, with the screech of a dying animal, the roof behind them let go.

It did not end there. The explosion shattered the brittle rock like a sledgehammer blow to a block of ice. An avalanche of falling roof raced up the lava tube toward them. When it reached the Atrium, the cracks spread out across the entire roof. Sections of the rusted metal supports for the glass dome in the roof broke away, as did pieces of the surrounding rock. Slabs of rock fell onto the buildings, crushing them. The metal framework for the elevator shook itself apart and collapsed in a heap of metal beams and a smashed cage.

The opening in the ceiling grew larger. Dust from the dunes above cascaded down. The entire complex was collapsing in on itself. A cloud of dust enveloped them, mixing with the storm-driven dust blowing in from outside. Dax could barely see to guide the sledge.

Gradually, the sledge pulled ahead of the dust. He shot between the failed protective walls and up the ramp as it crumbled beneath them. He saw *Fortune's Luck* through the dust and swore at Plia that they were still there, but glad she had not left them behind. As he drew abreast of the ship, he saw the rip in the hull of the engine room and guessed why the *Luck* was still on the ground. He grabbed the walkie-talkie.

"Open up, we're coming in," he shouted.

Seconds later, the cargo hatch opened. He didn't bother hitting the brakes. He released the accelerator going up the ramp. The sledge went airborne and landed with a bounce and a thud in the middle of the cargo bay. One of the tracks snapped and slung across the bay. He turned the wheel sharply to the right to avoid

Plia standing at the door control console, and slammed into the ATVs.

He leaped out of the seat. “Ivers, take the pilot’s seat. I’ll check the engines.”

“Dax,” Plia said, “the Skip engine ....”

“Later. We have to go. Now!”

Ivers rushed to the bridge. Dax raced to the engine room, saw the damage, and cursed his luck. They couldn’t Skip, and they couldn’t leave the atmosphere with a two-meter long gash in the hull. He wasn’t certain they could take off, but they had to try. He made a quick survey, determined the damage mainly affected the Skip engines, and brought the main engines online. He had no time for the long pre-flight checklist. Either they worked or everyone died. There was no in between.

He hit the intercom. “Everyone brace themselves. Ivers, get us off the ground.” He held on as Ivers fired the engines. “Come on, *Luck*, baby. One more trip for papa, okay?”

# 13

The lift-off had been rougher than Cici expected. The crosswinds and rising thermals ahead of the storm front tossed the ship around like a kite on a short string. She clenched the chair armrests so tightly her hands ached. She had once ridden the station's shuttle along the edges of a dust storm, but it had been nothing compared to the shaking of *Fortune's Luck.* The high-pitched scream of shearing metal that had echoed throughout the ship just after takeoff had not been a normal sound. She did not know much about ships, but the sound was enough to concern her.

She watched the take-off on the wardroom's view screen. Through the swirling haze of dust, the ground around the station trembled and subsided, collapsing into the lava tubes. First, the outer reaches of the ruined city disappeared block by block; then, the station domes and shacks, her home for over nine months, followed, swallowed by the expanding yawning chasm. Geysers of dust jetted into the air to join the thickening cloud shrouding the city. Station K124 and everything they had built, even the ruins they had come to explore, were gone. At least the bodies of her friends and colleagues were getting a proper burial. She hoped it meant the end of the Ravers, though she doubted it. They had already proven more resourceful than anyone had thought possible.

She was overjoyed that Dax and Sergeant Ivers had made it. Enough people had died on Loki. She felt out of place sitting helplessly while the others tried to get the ship operational; however, she knew she would only be in the way. She could not question Rathiri about events at the station. He had fallen asleep almost as soon as she had strapped him into a seat, even before he had his tea. Days with no sleep, no food or water, and the constant tension had drained him. She let him sleep and concentrated on her field, xenobiology.

She had not been able to perform a microscopic examination of the creatures, but her visual inspection of the dead Raver had revealed much. She was more certain than ever that they were engineered creatures, a combination of advanced gene manipulation and technology. She had performed a spectral analysis of one of the ebony shards of the creature's scales and discovered that the Ravers had not secreted them like normal keratin. The material resembled a crystallized metallic compound cast as one piece and attached to the creature by a strong organic bonding agent.

Given Ivers' account of the creatures surviving in a vacuum and deep-freeze temperatures, and Dr. Rathiri's revelation to the crew of the *Abraxas* that the Raver DNA did not match any DNA found in the few *Huresh* remains, they could not be native to Loki. But who had created them? She regretted her inability to access any of the computers at the station. She hoped that once she reached KB, she could download copies of files from the backup server in the orbiting satellite. Until the discovery of the Ravers, her nine months on Loki had been unremarkable and not very productive. Now that she had a subject worthy of study, she would have to leave the planet. She consoled herself with the fact that she was still alive when so many of her companions were not.

Fifteen minutes into the trip, alarms began sounding throughout the ship, raising more concerns in her already troubled mind. A few seconds later, Romeo stuck his head in the door of the wardroom and said, "We may have to land. Dax said to suit up. Andy's suit should just about fit you." He looked at Rathiri. "Wake him. He needs to suit up, too. We have a spare suit that should fit him. I'll help you."

"What's wrong?" she asked. Her heart pounded. "Are we crashing?"

"Ivers took out the station's com antennae when he lifted off. Part of the mast lodged in the port forward thruster. We'll never be able to land at K124B. She's too unstable. Dax is trying to set down on a flat plain and repair the thruster. If not, we'll have to hike in."

"How short of KB are we?"

"About fifty clicks, er fifty kilometers."

Walking fifty kilometers in a raging dust storm, even wearing an excursion suit, sounded suicidal. She knew from experience that most of the suit's visor filters and radar would be useless. The area in which the *Fortune's Luck's* captain had chosen to land was crisscrossed with fractures ranging from half-meter-wide cracks to two-hundred-meter-deep chasms fifty meters across. Avoiding them in near-zero visibility would be a challenge.

She roused Rathiri. At first, he looked confused; then, realizing where he was, his features contorted into a mask of fear. "What's wrong?"

"We're landing to make repairs. You'll need to suit up."

He nodded, but needed her help to stand. "I'm sorry. I feel rather weak. I haven't eaten in quite some time."

She noted how pale he looked. As she held his hand, she felt his rapid heartbeat. His ordeal had taken a heavy toll on him. He looked much older than his fifty-six years. "There will be a nutrient drink in the suit. Sip on it until we can eat a real meal."

He nodded. "Yes, thank you."

She felt a twinge of guilt when she saw the name Andy on the suit Romeo handed her. Romeo held it upright while she slipped her legs and arms into the one-piece suit. She was several centimeters shorter than its former occupant was. She could barely see over the lower lip of the faceplate, and the joints rubbed the underside of her armpits. She was thoroughly uncomfortable, but she did not let Romeo see her discomfort. She had worn a suit before on the trip out, but that had been over nine months ago. She did not like it then and liked it even less now.

"Thank you," she told him.

He smiled at her. "My pleasure. You had better strap in again. It's going to be a rough landing, I think."

After he left, she helped Rathiri into his suit, following the same procedure Romeo had shown her. Just as they returned to the wardroom, Dax announced over the intercom, "We're landing in two minutes. I'll channel power to the other thrusters to compensate for the damaged one, but it might get a bit shaky. Hold on."

Hearing his voice brought a thrill to her. She had thought he had chosen a hero's death to save his crew and her. Ivers had decided to return to help him. Her first estimates of the captain of *Fortune's Luck* had been off the mark. Dax had struck her as self-centered, cowardly, and untrustworthy. He had proven her wrong on all accounts.

Tish had been beside herself with joy since she heard Dax's voice on the walkie-talkie. It was all they could do to keep her from rushing out to meet him. Since the take-off, Dax had acted like another person. His concern for his stricken ship rivaled his concern for his crew. Having lost two of them, he doubled his efforts to save his ship.

She tightened both her and Rathiri's harnesses as taut as possible and held on with both hands. Without warning, the ship fell from beneath her. For a moment, it felt as if the ship were standing on its nose, but then it leveled off. She heard the engines powering down from a thunderous roar to a painful scream. The ship slewed to the right and tilted twenty degrees. It had barely righted when it hit the ground like a stone skipping a cross a lake, jarring her teeth. The ship's keel gouged out a deep furrow in the hard earth; then, lifted back into the air. Like an awkward gooney bird trying to land, it hit harder the second time and spun to one side. The deck canted onto its side until Cici was lying parallel to the hull, which had become the new deck. A large steel stewing pot flew from the galley and bounced by her head, barely missing it. The metal deck shuddered and popped until the ship expended its forward momentum. With the groan of an old man rising from his chair, it settled back down on her keel.

She almost expected to hear, "Thank you for travelling Captain Dax Airlines," over the intercom. Instead, she heard a glaring silence. Slowly, as they overcame their fear of movement, people began stirring. Romeo came in and saw the dented steel pot on the floor. He grinned.

"Sorry. The cabinet door doesn't shut properly. Are you all right?"

She loosened her harness and stood, shakily at first, but after a few steps, her balance returned. “Yes, I’m fine.” She went to Rathiri and helped him up. He was shaky but unharmed.

Romeo walked up to the director and stared into his visor. “You okay in there?” Rathiri nodded. Romeo disappeared into the galley. “I’ll start some coffee brewing,” he announced through the open door. “The captain needs his coffee.”

“How did the ship weather the landing? Is weather the right word?”

“Yes, it is. The *Luck* is in more or less in one piece. The captain decided not to lower the landing skids. If he had, we would probably be upside down. The captain, Plia, and Tish are checking the damaged thruster right now.”

“You’re the only one who doesn’t call him by his first name,” she observed.

“He’s the captain. He’s earned the title, so I use it. You see, it’s the little things that mean anything. The others call him ‘Captain’ in port out of respect. I choose to use his rank at all times. He says he doesn’t mind, but I can see his back straighten slightly when anyone calls him captain.”

She nodded. It seemed Captain Dax Wyldd was more complex man than she thought, and he had earned the respect of his crew.

* * * *

“I’ve seen worse,” Plia said.

Looking at the mangled thruster housing, Dax doubted it. A piece of the antennae mast protruded from the hull beside the thruster. It hadn’t penetrated the inner bulkhead, but it had severed power couplings, fuel lines, and attitude controls to the thruster.

“How long?” he rasped. His throat burned with every word.

“In this?” She waved her hand at the dust swirling around them. “We’ll have to yank out the antennae splinter without doing even more damage and erect a tent around the thruster. Otherwise, the dust will infiltrate everything and contaminate fluids and bearings. I’ll have to mill a new gimbal. I’d say eight hours.”

He didn’t want to hear that dire news. He winced at the mention of milling a new part. That had been Nate’s job. Many things would have to change until he could find a new engineer. “That’s too long.”

"Even if everyone pitches in on the removal and installation, it will still take two or three hours to mill a new gimbal. It's a precision part, and we don't carry a spare. It would be impossible shave off more than half an hour, and I doubt that that much. We either work in our suits, which are cumbersome, or wear respirators. We can't breathe in this dust."

Dax sighed. In a couple of hours, the storm would be fully upon them. Working in those conditions would be nearly impossible, even wearing a suit. A tent could never remain intact in such conditions. Ivers had crippled his already damaged ship, although given the circumstances, he didn't know if he could have fared any better than the Marine sergeant had. Not that he would ever admit that to Ivers. He would let him stew in his guilt for a while. Dax suspected his own rough landing had not helped matters. He hoped he hadn't ruptured the *Luck's* belly by not using the skids. He had probably driven the antennae deeper into the ship's wound.

He worried about Ravers. Rathiri had said a group had left K124 for the remote station almost three days earlier. He didn't even want to try to guess how they knew humans were at the remote station. It seemed impossible, but they had surprised him before. He didn't know how fast they could move, but he suspected it was damn fast. They had managed to keep up with the ATVs. Their creators had engineered them to be perfect weapons, like shock troops.

Dax had tried to land the ship south of the estimated path of the Ravers. However, because of the broken ground and the canyons they would have to negotiate, it was only a guess. If they could detect humans from 2,000 kilometers away, they could find the *Luck*. He had seen how quickly they moved in short bursts, but he suspected they had endurance as well. Those backward-jointed legs looked efficient. He wouldn't put 60 kph past their ability. That placed them near the ship long before they could complete the repairs. He hoped the dust storm slowed them.

They could abandon the ship and hike to the station, but they would be no better off once they got there. The small station was less secure than the main base. Their only hope lay in getting *Fortune's Luck* back in the air as quickly as possible.

"Let's get started. I'll work on sealing the hull breach in the engine room so we can reach orbit."

He didn't mention that without a working Skip engine, they were not going home. As a civilian cargo vessel, it could be months before anyone came looking for them. Even when the Navy received their message, it would take its sweet time. They would do a thorough search for the *Abraxas* at her last reported position before venturing to Loki. The idea of planet hopping to stay ahead of the Ravers did not appeal to him. He wasn't sure the ship could take it. They had to reach orbit.

"I miss Nate. He was better at this than I am."

Plia's statement felt like a jab in the heart with a knife. A sudden image of Nate flying across the cargo bay of the *Abraxas* popped into his mind. "I miss him too, and Andy. I killed both of them."

"It's not your fault, Dax. It just happened."

"They followed me to places I shouldn't have led them because I was their captain. Now they're dead." He patted the hull and swore he could feel his ship's pain. "I can't even keep my ship safe."

He knew he was being overly morose, but he couldn't shake the feeling that his world was collapsing around him. He was no longer in control. He had pissed off some god of the void, and payback was a motherfucker. He left Plia to go pull the welder out of the tool locker. She could organize whoever she needed to replace the damaged thruster. Romeo met him in the cargo bay with a cup of coffee as soon as he cycled through the airlock.

"Here, Captain. Just like you like it."

Dax opened his faceplate and took a sip. The coffee was hot and sent his scalded throat into spasms going down, but he needed the caffeine. Something about coffee transcended its use as a simple beverage. It had psychological healing properties. It was a mood enhancer. It could perk a person up, keep them awake and alert, or relax them. He had never smoked tobacco, but he imagined that was how tobacco made users feel.

"Ah, the beverage of the gods," he whispered.

Romeo handed Dax a suit ration tube. "I filled this for you. You might need it while you're working outside."

Dax nodded, touched by the cook's foresight and concern.

"Do you need me to suit up?" he asked.

He considered it, but didn't like the idea of leaving strangers alone on his ship. "No, Tish, Plia, and Ivers should be enough." He held out the empty cup. "You work your magic and keep the coffee coming. Make some sandwiches while you're at it. We'll eat before we start."

Romeo grinned. "Will do."

"How is Dr. Adar?" he asked.

His quick grin almost made Dax chuckle. "She's a trooper. I'll see if she wants to help me. She needs to keep busy. You know, with her friend Dr. Benson dying and all."

*And almost everyone she had known and worked with for a year*, he thought bitterly. "Yeah, we all do. How is the director?"

Romeo grimaced, held his hand out horizontally, and wiggled it. "So-so. I told him to take a shower, and I would feed him. He needs a few good meals, lots of fluids, and a day or two of sleep, but I think he'll recover. It probably wouldn't be a bad idea to sedate him and start a glucose IV."

"Go ahead. Have Tish do it. She's good at it. Keep an eye on them both."

Romeo grinned. "You betcha." He eyed Dax. "You could use some medical attention, Captain. You look like shit. I've overcooked roasts that have less crispy skin."

Dax doubted Romeo had ever overcooked anything in his life. "Later."

Each lungful of air burned. He had increased the $O_2$ in his suit mixture to compensate for his poor breathing, but the burn ointment from the first aid kit could only do so much to alleviate the pain in his hands, neck, and head. The suit gloves were rubbing his blistered and swollen hands raw, and his undersuit was sticking to his body, but he had no choice but to shrug off the pain and keep working. He had no time to rest and no time to feel sorry for himself.

By the time he began welding the gash in the hull, visibility had dropped to near zero. Welding steel plates over the rent would solve the air leak problem, but the dust that had blown into the space between the inner and outer hull would plague the ship for years, working its way into the ship's air ducts, corroding wiring, and holding moisture for mold to grow in. He vacuumed out what he could get to, but had to leave the rest.

Luckily, he didn't need to see what he was doing to weld. He could feel the edge of the metal plate he had tacked onto the hull. It was a simple matter of running a strong bead where the two met with the TIG welder. The blowing sand caught in the welding bead would weaken the weld, but it was not a structural piece. He just needed it not to fall off before they reached orbit. He could do a better job later when ship and crew were safe.

He lost himself in the simplicity of the job, mesmerized by the bright actinic light hot enough to melt and fuse metal. When his right hand cramped from grasping the welder, he switched hands. After a while, he developed a rhythm and made good progress. He reached a Zen state of consciousness, knowing exactly when enough metal had melted to provide a strong weld and to move the bead forward.

It wasn't a pretty job, but it was fast. He pushed his OCD to the back of his mind. If he took the time to even out every weld to satisfy his obsession, he would be there all day. He was running his last bead before he remembered the coffee tube. He sipped it through the suit straw and felt the hot caffeine reawaken his dulled senses. Welding had taken a lot out of him.

Ivers' hand on his shoulder caught him by surprise. "We're going inside. Plia is already milling the new parts. We placed a temporary patch over the hole to keep out the dust. The tent blew away."

Dax touched the welding rod to the hull in a couple of spots. "Yeah, I'm finished here too." He stood and almost fell over, his aching muscles rebelling about crouching for so long. Ivers steadied him. "Whoa, I'm getting ground-pounder legs."

"Sorry I holed your ship. I guess I'm a little rusty."

"It was a fast lift off in a tight spot. We lived." Seeing he was becoming too maudlin, he added, "It wasn't bad lift off for a Marine, especially with the entire surface collapsing beneath us."

In the airlock, he hit the decontamination button for a jet of mist to wash away the dust from his suit. He peeled off his suit gingerly, but large patches of blistered skin came with it, sending his nerve ending into a frenzied rampage. In spite of the agony, it felt good to shed the confining suit. He took a deep whiff and finally decided the odor he smelled came from him rather than something Romeo was cooking in the galley. A quick shower was in order.

On his way to the communal bath, he passed the machine shop. He heard the lathe running as Plia milled the parts for the new gimbal that allowed the thruster to pivot. He felt sorry for her. She had to be exhausted, yet she still faced hours of continuously monitoring the lathe as it slowly shaped the metal millimeter by millimeter to exact specifications. If it had been almost any other part, they could have manufactured one with the 3-D printer, but the thruster became too hot for anything but a high-density steel alloy.

He checked his chronometer and saw that he had been outside welding for nearly three hours. It was no wonder his muscles ached. As he entered the bath, Cici stepped out of the shower. Her wet, long brown hair hung down, not quite covering her breasts. His view of them was much better than while waiting in the cul-de-sac. They were more magnificent than he had imagined, firmer and more conical than pendulous. Her supple legs met at the smooth curvature of her hips. He had just a moment to admire her luscious body before she noticed him, grabbed a towel from a bench, and wrapped it around her body.

"Sorry," he said. "I came in to clean up. I should have knocked."

"It's your ship."

He noticed she did not flinch in embarrassment or try to hide from his gaze. She did not seem as angry with him as she had been. He wasn't sure how he felt about her. She was intelligent, a knockout in the looks department, and didn't scare easily, but they seemed to rub each other the wrong way. They had spent most of the time since they met arguing. He grinned, realizing he was describing his and Tish's tumultuous affair.

"True, but we have guests."

"I hope I didn't use too much water. Showers were restricted at the remote station; transporting water cost fuel. This was a luxury."

"Good coffee and hot showers are all the old girl has to offer, but we have plenty of both. Uh, are you okay?" He grimaced at his hesitation. He wasn't sure what to say to her if they weren't arguing.

Her shoulders sagged. Dax thought she would drop the towel. "I still can't believe it's real. All my friends."

"It's real enough, and it's not over yet."

She cocked her head to one side and stared at him. "What do you mean?"

"Your boss said half a dozen Ravers had headed toward the remote station."

Her jaw slackened as realization hit her. "They would have come for us." She considered the implications for a moment, and then asked, "Where are they now?"

"They'll be knocking on the door soon."

She paled, but said nothing. They stood staring at each other for an uncomfortably long time. Finally, she said. "You came in to take a shower."

His face reddened, though it was probably not visible on his blistered face. "Uh, yeah. Uh, I want to apologize."

"For seeing me naked?"

He grinned. "No, that was a bonus. I want to apologize for being so hard on you. I didn't think we would find anyone alive in the tunnels. I thought it was a foolish risk. I was wrong."

"We were both wrong. I got your crewman and Myles killed in the process."

She was feeling the same guilt he felt over Nate. There was no reason for two people to feel guilty. "No, it all falls into my lap. I got all gung ho and wanted to kill those things. If I had insisted we make a run for it, take our chances, we might have all made it out alive."

"That was Sergeant Ivers' decision, not yours."

"My decision to investigate the *Abraxas* resulted in my engineer's death. I abdicated my responsibility to Ivers because I didn't want to make any more bad decisions. Even that decision was wrong."

After another awkward pause, she said, "I had better dress. Tish might walk in on us. I wouldn't want her to think …"

"No, God forbid I make her angrier than she already is."

She picked up one of Andy's spare jumpsuits and left. He peeled off the sweaty bodysuit he wore under his excursion suit and stepped into the shower. The misters soaked his body with jets of steam. The hot water exacerbated the burns on his neck, head, back, and shoulders. His hands felt as though he was holding them in boiling water. He ignored the pain and leaned into the jets to let them massage his aching shoulders. *Fortune's Luck* had a first-class recycler, so he did not rue the loss of water. He stayed much longer than his normal shower time. Finally, satisfied he was clean if not completely refreshed, he dried himself gingerly and sprayed a liberal amount of skin growth promoter on his hands and upper body. The enzyme mixture contained a local anesthetic to numb the skin. He touched a particularly bad burn spot and felt only a little pain.

He donned a clean ship's jumper from his locker. He glanced in the mirror at his blistered face and badly singed hair. He couldn't do much about his hair without shaving his head, and that would have hurt too much at the present time. He covered it with a clean cap, biting his lip to keep from yelling when he pulled the cap down on his head.

"Just a little tanned, that's all," he muttered. "Like falling asleep at the beach."

Ivers waited for him on the bridge. The video scanners were operating, but they revealed nothing but strong winds and blinding dust. The dour expression on his burned face was ominous. Dax braced himself for more bad news.

"I linked to the satellite, but the image isn't much better. However, I did pick up this." He touched the screen to back up the image; then, stopped. He pointed to the screen. "I'll run it in slow motion."

The image advanced, but Dax saw nothing but the dust storm as seen from a bird's-eye view. *Fortune's Luck* sat somewhere along the storm's southeastern edge being sandblasted. Then, in a brief moment during a thinning of the dust swirls, he saw what Ivers had seen – six or seven objects moving rapidly in their direction. The clarity was poor, but he didn't need a long look to know what they were – Ravers.

"I guess Rathiri was right. How far away are they?"

"Forty clicks."

"Less than an hour. We're not leaving before they get here."

"Can we get the ship in the air long enough to move far enough to give us a breather?"

"Not a chance in hell. If I managed to her get off the ground without killing us, the next landing would probably crack her up."

Ivers tapped the screen with his finger. "I guess we fight."

Dax was incredulous. "Six or seven Ravers. With what? Sticks and stones? Your disruptor is almost out of power. The lasers aren't very effective. In this dust, maybe not at all. We keep killing them, and they keep coming. These things conquered a planet and wiped out an entire species. What chance do we have?"

"What do you suggest, give up? We can't run and we can't hide. We can't do anything from inside the ship, but if we stay here, they'll make it inside eventually."

"Are you suggesting we meet them outside?" It sounded too much like certain suicide for him. He had tempted fate too often in the last few hours. He was sure once more would be the last one.

"You, me, and Romeo. The rest remain inside. Dr. Adar is no help, and Tish can help Plia. Plia keeps working on the gimbal; then, we protect her while she installs it."

"That means taking the fight to the Ravers. The lasers are like big flashlights to those things. Unless, we got in a lucky shot, they're useless."

"I'll see if I can make some adjustments. With Plia's help, I think I can recharge the power packs from ship's power. We'll get fewer shots, but they'll pack more punch."

"What if we're separated from the ship?"

"It goes without us. Plia can reach orbit, can't she?"

Dax nodded. "I insisted all my crew be able to get the ship off the ground. It doesn't mean I'm ready to hand her over."

"I can try this alone, but I doubt I would last long." He shrugged. "It's your choice."

"It quit being my choice when I decided to continue to Loki instead of turning around. Since then, I've been rolling with the punches. This sounds like the final KO."

Ivers grinned. "Afraid of dying?"

"No. I'm afraid of being eaten alive, and then dying." He sighed. "Damn. I guess I don't have any choice. I think I can rig a few bombs from some items from ship's stores and fuel from the grasshopper. The suits have a small torch in the tool belt. It might be difficult lighting a fuse in that wind. They might go off immediately and blow our asses up, but I guess it doesn't really matter that much does it. I'll get started."

Ivers nodded. "After I recalibrate the weapons, I'll suit up and wait outside in case they move faster than we thought."

"Thirty minutes."

"Dax, I'm sorry how this turned out. From the beginning, I didn't want you or your crew involved other than getting me here. If there were any other way …"

"Believe me, I've been mulling every decision over in my mind and can't see a way I could have changed things. My crew is my main concern. My job is to get them off this damn planet in one piece. You and I … well, we're collateral damage."

"I've had a good run."

Dax looked at Ivers and saw the pain in his eyes. Ivers had been closer to the flash of the mine than he had. His skin was bubbly with blisters. "You had better apply some salve to those burns. It helps."

"I'll take care of my wounds later. They help me focus. I don't have time to hurt."

*I hope you have time to die*. Dax tried to shake the feeling of gloom and despair descending over him, but for once in his life, he saw no rosy side. *We're going to die*.

# 14

Dax was no ordinance specialist, but he knew enough about chemicals to know which ones were dangerous in the wrong combinations. He filled thermos bottles with hydrazine from the grasshopper, a mixture of corrosive cleaning solution, bits of magnesium metal shavings, and then added ball bearings to create simple fragmentary grenades. For fuses, he used cotton yarn impregnated with gunpowder from .338 caliber shells. He tested a couple of fuses and got a wide range of times from three seconds to ten. He didn't have time to refine them. His half hour was up. In the end, he had six bombs of dubious reliability.

He stopped by the machine shop to speak with Plia and found Tish there as well. He didn't have time for teary goodbyes. "As soon as the thruster is in, take off. You can try to use the com to let us know, but in this dust, it will be iffy. When we hear the engines, if we can get back, we will. If not, you're in charge. We came here to save lives. Don't waste any more."

Plia nodded, but kept her eye on the turning gimbal.

"Tish, it's been fun. I guess it won't hurt to tell you I love you."

"Oh, Dax."

"Don't go all teary-eyed on me. We might just win, and you'll be stuck with me."

"Please, Dax."

"Don't. I have to do this. For you. For all of you." He turned to leave.

"I love you, Dax," she said.

He paused for a second; then joined Romeo in the cargo bay. "Let's suit up."

A few minutes later, he and Romeo joined Ivers outside. The wind-driven dust slammed him like a sledgehammer. Visibility was less than five paces, and he had to wipe his visor constantly to keep it clean. Ivers stood, legs spread wide for better stability, with his ion disruptor held down beside his waist. Dax handed him one of the bombs.

"No guarantees. Light it and throw it fast."

Ivers stuffed it into a utility pocket on his suit. "I figured we would spread out on this side of the ship where we can watch over Plia. We can't protect the whole ship. If we separate too far, a Raver might slip by us."

Dax didn't think a Raver would ignore them to go after Plia. It might go through them, but it would not ignore them. "Sounds good. I linked the satellite image to my suit screen for a heads up. The ship sensors are at maximum range, but in this dust storm, they're practically useless." He didn't really think the lack of visibility would give them much warning, but every second counted against a creature as large and a quick as a Raver.

He paced along the length of the ship keeping his eye to the west, the direction from which he thought the Ravers would attack; although, it was equally likely they would use the storm moving in from the north as cover. Romeo stood nervously near the rear of the ship. Ivers, like him, paced, but his circuit took him farther out into the storm before returning to the ship. There was a slim chance the Ravers would pass them by and continue to the station, but he doubted they would be that lucky. Whatever senses allowed the creatures to locate their prey or a station two thousand kilometers away would easily pinpoint a ship in the desert and humans standing around it like mobile snacks.

He almost pissed his pants when the proximity alarm began beeping in his earphones. He stopped moving, peered into the blinding dust, and raised his laser rifle.

"We've got company," Ivers warned.

Dax's senses went on high alert. *Glad they still work.* He peered into the blinding dust storm hoping for some indication a Raver was there, a familiar shape, a moving mass too dense for dust, anything he could shoot at. Knowing their speed and their capacity for leaping, he knew one could attack him from nowhere before he had a chance to defend himself, and there were at least six out there in the storm. Behind him, he heard Plia and Tish pounding to force the new gimbal bearing into place. He didn't worry about the sound they made; the creatures knew where they were.

"I see something about your two o'clock," Ivers said to him.

His voice sounded high pitched over the com link, as if the prospect of a fight excited him. Dax shared none of his enthusiasm. Dax looked in the direction Ivers had pointed out and saw a dim shape through the swirling dust haze. He raised his rifle and waited. Ivers had adjusted the output of the lasers to produce twenty percent more power. He hoped it was enough.

The Raver was on him in a blur or motion. He fired one shot and rolled away. The creature screamed in pain. The bolt had struck the creature in the throat, a less protected area of its body. It had not expected the strength of the laser. It would be more cautious now.

"There's another amidships twenty meters out," Ivers reported. "No two."

Dax heard the whine of the ion disruptor and another loud scream from a Raver. He saw motion toward the rear of the ship. "Watch it, Romeo," he warned. Seconds later, a large explosion ripped the air, the sound quickly ripped away by the wind.

"I think I got one," Romeo reported. He sounded half-excited, half-afraid.

Sharp chirps and growls came from several different points, as the Ravers compared notes. *Maybe it's a pep talk,* Dax thought dryly. *Bastards are smart.* A Raver rushed at him. This time, Dax held his ground. He continued to pour blasts from the laser into the Raver. Chips from its ebony armor flew in all directions, but it did not slow. He knew he had waited too late to run. He held the trigger and aimed at the creature's face, hoping to confuse its senses. Seconds before it reached him, the side of its head exploded in a spray of blood and flame. It hit the ground, bounced, and struggled to rise. Dax walked up to it and fired point-blank into its head, killing it. He looked over and saw Ivers standing there with his disruptor.

"Thanks."

"That's two down," he replied.

"We're finished, Dax," Plia said over the com link. "We're headed in."

"Great. I'll guard the door."

He strode to the cargo door and saw Plia and Tish moving toward it. A Raver appeared as if by magic from the dust behind them. "Drop to the ground!" he yelled. He pulled one of his bombs from his suit belt, hit the switch on the torch on his suit, and lit the fuse. It caught slowly in the stiff breeze, but the flame raced down the fuse at an alarming rate. He tossed the bomb just as both Plia and Tish hit the ground. The Raver snatched the bomb out of midair and stared at it. It exploded, sending a dozen ball bearings and shrapnel from the thermos into the creature's head. The Raver screamed once and fell dead, half its head torn away by the blast.

The cargo hatch opened. "Get inside," he told them. He saw a figure in the open hatch and for a moment thought it was Andy; then he realized it was Cici in Andy's suit opening the door for them. Director Rathiri walked up beside her. He was not wearing a suit. Dax wasn't sure why the director was there. He still should have been under sedation. He was so weak he could barely walk, and the swirling dust would have blinded him. All of them failed to see the Raver on top of *Fortune's Luck* until it reached inside and snatched Rathiri out of the cargo bay, as if picking a snack from a refrigerator. He hung suspended, struggling uselessly, until the creature raked its talons across his stomach, disemboweling him. He stared at his intestines falling to the dirt, mystified by what was happening. The Raver dropped him beside the ship in front of Plia and Tish. He was dead.

Dax fired his laser, but the creature leaped down to the ground and faced him. Its mouth hung open, baring its teeth. If it had eyes, it would have stared at him hungrily. Instead, its nose flaps fluttered in what he imagined was the Raver equivalent of licking its lips. Once again, Ivers saved him. He had no good shot at it because of Dax. Instead, he fired the disrupter at the ground at the Raver's feet, giving it a hot foot. When it turned to confront Ivers,

Dax dropped to the ground and fired his laser at the same time Ivers fired. At close range, the disruptor and the jacked-up laser were devastating. It fell with two holes drilled in its head. *That's four down.*

Dax's laser began to overheat. He felt the heat through his gloved hand. Supercharging the power output made it more effective, but overloaded its cooling capacity. He doubted he would get one more shot out of it before it exploded in his hands.

Another bomb exploded a few meters behind him. Ball bearings whizzed by overhead. He turned to see Romeo rush by him. "Missed," he said. "There are two of them back there."

Dax looked and saw that Plia and Tish were inside the cargo bay. They had accomplished their mission. The *Luck* could fly. "Back inside the ship," he said.

Romeo rushed up the ramp ahead of him. Dax waited on Ivers. They walked up the ramp backwards, keeping their weapons trained on the Ravers lurking just inside the swirling dust but remaining carefully just out of range. Cici closed the door behind them. Seconds later, the Ravers attacked the ship, pounding and clawing at the door. It wouldn't take them long to get inside or rip a new hole in the *Luck.*

"If we don't go now, we might not go at all," he said, as he rushed for the bridge. "Find a seat."

He didn't wait for anyone to strap in. He fell into the pilot's seat and fired the thrusters. The ship shuddered and hopped along the ground on its belly until the new gimbal swung into position. The ship began to lift. He hoped he landed on one of the Ravers as the ship bounced along. He increased power to the thrusters and fired the main engines. The ship trembled violently before settling down to a dull rattle. The fuel flow to the thrusters was slightly misaligned, but they all worked. He lifted the nose and powered up the engines. *Fortune's Luck* drilled a path through the blowing sand, sounding as if a dozen grinders were reshaping her exterior. He didn't let up until the ship punched through the top of the storm. He leveled the ship, relishing the feel of sunlight on his face after hours underground or enveloped by the dust storm.

"Everyone strap in while you have the chance. It's going to get rough when we hit the upper atmosphere."

A surge of relief swept through him. They were off the ground, out of reach of the Ravers. They could sit in orbit and repair the Skip engines until the Navy arrived. If he and Plia couldn't do the job, the Navy at least owed him the use of a Navy Skip technician.

A blinking light on the instrument panel caught his eye. He frowned when he saw the temperature spike in the engine power relays. The engines cut out for a millisecond before kicking in again. The ship dropped sharply. He swore at himself. His adjustments to the relays to tweak the engines to reach Loki faster, coupled with all the jarring of the rough landing and takeoff, had knocked the power relays out of alignment, causing them to overheat. Modern ships had a secondary system to allow repairs while in flight. Ships as old as *Fortune's Luck* did not. Nate had suggested he spring for one, but he had seen no reason for the added expense, an oversight he now regretted.

He wasn't overly concerned. Once they reached orbit, he could cut the engines and make the necessary repairs. All he needed was five more minutes. He kept a close eye on the temperature panel as he pushed the engines harder to compensate. As the red temperature bar continued to creep higher, the power level in the starboard engine dropped. He had to ease back the port engine to maintain balance. The *Luck* struggled to gain altitude. He knew the ship was in trouble. The engines had a built-in failsafe to prevent an explosion. Before the temperature reached critical stage, the engines would shut down, not much of a problem in space, but on takeoff, it could be fatal.

He checked the altimeter. They were not going to make orbit. He calculated he had less than three minutes before the engines shut down completely. If they weren't on the ground by then, they would wind up a permanent part of the landscape. The storm still swirled below them. He could see no ground features, and the radar was useless. He could slam the *Luck* into a five-thousand-meter-high mesa or plunge it into one of the kilometers-deep canyons.

If he had a functioning Skip Drive, he would have been tempted to attempt a Skip in the atmosphere. As far as he knew, it had never been tried and for good reason. The odds of it succeeding were slim to none. Without a Skip engine, he had no choice. He slipped into his seat harness, pushed the yoke forward, and brought the *Luck* into a steep dive. It was a risky maneuver, but it got them on the ground quicker. He reentered the top of the raging dust storm. The dust was as dense as porridge, almost thick enough to float the *Luck*. He prayed he spotted a place he could land. They had travelled less than two hundred kilometers. He tried to visualize the topography from memory, but it became a jumble of peaks and valleys in his mind. He had paid little attention on the four previous trips he had made to Loki. He recalled there were no good places to set down. The engines began sputtering as the relays overheated and reached the critical point. He held his breath, fighting the urge to level off. Doing so too quickly would leave them too high above the surface.

At two thousand meters, he broke out of the dust only to see a jagged peak directly in front of him. He fought the steering yoke to veer away, brought the *Luck* in a tight banking turn to kill speed, and lined up with a narrow canyon below him. The terrain one either side was too broken for a landing. The deep canyon offered a flat, kilometer-long stretch of sand and packed earth. He saw no large rocks or outcroppings, making it as safe a landing site as any he was likely to find. He could not bring the ship in for a vertical landing; he had too much momentum. As the ship dropped below the rim of the canyon, the engines died completely.

Cursing, he fought to keep the nose up. It was like flying a brick. He waited as long as he dared before firing the thrusters. They would dampen his forward momentum, but not enough for a soft landing. He lowered the landing skids hoping they would act as skis on the hard-packed sand. He checked his air speed. 450 kph – too fast. He lifted the nose to stand the ship on its tail, facing the thrusters forward perpendicular to his flight path. He had to be careful; too far and the *Luck* would flip over and land on her back, and like a turtle, she would never fly again.

He dropped the nose again. The ground rushed at him, but his speed was now 320 kph. He had run out of tricks from his bag. *Fortune's Luck* was going in hard no matter what he did. He braced himself for impact. The ground rushed up at him. The ship hit and bounced; then bounced again, eating up more of her momentum. She hit a third time with a bone-rattling thud, staying on the ground this time, losing speed as the skids dug deeper into the sand.

190 kph – they were going to make it. Just as he began to relax, his scalp broke into a frenzy of itching. Ahead, he saw a small protrusion in the sand in *Fortune's Luck's* path. He tried to will the ship to veer aside but to no avail. Ship and rock were inexorably doomed to meet. He braced for impact. The shrill screech of ripping metal reverberated through the ship. The *Luck* lurched drunkenly, as the sharp rock protruding from the sand ripped open her exposed belly. So close was his affinity with *Fortune's Luck*, his own belly felt as if it had been stabbed.

The ship slowed and stopped, creaking from the strain and heat from friction with the sand. Another sound impinged on his consciousness, a cry for help – Tish. He recognized her voice. His legs were wobbly as he strode down the corridor. Locker doors had opened from impact, spilling their contents around the deck. Smoke billowed from the engine room. One of the ATVs had broken loose and jammed in the cargo bay door halfway into the corridor.

He passed Cici and Plia struggling to release their harnesses, saw that they were okay. He found Tish in her cabin. The safety harness over her bed had wrenched from the wall on impact. She had slammed into the bulkhead when the ship bounced. Blood dripped from her mouth and streamed from a laceration on her forehead. She lay groaning on the floor. His heart broke at the sight of her broken and bleeding body.

"Tish!" He knelt beside her and cradled her head in his lap. Her eyes barely focused on him, but she recognized his voice.

"Dax," she moaned. "I hurt."

"I'll get the med kit." He started to lay her head back on the deck.

She gripped his arm tightly and squeezed. "No, please don't leave me."

"Okay," he promised. He yelled for help. "Someone bring the med kit to Tish's quarters!"

Her breathing was ragged, and blood spilled from the corners of her mouth each time she coughed. Her flesh was so cold to the touch it frightened him. The gash on her forehead looked bad, but he suspected her pain came from internal injuries. He prayed they were not too serious for the ship's limited auto-surgeon to repair.

"I have to get you to the automed," he said. "We'll fix you right up."

She shook her head. "I'm not hurting now." She coughed up bright red blood and shivered. A sharp grimace belied her claim of no pain. "I'm cold, Dax."

"I'll get a blanket." He looked at the color of the blood with dismay. Even with his limited medical knowledge, he knew it was arterial blood. At the very least, she had a punctured lung. The automed could not deal with such severe trauma.

"No, don't let go," she begged. "Hold me, Dax."

She passed out, going limp in his arms. Her color drained away, and her breathing grew shallow. He checked her wrist, but her pulse was too weak to detect. She was rapidly slipping away from him. He had so much he wanted to tell her, but it was too late. She would never hear him. Romeo walked in with the med kit and knelt beside her. Dax shook his head. He held Tish until she gasped out her last breath, and continued to hold her until Romeo finally touched his shoulder.

"Come on, Dax. The *Luck's* hurt, too."

He nodded. He lifted her lifeless body from the floor and lowered her gently to her bed. He covered her with a blanket from her bed, the silly one covered in smiling Teddy bears he had bought for her in a shop at Kinta Station. "Goodbye, Tish," he whispered in her ear; then kissed her cold forehead.

Romeo, Cici, and Plia gathered just outside the door. Romeo and Cici wept openly. Plia clenched her fists by her side and bit down on her lower lip.

"Where's Ivers?" he demanded.

"Outside checking the damage," Plia answered.

"That's where you should be," he snapped. "Me too. Come on. Let's go see if the *Luck* will ever fly again."

# 15

As he looked at his battered ship, Dax knew he should have felt something, some sense of loss. He had killed Nate, Andy, and Tish – half his crew – and now his ship, but he was numb inside. *Emotional burnout. That's what they call it.* He had suffered too much for too long. His mind could not cope with the stress. Later, it might get a handle on it; try to pigeonhole his feelings, but not now. He didn't know if he could deal with it. Plia still crawled around beneath the ship, checking the bent landing struts, the half-buried thrusters, and the cracked nacelle for the Skip Drive; as if she held out hope, she could make the repairs. Even her considerable skills would not suffice. *Fortune's Luck* wasn't going to fly again without a major refit. He had no way to get her to a shipyard, even if he had the credits to pay for it. That meant she was now just so much scrap metal.

The tortured metal popped as it cooled, punctuating his pangs of mental anguish. A steady stream of water leaked from the freshwater tank through the cracked hull. The desert sand lapped up the water eagerly, an unexpected feast in a ravaged land. He should have ordered Plia to find something to catch the precious water, but he could not bring himself to issue another order. He was through giving orders. He was unfit for command.

He didn't have to issue an order. Plia crawled from beneath the ship. "Do you want me to catch the water?"

When he didn't respond, she stared at him a moment with something akin to sympathy in her eyes before saying, "I'll go get a container, and then see if I can stop the leak."

When she walked away, Ivers came over. He had come to the same conclusion about the *Luck* as Dax had. “Any idea where we are?” he asked.

“Does it matter?” he answered sharply. Ivers stared at him. Dax sighed. “I took a reading of K124 B’s beacon when we cleared the storm. We’re roughly ninety kilometers east and a little south of the station.” He pointed to the towering cliffs on each side, an unbroken wall of layered ocher, white, and red sandstone that continued for kilometers. “This is the same canyon that runs beside it. It’s a long walk, and we didn’t kill all the Ravers. Remember what I said earlier about our situation?”

“That we’re fucked.”

Dax kicked at the sand with his boot. “Well, we’re fucked-er, if that’s a word.”

“I don’t think it is.”

“It should be.”

Ivers cast once last glance at *Fortune’s Luck* and scanned the canyon bluffs. “We’ll never scale those. Do we wait here or try for the station? We still have the ATVs.”

“One of them. The other one is lodged in the cargo bay door. I wouldn’t give it a 50-50 chance of still being operational.”

“One will do.”

Dax grimaced. “Thanks for reminding me of how few we are.”

Ivers looked away nervously. Dax didn’t expect any comforting platitudes from him. Ivers had lost men under his command without breaking. He accepted the responsibility and expected Dax to as well. The difference was that Ivers had lost soldiers; Dax had lost friends.

“I’m sorry about Tish, Dax. She was good people.”

Dax sighed. “You didn’t kill her. I did. Chalk up one more tombstone for ex-Captain Dax Wyldd.”

“The Navy won’t be here for a day or two,” he said. “Station B has a radio.”

Going back to Station B sounded foolish to Dax. “We would be headed straight back toward the Ravers.” He looked eastward down the canyon. “I say we go that way, stay ahead of the Ravers until the Navy arrives." Unlike Ivers, he thought they would be on their own for more than a couple of days.

"We'll have to stop to recharge the batteries at some point. What then?"

Ivers had a point. They could never outrun the creatures. They would not stop until they caught up. They were like the proverbial Sword of Damocles hanging over their head. The creatures never seemed to tire, and having just awakened from a 2,000-year nap, they had no need for sleep. *And the bastards can think*, he added mentally.

He wasn't thinking straight. His mind hurt. As much as it pained him, he had to forget about Tish for the moment and concentrate on saving the others. He could commemorate Tish another time. "We might as well wait for them. At least we won't have a long trip to deal with."

Ivers nodded. "My sentiments exactly. Maybe they won't come. Their goal might have been the station, drawn by detecting the power grid or something. We power down the ship and hope they ignore us."

"Fat chance of that."

Ivers scratched his head and grimaced. "Yeah, well …"

Romeo stuck his head out the cargo hatch. "I made some coffee and sandwiches. Better eat them now. The refrigerator's busted."

*Another casualty to place at my feet.*

"Make more of both. We're going to power down and play hide and seek."

Romeo frowned and disappeared back into the ship.

Dax said, "We had better inform them of the situation. They get a vote. I'm not making the decision for them." He glanced at the *Luck*. "I'm not in command anymore. I'm a captain without a ship, a ground-pounder."

* * * *

They sat around the wardroom table in an air of stunned silence. The empty seats where Nate, Andy, and Tish usually sat haunted Dax. He added Myles and Director Rathiri to the litany of the missing. Cups of coffee and half-eaten sandwiches lay on plates in front of them. Like him, they had no appetite. He could barely look into their faces as he apprised them of the situation. Plia, as usual, maintained her air of stoic acceptance. Her face was unreadable, but he suspected even she had her limits. Romeo looked frightened, but he said nothing. He trusted his captain. Dax regretted that act of blind faith. He did not deserve it. Of them all, Cici surprised him most. She took their situation in stride.

"KB is an inflatable dome sprayed with a thin shell of concrete. It can handle a normal sandstorm, but it wouldn't keep out a Raver for two minutes. At least the ship is metal."

"It won't keep them out for long," Dax reminded her.

"I vote we stay," she said.

He nodded. "Okay. Romeo?"

Romeo shrugged his thin shoulders. "Whatever you say, captain."

Dax winced and shook his head. "No, not this time."

Romeo looked uncomfortable. "Oh, okay. I vote we stay with the *Luck*. She's my home."

"Plia?"

Her face became grim. Her dark eyes flashed angrily. She shook her head. Through lips thinned to a tight straight line, she said, "I'm not leaving. I'll face them here."

Ivers spoke for him. "I guess it's decided. We stay. Cici, will you see if you can access the satellite and spot the Ravers, see how much time we have? Plia, round up all the weapons and ammo and recharge the lasers and the disruptor. The cargo hatch is the weakest point. We'll meet them there and fall back to the bridge. The bulkhead steel is thickest there."

Plia looked at Dax for confirmation. He stared at each of them, moving from face to face. "Look, I won't lie to you. We're in a bad situation here. We've got nowhere to run and nowhere to hide. You know what these things are capable of. The Navy won't be here for days at the earliest. The *Luck's* bad busted. She's not flying again."

He was surprised how much it hurt to utter that declaration. It seemed to negate his entire life. "We're stuck here. If the Ravers get inside, we're dead." He decided he was being too grim even for him. They all knew the odds. He forced a grin. "I'm planning on taking a few of the shiny little bastards down before I let them screw around with my coffee."

Cici pulled down a satellite image on her computer. She zoomed in and pointed to a dot in a long, winding canyon – *Fortune's Luck*. "We're here." She moved her finger across the screen and pointed to a small dot on the edge of the cliff. "KB is here."

Dax gazed at the map. The storm was still blowing. Within the hour, it would engulf K124B. It might miss them, but with their luck, it probably wouldn't.

"Zoom in on K124B," Ivers said. Cici increased the magnification as far as she could. He could see the remote station's ATV and even a folding table and two chairs. "Something's wrong here," he said.

"What?" she asked.

Curious, Dax leaned in closer as well.

"Where are the Ravers? They should have reached KB by now, but it's still intact." He pointed to a spot west of KB covered by the dust storm. "That's where we first landed for repairs, correct, Captain?"

Dax looked at the image and nodded. "Near enough." As Ivers scanned the area around K124B, Dax took a closer look at the map. Something bothered him. He drew a mental line from K124 to the landing site, and the remote station. "Zoom in on the head of the canyon," he told Cici. Ivers gave him a questioning look, which he ignored. The image changed. Dax immediately recognized three dots moving down the canyon a few kilometers east of the station as the Ravers headed directly for the *Luck*. "They bypassed the remote station. Why?"

"They know we're here," Cici said.

"No. They spent three days travelling to the remote station; and yet they changed course. Hmm." He used one of Andy's vid entertainment magazines as a straight edge and laid it along the dots from K124 to K124B. The point where they had first landed for repairs was well south of the line. Next, he laid it along the path between K124 and the *Luck's* present position. The line split their first landing site and their present one down the middle, the same line the Ravers now followed.

"They weren't headed for the remote station," he said with sudden realization. He looked at Cici. "What's out this direction?"

She looked pensive for a moment. "Nothing, a small ruin we haven't investigated yet. It's so far out and sits by itself; we didn't think it was important."

Dax hated coincidences. This rang of a big coincidence. "Where is it?"

She pointed to the image. "About here, maybe twenty kilometers east of us, at the bottom of the canyon." When she looked up at him, her eyes reminded him of Tish's when she thought he was on to something. "Do you think it's important?"

"The Ravers do." He thought a minute, trying to drive the doldrums from his head. He needed to think clearly. "Was there anything different about this ruin?"

"I haven't seen it in person. We sent a drone out to photograph it. I'm just a xenobiologist, but it seemed much older than any of the other ruins were. The architecture is different, more decoration. Ambrose ..." Her voice cracked at the mention of the dead director's name. "Ambrose planned on exploring it more thoroughly later this year. He, Doctor Hokomida, and Bob Rosenthal, two of our archaeologists, visited the site two months ago in the shuttle for a few hours. They seemed excited when they returned, but we already had so much to do that took precedence. Do you think the ruins are important?"

Dax rubbed his chin, wincing when he popped a blister on his finger. "I'm not sure. I'm just grasping at straws." Dax noticed the expression of bewilderment on Cici's face. "Why, do you know anything about them?"

"I know the three of them discussed the site a few times in private, which seemed odd given the amount of work before us. Ambrose ... Doctor Rathiri wanted to tell me something important about the *Huresh* and the Ravers. He wanted to tell you too, but he was so weak and somewhat delirious, I ignored him." She put a knuckle in her mouth and bit down. "I should have listened to him."

Ivers had been listening closely to the exchange between him and Cici. "What do you have in mind?"

"I think we should check out these ruins. Even more so with what you just told me," he said to Cici.

"You mean go out there where they are?" Romeo sputtered.

Romeo's last close encounter with the Ravers had been enough for him. Dax didn't blame him. Leaving the ship was a risk, but the odd behavior of the Ravers concerned him. If the director and the archaeologists had found something at the new site … He bit down on his blistered lip. He was doing it again. He had just abdicated taking responsibility, and once again, he was making decisions for the group. He turned to Ivers.

"It's up to you, Sergeant, but I don't believe in coincidences."

Ivers nodded, but the corners of his eyes wrinkled, as if he realized what Dax was doing. "If we're going, we had best do it soon. We don't have much time." He looked around the table. "Everyone suit up. Load food, water, and weapons in the serviceable ATV. We don't have time to repair the other one."

"It holds four people," Romeo said. "Do you want someone to stay here with the ship?"

"No," Dax replied, noting Romeo's disappointment at his answer. "We stick together. Switch on our beacon and leave a message indicating where we're going. If we don't get back to the ship, the Navy will know where to look for us."

He didn't know if the new site had a sanctuary or walls more solid than the *Luck*, but he would not let the Ravers trap him without food or water again. His gut told him the site was important. Rathiri's comment to Cici only heightened his resolve to investigate. The key to understanding the creatures might be at the new site. If he was wrong, they would die slightly earlier than if they remained with *Fortune's Luck.* He considered the odds acceptable.

"Do we have time to bury Tish?" Romeo asked.

Dax suppressed a shudder at the reminder that she was gone. She deserved better than she had gotten. She deserved someone better than him. "No, we don't have time for a funeral. She won't mind. We'll conduct a proper ceremony later." *If we're still alive,* he added silently.

Thirty minutes later, the five of them jammed into the ATV with all the supplies they could carry lashed to the top, and drove eastward down the valley. He glanced back at his crippled ship glinting in the sun. *Fortune's Luck* would eventually become part of the landscape. In two thousand years, she would be rusted hulk buried beneath the sand waiting for another team of archaeologists to unearth her. What would they determine about her crew? That they enjoyed good coffee. That they were a happy crew until their captain killed them. The *Luck* had been a good ship with good memories. Now, the ghosts of her dead crew haunted her tainted corridors. She should remain buried. The earth was a fitting last resting place for her.

The first thing he noticed about the ruins was their placement on a rocky shelf ten meters above the canyon floor. Two millennia ago, it was probably a riverside building, though why its builders would place it in such an inaccessible spot, he couldn't figure. The dilapidated ruins possessed symmetry different from the other ruins, reminding him of a flattened Mayan pyramid. He had not studied the *Huresh* cities, but the ruins appeared older, megalithic, a structure designed to last for millennia. The shaped stones looked Neolithic, but it had taken modern technology to shape the massive stones and place them atop of one another. The smallest stone was three times as heavy as the fifteen-ton red granite blocks used inside the Khufu Pyramid at Giza. Manpower and earthen ramps would not have sufficed.

The blocks were not sandstone as were most of the *Huresh* buildings, subject to erosion and decay. The lightly veined opalescent stone resembled marble but had the durability of granite. It retained its luster after eons of sandblasting by the relentless winds. The building abutted the cliff rather than stood apart from it, as if its builders had used the multi-hued sandstone layers as a backdrop for their creation. The building was not ornamented by massive columns or statues, as if the building itself expressed the will of its builders, simplistic, yet powerful.

"They don't look *Huresh*," Cici said. "I suppose it could be from a much earlier period, but why was it constructed way out here? The nearest city is at K124."

As Dax watched the structure loom larger as they approached, he wondered that as well. He believed the answer to that question was part of overall answer concerning Loki.

Plia parked the ATV as close to what appeared to be the entrance as possible. The triangular entrance sat at the top of set of wide steps whose bottom was half-buried in the sand. The ten-meter-wide stairway had two-meter-deep treads and meter-high risers. It consisted of three platforms of diminishing widths until they became the same width as the five-meter-wide, six-meter-high entrance. Two large stones, carved to fit together so tightly they resembled a single stone, formed the entrance. Unlike any other *Huresh* buildings, the entrance stones bore carved, intertwining vines with triangular leaves gracefully winding up their faces.

"That's different. I've never seen that motif before. It's beautiful."

The oddly spaced steps were difficult to negotiate. Dax felt like Jack confronted with the Giant's castle staircase. Clambering up each step wearing his suit, lugging his rifle, a pack with food, water, and extra power cells for the laser wore him out. He stopped at each landing for a quick breather. He noticed Ivers, Cici, and Plia had no difficulty. Romeo, like him, sweated profusely in spite of the cooling unit in his suit and gasped for breath halfway up.

Just inside the entrance lay an open portico formed by rows of square stone columns that had once supported a raised wooden roof. The columns, like the door lintels, bore engravings of vines, some with vestiges of the metal used to ornament the grooves. Many of the columns had collapsed, creating a narrow passageway that wormed through the pile of stones.

"We'll leave our packs here," Dax said. "Bring your weapons." The building set his nerves on edge. He did not like it. His itching scalp argued against entering, but he had no choice.

They crawled on hands and knees through the portico rubble before eventually reaching a long, wide corridor. The corridor ended in a large room. Part of the roof had collapsed, and sand had accumulated over the centuries, filling the room to a depth of three meters in some spots. Whatever the room might have once contained had long since turned to dust. The room was windowless and had only the single entrance. He thought it odd the top of the pyramid had a single room. Two shallow holes, partially refilled with blowing sand, marked spots where Rathiri's expedition had excavated.

"This part of the building is built into the cliff face," Cici said.

Dax glanced up at the opening in the roof. The cliff loomed dizzyingly only a few meters away. He walked around the room slowly, examining the walls and floor for anything out of the ordinary. His scalp itched. He knew something was there, something he was not going to like. After ten minutes, he found what he was searching for.

"Look at this," he said.

Ivers walked over and saw Dax staring at a depression in the sand near one wall. "There's nothing there, just another hole."

"No," he insisted. "Watch."

Ivers stared at the spot. After a minute, he saw what Dax had noticed. "I'll be damned."

"What?" Cici asked joining them.

"The sand," Dax told her. "It's moving."

"Moving?"

"The sand is trickling down a hole, and sand from the room is moving to replace it, like water down a drain. It's hard to spot. I understand why Rathiri missed it." He looked at Cici. "If he missed it. Sand blows in to replace the missing sand. There's something, an opening beneath the sand."

"It might take longer than we have to dig down to it," Ivers pointed out.

"Not if we blast," he said with a grin. "Romeo, bring a homemade bomb."

Cici was appalled at his idea. "You can't use explosives. This is an archaeological site. You might damage it."

"I intend to." He pointed to the floor. "Whatever the Ravers are after is down there. I want to find it first."

A rush of possibilities coursed through Dax's veins. After so many days of reacting to events, of watching friends die, he was now prepared to break the tragic cycle before more died. He knew he was right about the building and its connection to the Ravers. He could feel it like a tiny voice whispering in his ear telling him what to do. The secret lay below their feet. Director Rathiri suspected some connection but died before he could reveal what he had learned. *Unless we're both insane*, he thought.

Romeo brought the bomb and handed it to Dax. "Everyone had better leave," he said. With the short fuse, he would have very little time to get far enough away from the explosion, especially if he brought the entire structure down on top of him, which looked like a distinct possibility. He no longer cared. His life needed resolution even if that final resolve was death. He gave everyone time to clear the area, dug down against the wall, and placed the bomb. The fuse was short, and he was no speed demon. He shredded up some papers from his utility belt and placed them in a pile on the sand. He then laid the fuse on one side of the pile to give him a few seconds extra head start.

He lit one side of the papers and ran. Slogging through the loose sand in his suit boots felt as if he were trudging through a quagmire. He heard the fuse ignite before he crossed the room. Reaching the corridor, he knew he was out of time. He hit the ground, covering his head with his arms. Seconds later, the bomb exploded. The floor quaked violently. The giant stones groaned in protest of awakening from their millennia of slumber, sifting dust down over him, but they held. He expected the floor to give way beneath him, but it did not. As the echo died away, he returned to examine his handiwork.

The explosion had blasted away several meters of sand, revealing the top of a triangular opening and several stone steps similar to the ones out front leading beneath the wall. It was a start. The others joined him.

"It's a doorway," Cici gasped in amazement.

"But where does it go?" Romeo asked.

Dax got down on his hands and knees and began digging. "We'll find out." As his blistered hands dug into the sand, he wished he had brought a shovel. He considered sending someone back to *Fortune's Luck* for one, but he did not want to split the group. They all joined him, digging like a pack of dogs searching for a lost buried bone.

Within an hour, they had excavated the hole sufficiently to determine the steps led to another room or passageway. He had feared sifting sand filled the entire space, but their digging revealed a void. He squeezed through the opening on his hands and knees and discovered a space large enough to stand beyond it. Switching on his suit lights, he gawked in wonder.

He stood at the top of a long tier of steps descending into a cavernous space. Sand covered the steps, creating the slip face of a dune ten meters high. His light could not illuminate the far end of the room. The walls and ceiling, carved from the native rock, met fifty meters above his head, forming the point of an enormous inverted V. Rows of statues lined niches along each side of the room, disappearing into the darkness. Those nearest him revealed only their heads. The subjects of the statues caused palpitations in Dax's heart.

"This isn't *Huresh*," Cici said.

"Not unless they liked statues of Ravers."

Each of the statues was a Raver, all bearing the same pose, standing straight and tall with their arms folded over their chests and heads bowed.

"They look different," Ivers said. "They have eyes."

"They're wearing clothes," Romeo snorted. Dax saw that Romeo was right. Each Raver wore a sort of cloak with pockets.

"They're smaller than Ravers," Cici observed, "and more defined. Look at their hands. Instead of long talons, they have fingers designed for grasping. Their legs are less elongated."

"And that's not armor under those togas," Ivers noted. "They have scales, but more like a lizard."

Dax listened to their observations, but his mind had already leaped to the most logical conclusion. The pieces of the puzzle fit so neatly he did not doubt his outré presumption. "This is the race that created the Ravers."

Cici stared at Dax. "What do you mean?"

"This reptilian race was the original inhabitants of Loki. The *Huresh*, who we called Lokians, the builders of the cities, invaded and terraformed the planet, wiping out the reptilian race. Before they died out, they created a doomsday weapon, one that ensured their world would never be colonized by anyone else – the Ravers."

Cici wrinkled her brow. "It makes sense in a macabre kind of way, but why are the Ravers coming here? A homing instinct?"

"We'll find the answer down there," Dax said. She still did not see the significance of the pyramid. He suspected he did, and the thought troubled him. He began walking and sliding down the dune, using one gloved hand thrust into the sand to brace himself.

As he walked down the room, Dax counted the statues – fifty-four, perhaps six more buried beneath the sand. Was the number significant to the race they sculpted them? He glanced back to see the others still standing on the steps. "Anyone else curious?"

"I'll bring the weapons," Plia said.

# 16

The flat pyramid and the room built into the cliff predated the *Huresh* ruins by a thousand years. The members of the unnamed native race were master craftsmen. They had carved the niches and statues from the dense sandstone as they excavated the room. Slabs of the same marble-like stone as the exterior lined the walls and ceiling of the room. The floor was highly ornamented. A mosaic of smaller polished stones created a river winding through a landscape lined with forests, hills, and expanses of grasslands – Loki as it had once looked. To Dax, the loss of such a world was sufficient cause to wish its despoilers eliminated. The base of the wall beneath the niches bore colorful bas-relief images of animals, birds, and sea creatures, the vanished flora and fauna of Loki.

"It's beautiful," Cici observed.

Dax had to agree. "It was." It looked as Earth had looked before mankind had dirtied the air, fouled the oceans, and driven the wildlife into near extinction. A flash of light along one wall gave him a start. He stopped and aimed his laser, but he saw nothing. After a few seconds, a soft glow slowly illuminated the room from a source set high in the walls.

"Power, after all this time," Plia said. Her voice held a degree of admiration for the builders. She had shown little interest in their find. He was glad she had discovered something that could break her shell of icy stoicism.

Walking down the twin rows of Raver statues gave Dax the shivers, as if he expected one to come to live and attack him. In spite of how the neat even rows pleased his sense of balance and his OCD, the statues repelled him. As he studied one of the statue's faces, he noted the differences between the creators and their creations, the Ravers, as he knew them. The beings depicted on the statues were not blind. Their large round eyes gazed outward filled with intelligence and pride. Their mouths revealed rows of normal-sized teeth, not the black, razor-sharp teeth of Ravers. Their bearing denoted dignity.

"This must have been some kind of religious complex, a temple," he proposed. "Maybe these statues represent former high priests or leaders."

"Did these people devolve into the Ravers?" Romeo asked.

"Not enough time has passed for that much evolutionary change," Cici replied.

"No, they created Ravers from their own kind," Ivers said. "By some process, part genetics, part bioengineering, they turned citizens into super soldiers, rampaging beasts designed to kill anything it encountered. They knew they were dying, wiped out by the invaders, and directed all their efforts into extracting revenge."

"I feel sorry for them," Cici admitted. "To lose your world … it's more than I could have born."

"Don't," Dax snapped. Cici's sympathy for the builders annoyed him. They were the victims of an invasion, and for that, he felt sorry for them, but they had descended into racial madness, choosing an unthinkable form of retaliation. He doubted the subjects for bestial transformation were all volunteers. "Whatever their motivation, their creatures are loose out there. They killed our friends. We have to stop them."

He quickened his steps. Somewhere in the underground complex lay the answer. They had to find it if they wanted to survive. Cici was right about one thing. Despite his anger at them, he understood their reasoning. Bereft of their world, wiped out like the buffalo on Earth or the Bey's Helix Elk on Glorious, the indigenous race chose not to go out meekly. They set loose a horde of monsters created from their own flesh. The *Huresh* were not an invading army; that assault had already taken place before their arrival, the terraforming process that had changed the landscape and exterminated a species. They were colonists, planted and left to thrive or fail on their own. They weren't soldiers, but farmers, builders, businessmen. They could not face the Raver threat. The Ravers had done their job, but now, having reawakened, they did not know that job was over. Humans were the new threat, and they would face the same fate.

The grand hall was over four-hundred-meters long. The far wall was blank except for two metal doors. Plia carefully examined the door on the right. "It has an electronic lock, but I think I can bypass it," she said. She placed a small black disc over the door lock and plugged it into a port on her suit. Using her suit computer, she ran a decryption code. After twenty seconds, the door emitted a loud click. "There." She pushed the door. It split into two diagonal halves, which slid into opposite recesses in the wall.

The short corridor revealed beyond the door led to a series of interconnected rooms. Time had long ago decayed whatever organic materials they contained, but several of the rooms contained the rusted remains of scientific apparatus, most of whose purpose was indecipherable. Time had taken its toll on it as well, but several large slabs of stone contained the remnants of restraining devices where the victims, willing or unwilling, underwent the transformation process. Dax tried to imagine the pain and agony the stones of the room had absorbed, but failed. It was beyond his comprehension.

"I'm sure the science people will be interested in this," Ivers said.

Dax sneered. "Yeah, like I trust the military with monster-making equipment."

He had seen enough. He turned abruptly and retraced his steps to the other door.

The left-hand door revealed a sloping ramp descending deeper into the bluff, illuminated by sparsely spaced lights in the ceiling. They emerged into a second cavernous space. He heard Cici's sharp drawn breath as the lights flickered on as they entered.

Like the first hall, the long walls contained rows of niches; however, the recesses did not contain statues. Instead, each of the hundreds of vertical glass-enclosed cavities held a Raver in suspended animation, duplicates of the Ravers in the lava tubes.

This was what attracted the Ravers like a magnet – their kin awaiting reawakening in the cryo chamber.

"Oh, my God!" Cici exclaimed, as her gaze fell on the rows of glass crypts. "There are so many."

"An army," Ivers replied. Ivers' voice was cold. He saw the creatures as a threat to humanity. If they ever got off planet, they would be.

Dax didn't understand what they were doing there. "But why didn't the indigenous population release them?"

"Maybe they didn't need them, or maybe they died before they could," Ivers suggested.

Cici's face was ashen, he eyes wide and wild with fear. "Are they alive?"

"Yes. They're just sleeping." Ivers ran his gaze the length of the room. His expression was grim. "We have to destroy them."

While Dax agreed with Ivers, he thought it more likely they would only succeed in awakening them. "We'll never kill them one at a time. We don't have time. Our company should arrive soon."

Ivers would not be deterred. He had come to Loki to kill the Ravers. It did not matter how many there were. "There must be a kill switch somewhere, a means to shut down the power to the crypts. Without life support, they'll die."

"Or awaken. The ones in the lava tubes didn't need any fancy technical support. They simply dug a hole and went to sleep. What if killing the power brings them out of stasis all at once?" The thought made Dax shudder. He turned to Romeo. "Go outside and keep watch. As soon as you spot a Raver, call us on the com link."

"You mean alone?" he asked.

His fearful expression made Dax reconsider his suggestion. He wouldn't order anyone else to risk their life. "Okay, you stay here. I'll go."

Romeo sighed deeply and shook his head. "No, I'll go. You know what you're doing here. I don't."

"If you see anything, hurry back here."

"You betcha I will," he said as he climbed up the sand dune and left.

Plia walked farther down the chamber. "Dax, there are several corridors off here. One might lead to a control room or power facility."

"We're doing nothing standing here," he said.

They followed one corridor, but it quickly branched off. Dax chose one at random. The next corridor divided again. "It's a damn maze down here," Dax griped, frustrated with the progress.

"Maybe we should split up," Plia suggested.

"No. We stay together. Less chance of getting lost and splitting up divides our firepower."

"Maybe the real Lokians, the lizard race, had weapons powerful enough to kill Ravers. I mean, the Ravers must have been dangerous to them, too, right?"

Dax looked at Cici and grinned. "Good thinking." Now they had two things to search for: weapons and a way to shut down the power. He took out his knife and scratched an arrow on the wall to blaze their trail.

"We were so wrong about this planet," Cici said. She shook her head slowly as she walked. Her face betrayed her anguish and confusion. "My sympathy was with the *Huresh*: at first, because of the change in the environment; then, because of the Ravers. Now, we learn they were the invaders. It's difficult to erase all that preconceived emotional baggage. The real Lokians, who I should feel sorry for, created monsters that killed men, women, and children – farmers and businessmen, not military. Who was in the right?"

"The settlers might not have known the history of the planet they settled. Their leaders might not have bothered telling them. The fact that they vanished tells me they received no support after the colony was established. They left on their own to thrive or die. They might have thought the Ravers were wild animals not exterminated by the terraforming." He shook his head, confused. "I don't know, Cici. Like most wars, it depends on which side you're on. Whatever their sins, the people in the cities did not deserve to die in the manner they did."

"Right now, it's us against the Ravers," Ivers pointed out. "Who and why doesn't matter. Let the historians and the philosophers figure it out.

Dax conceded Ivers' point. "Right. Let's keep searching."

After several dead ends and returning to their starting point to retrace their steps, they entered what at one time had been living quarters, a large space with rows of low stone partitions dividing the room into individual quarters. Piles of rusted metal that might have been bed frames, and the dust of personal effects filled the spaces. Holes in the floor marked a communal lavatory. Dax counted the stalls.

"No more than a few hundred survivors out of an entire race of people," he said.

"All dedicated to creating monsters," Ivers added. "I wonder how many of these people became Ravers?"

"I get the feeling it was like a cult," Cici offered. "The remnant of the survivors banding together and dedicating themselves to one last great act of revenge, offering their bodies as the raw material for weapons."

"Kind of like 'last person to leave turns off the lights'," Dax said. "Maybe just a handful remained unchanged to continue the process. Either something happened before they could release all of the Ravers, or they had a change of heart."

Ivers had a different opinion. "Considering they managed to wipe out the invaders without the Ravers in hibernation, they might have decided to save them for a second wave of invaders."

"You mean us," Cici said.

Ivers shrugged. "Well, we're not really invaders, but they might consider us unwanted visitors."

Ivers' statement intrigued Dax. "So you think the Ravers are intelligent."

"Don't you? You saw how smart they are. They know how to disable a spacecraft. They engage in tactics. I suspect they retain a great deal if not all of their former intelligence."

Cici made a face. "Oh my God, an intelligent being trapped in a monster's body. That's awful."

"That's the price of revenge," Dax said.

"Take a look at this," Plia said.

She stood farther down the room by another set of stalls. Dax went to join her. She stared at three reptilian skeletons. They lay side by side amid a pile of what might once have been a bed.

Judging by their stature and backward-jointed legs, they were Lokians.

"It looks as if they simply lay down and went to sleep," she said.

"Or took their own lives," Cici said. "These may be the last Lokians. Maybe they decided against releasing the remaining Ravers."

"We'll never know," Dax said. "It doesn't much matter now."

Ivers was getting restless. "We're finding nothing here. It's a maze. We need to check out the other door while we have time. We can come back here if necessary."

"Do you think the Ravers know how to release their fellow creatures?" Cici asked.

Ivers turned to leave. "I don't want to find out."

They returned to the hibernation room. Plia repeated the lock-picking process on the second door. A high-pitched whine greeted them when the door opened and became louder as they travelled the narrow corridor behind it. The sounded grated on Dax's nerves and made his teeth tingle. It was the sound of machinery. The tunnel ended at a metal door. He placed his hand on the door and felt it vibrating.

"Plia?"

Plia examined the door for a few minutes, running her hand along its width. "There's no lock, but this door is different." Finally, she pressed her hand against the center of the door and stepped back, as the door split into four sections and withdrew into the wall. The hum became a screech.

They exited the tunnel onto a narrow walkway circling a deep cylindrical shaft ten meters in diameter. The center of the shaft contained a slim metal rod half-a-meter thick. It ran from somewhere above them down into the depths of the black abyss. A gust of hot air rose from the chasm. As they watched, a blue halo of light rose along the length of the rod. As it passed them, the hairs on Dax's arm rose, and the displays on his suit monitors flickered. The light ring continued for several hundred meters above them before dissipating. Set at intervals along the walls of the shaft, glowing metal rings became brighter as the halo passed.

"It's some kind of geothermal generator," Plia said. "The apparatus converts heat energy to electrical energy. The induction rings in the wall act as transformers increasing the power and siphoning off the energy. The shaft must go for kilometers down to the mantle." She looked at Dax and smiled. "This machinery had operated unattended for centuries. The builders knew what they were doing. After the initial investment of time and equipment, it produces power at practically no cost as long as there is magma at the planet's core. We couldn't do this, not on this scale."

It took a lot to amaze Plia. Dax had no doubt she was right. "The problem is we have no idea how to shut it down."

"I seriously doubt we could," Plia answered. "If we simply shut it down, it might crack the mantle and destroy the planet."

"There must be a way to shut down the power to the cryocrypts," Ivers said. "I don't want to destroy the planet, just the Ravers."

Dax leaned over the rail and stared into the depths. "The builders of this contraption strike me as the kind of people who would rather destroy their world than let anyone else have it or benefit from their technology."

His suit com hissed. He switched it on. "What?"

Romeo's voice was more animated than Dax had ever heard it. "They're coming, about ten clicks out."

"Damn. Okay, join us in the main hall."

"I'm almost there now."

Dax looked at Ivers. They had failed in both their quests. "What now?"

The halo of light, much dimmer than before, slowly descended the rod like Time Square's Big Apple at midnight on New Year's Eve. Ivers gritted his teeth, raised his ion disruptor, and before Dax could stop him, fired at the halo. A brilliant blue arc of light leapt from the rod to the disruptor, knocking Ivers off his feet and sending him into the wall. The disruptor laid smoking beside him. Ivers was alive, but stunned. The halo continued uninterrupted down the shaft.

"That was a damn fool thing to do," Dax barked. "You could have killed us all. You almost did kill yourself."

Ivers slowly rose to his feet. He was unsteady and held onto the rail. "I had to try something." Gingerly, still bracing himself on the rail, he bent over to retrieve the disruptor. He gave it a quick examination. "Damn, I fried it. Useless." He tossed it to the ground.

"Great. It was our only effective weapon. When I asked what now, I expected an answer, not a suicide attempt."

"What do you want me to tell you? We have, had, a disruptor and three lasers. We could never hold off the three Ravers that are coming. If they awaken the rest, we're outnumbered a couple of hundred to five." He shook his head. "Those aren't odds we can work with."

"So you tried to blow up the planet?"

He glared at Dax. "Yes. We're going to die. I wanted to make our deaths count for something."

"Maybe we should die."

Dax turned to stare at Cici. "Why would you say that?"

"The race that spawned the Ravers did so to defend their world. Why shouldn't we allow them to retain it for themselves? They wiped out the invaders. They are going to wipe us out. It's their world. Leave it to them. In the end, they win."

"I'm not ready to die to quiet their restless ghosts."

They entered the cryochamber room. Romeo waited for them, out of breath. Dax looked at the rows of caskets. He did not see the remnants of a civilization. He saw animal pens. The race that spawned the Ravers was long gone. So, too, should be the monsters they created.

He turned to Plia. "How much shielding do you think this rock can provide?"

"Against what?"

"An anomaly."

She gasped. "You want to activate the Skip Drive on the ground? That's … that's madness!"

"Yeah, I get it. I read the owner's manual. It states specifically on page one not to attempt a Skip while on the ground. It voids the warranty. I can activate the engines from here with the comp link. In their condition, it won't be difficult to induce an overload. The blast would be the equivalent of a five-megaton explosion. Can these walls withstand the blast?"

Plia froze. He hoped she was considering his question and that he hadn't broken her brain with his request. The others stared at him in confusion, all but Ivers. He understood. "You want to kill the Ravers outside without destroying the planet."

"It's a thought. Of course, I might just wake up the Ravers in here, but that's a chance we have to take. I take it you don't object."

"I'm in. If it takes care of the Ravers outside, we can let the Navy deal with the ones in here."

Plia began doing the computations on her suit computer. She spoke slowly as she considered the results. "I think the walls will hold. I'm not sure a deliberate Skip detonation has ever been attempted."

"Great, I'll go down in the history books."

"I'm not sure about the radiation," she added. "It might release some short-lived exotic particles that could pass through stone like tissue paper." She looked at Dax. "You might become sterile."

"Great, no little Wyldds running around. I'm counting on the door to the power core being radiation proof." He looked around at the group. "Are we agreed?"

Romeo swallowed hard. His Adam's apple quivered in his skinny throat. He nodded his head.

"I'm in," Cici said. "We shouldn't destroy their world after what they did to save it."

"It's slightly better odds than facing the Ravers," Plia said. "I'm in, although there is always the chance we will damage the power core. If that happens, we will all die anyway."

"My, aren't you a little ray of sunshine," Dax said.

"Hell, you know my answer," Ivers said. "Kill these fuckers and let's get out of here."

"Okay. Here goes." Dax entered his captain's code on his suit computer, and pulled up the screen for *Fortune's Luck's* engineering data. It took surprisingly little effort to start the Skip Drive. *Probably because no one anticipated the concept of initiating a countdown if you weren't prepared to Skip. I'm making history.*

"Two minutes," he said. "We had better move."

They took refuge in the shaft and sealed the door. The shrill whine was annoying, but they would have to tolerate it for a few minutes. If they failed, it wouldn't matter.

"Twenty seconds," he announced. Strangely, he didn't feel fear. He had been through too much to be afraid. He felt a sense of anticipation as he did before any normal Skip, but mostly he was relieved. He had thrown off the chronic morbidity that had threatened to turn him into a vegetable and had made an executive decision. Now, he would see if it was the right one.

At two seconds, he held onto the rail. For five seconds, nothing happened; then, the ground shook, a slight tremor at first, but it quickly turned into a Magnitude 6 quake. The tremor knocked him to the ground. He was glad he wore his suit to cushion his fall. The balcony rattled as if it were going to break free and plunge them into the shaft. He lay on his stomach, staring down into the abyss. The light halo rose upwards toward him. It briefly flared bright enough to cast shadows, and then flickered out, leaving them in absolute darkness. The tremors abated, but only for a few seconds. Then, the entire shaft groaned and rumbled. The heaving balcony bounced him across the floor before tilting at a steep angle. He slammed into the wall. He heard someone scream; Plia or Cici, he thought; then, realized it was him.

He passed out.

# 17

Cici's only proof that she was alive was the pain that racked her body. When the Skip engine exploded, she first felt a wave pass through her body that left her disoriented. *The anomaly boundary*, she realized. For a nanosecond, she had wavered between realities. She had no time to analyze the feeling. The balcony beneath her danced faster than her legs could follow. She hit the floor hard, holding on for fear it would bounce her over the side. The episode had lasted less than a minute, but it left them in total darkness. She fought a rising panic. She was alive, and as far as she could tell, not seriously injured, simply bruised and battered. She sat up, wincing at the pain in her elbow.

"Is everyone all right?" she asked.

Someone turned on his or her suit lights. She saw it was Ivers. He played his lights over the group. Dax appeared to be unconscious. The section of walkway on which he lay had broken free of the wall and canted at a twenty-degree angle. Only the rail had kept him from plunging into the shaft. Plia stood and brushed herself off as if nothing had happened, her face as expressionless as ever. Romeo sat with his back against the wall, looking bewildered.

"Yeah, I'm okay," Ivers answered. "The quake or the EMP must have knocked out the core."

She stood, holding onto the rail until her legs steadied beneath her. "Do you think it worked?"

"I doubt even a Raver could have survived that blast." He leaned over the broken section of walkway and shined the light in Dax's face. "I'm surprised we did."

"Is he all right?"

"Yeah, just stunned I think. He'll be okay." He grabbed one of Dax's arms and dragged him up the slope onto the section of walkway on which they stood.

"I don't detect any radiation," Plia announced, "but our suit meters aren't designed to detect everything."

Cici rubbed her head through her helmet, thankful she had it on. She felt as if she had gone twice around a Tilt-A-Whirl and been thrown out headfirst. Her head throbbed and her muscles ached. She was glad the incessant whine of the power core was gone. "Is it safe to open the door?"

Ivers stood by the door feeling it with his hand. "No heat. We were pretty far inside the mountain. I think it's safe."

Dax roused, groaning. He held his hand to the back of his head. "What happened?"

"You passed out," Ivers said. Cici thought he was gloating a little.

"Why is it so dark?"

"The power core failed," Plia replied.

"What's that going to do to the cryo units?" he asked.

Cici had forgotten about the Ravers sleeping just outside the door. A sense of unease crept over her. "Will they awaken?"

"Maybe it killed them," Romeo offered.

Dax stood, wobbling. He braced himself against the wall and shook his head to knock out the cobwebs. "Don't you think we had better find out?"

Ivers opened the door slowly. A blast of hot air rushed inside through the gap, bringing with it the odor of burnt sand and ozone. Cici sneezed and batted the cloud dust away from her nose with her hand. She hated dust. Her nine months on Loki had not changed her opinion of dust. Too late, she remembered the face shield of her helmet and lowered it. Without power, the tunnel was as dark as pitch. Ivers led the way with his suit lights and flashlight. When they had gone halfway down the tunnel, the power core groaned, produced a series of sharp loud clicks, and emitted a troubling noise that rose in frequency from a low grinding sound to an irritating high-pitched warbling. The blue halo of light resumed its journey up the rod, and the lights flickered before coming back on.

"At least we didn't destroy it," Ivers said.

Cici wasn't as certain. The high-pitched drone seemed less steady, undulating up and down the frequencies. The halo rose in a series of short jerks instead of its previous smooth transition up the rod. Fingers of blue light arced between the halo and the metal bands in the wall. "No, but we bent it a little, I think," she said in response to Ivers' statement.

When they entered the cryo chamber, the worst sight imaginable awaited them. The lids on the crypts were all open, revealing the Ravers inside. A mist rose from each of them. "Oh, my God!" she gasped. "They're waking up."

"The caskets must have a fail switch that begins the revival process when the power fails," Ivers said. He turned to Dax. "You were right."

"Hell of a time to be right."

"Back to the power chamber," Ivers said.

Plia said, "I would not recommend that."

Dax stared at her. "Why not?"

"The quake damaged the power core. It's arcing in an attempt to stabilize. Those arcs contain a couple of billion joules of energy. That's several billion Watts. If one hits us …."

Cici swallowed hard. Plia didn't have to elaborate. If one of the arcs struck them, it would vaporize them.

"Maybe we can leave before they wake up," Romeo suggested.

"And go where?" Dax replied. "It's ninety kilometers to K124B, and I doubt our ATV is waiting outside."

Cici realized Dax was right. They had nowhere to go, but the idea of willingly trapping themselves inside the complex ran counter to her concept of self-preservation, especially with hundreds of Ravers on the verge of awakening.

Ivers spoke up. "If we can't hide in the power core, and we can't run, that leaves the maze." He looked at the metal door. "That door won't stop them for very long."

"Maybe they won't know we're here," Cici suggested, more in hope than with any sense it might be true. "Maybe the EMP scrambled their senses."

Plia was skeptical. She voiced her doubt. "Perhaps, but I doubt it. The crypts probably shielded them from the worst of the pulse."

Dax removed the walkie-talkie from his belt. "In any case, I'll turn this on and leave it out here. We can eavesdrop. When it gets quiet out here, we can presume they've left. We have food and water for three or four days. With luck, the Navy will be here by then."

Dax's plan sounded insane but plausible, at least as likely to succeed as making a run for it. The idea of seeking refuge in the maze of tunnels frightened her, but they had little choice. With a great deal of trepidation, she nodded her agreement.

"Can you seal it?" Dax asked Plia of the door into the maze.

"Yes, but they might know the code."

It sounded implausible the creatures retained that much intelligence, but he didn't want to take chances. "Scramble it," he suggested.

Plia shut the door and plugged into the lock mechanism. "I can't fuse the lock. We need to get out again. I'll reset the code to a random repeating number that only my suit computer can match at the right time." She looked at those gathered around her watching. "Of course, they can simply slice through the lock with those talons."

"That's comforting to know," Cici said. "I guess we can only hope they are more interested in going outside than in coming after us." She had a bizarre thought. "Will they know how much time has passed?"

Ivers answered. "I've used a cryo chamber in the Marines when I was severely wounded. They used it to save my life and send me to a medical ship. I was out two weeks, but when I awoke, it seemed I had just nodded off for a moment."

"Great," Dax groaned. "They'll think the war is still on."

Ivers nodded. "Unfortunately, yes." He looked around the corridor. "We saw nothing with which to barricade the door. As Doctor Adar said, we can only hope they think the enemy is out there."

Cici re-evaluated their chances of survival. It did not look good.

* * * *

Dax was amazed they had survived the Skip Drive explosion. He only half-believed they would, but a 50/50 chance was better than no chance. *Fortune's Luck is gone for real now, vaporized.* Even though *Fortune's Luck* would never have gone into space again, not without more repairs than the ship was worth, it was there. It was still his ship. Now, he had no ship and a slim chance of ever getting another. Banks did not loan credit to captains who blew up their ships. If it came down to a Board of Inquiry, he would lucky to keep his captain's license.

To make matters worse, killing the three Ravers outside had awakened the hundreds inside. He had not counted on that bit of misfortune. Only a thin steel door stood between them and the creatures. He knew how useless that was. If the Ravers detected them using whatever seemingly magical sense they used, he and the others would die. He could see only one way to survive, and that depended on a lot of luck, which had not been running in his favor lately.

Unless the Ravers sensed the reptilian Lokians were kin and did not attack them, the Lokians had weapons effective against them or at least a means of controlling them. If the last few surviving Lokians died inside the mountain complex, any weapons they had were still there. They had to find them.

It surprised him that he still cared about living. He had killed Nate, Andy, and Tish. He could see no future for himself. All that mattered now was saving the remainder of his crew – Plia and Romeo. He could include Cici in that group.

His body ached and his head felt as if his brain was rattling around inside. The aftermath of the explosion had left him feeling fuzzy. He knew how close they had all come to becoming exotic particles whirling through space. He couldn't think far enough ahead to plan. He was going on instinct.

"The Lokians must have had weapons. Somewhere in here." He waved his hands around, bringing on a bout of nausea from the frantic motion. "We have to find them."

"If they had weapons, why did they create the Ravers?" Cici asked.

"In the beginning, they were fighting the terraforming process. They had no hope of winning that, but they anticipated an invasion. If they were intelligent, they must have had weapons. They just didn't have enough survivors to build an army except by transmuting themselves."

"We looked," Romeo said.

"We didn't search everywhere," Plia reminded them.

"Right. We ignored a few corridors. Let's make a thorough search." Their suit coms began picking up deep-throated wails from the newly awakened Ravers broadcast by the walkie-talkie. "We don't have much time."

"In pairs," Ivers suggested. "Plia and Romeo. Cici and Dax. I'll go solo."

Any other time, Dax would have been thrilled to be alone with Cici, but all he could think about was Tish dying in his arms. It felt like a betrayal to have carnal thoughts about anyone other than her. He and Cici chose one of the corridors they had bypassed originally. They explored small rooms that might have been storerooms but now contained only dust and slivers of rusted metal.

"What if we don't find anything?" Cici asked.

She walked pressed against Dax as if afraid to abandon physical contact with him. For his part, he did not mind.

"It was your suggestion, remember?"

She frowned and bit her lip. "I might be wrong."

"Don't give up yet. We might find something useful – a weapon or a control mechanism. I've given up twice already, but I keep getting pulled back in."

"You, Dax? You gave up?"

"When I took that mine from Ivers, I knew I was going to die. I had to save my crew. I had been wrong about survivors. It was the only thing I could think of. Ivers dragged me back in."

"When was the second time?"

"When I killed Tish."

Cici glanced away, ashamed at making him lay bare his soul to her. "I'm sorry."

"I wanted to give up. Hell, I did give up, but the Ravers puzzled me. The way they acted didn't make sense until you mentioned these ruins. Then, the pieces fell together. They're still as dangerous, but they don't seem as … as…" he struggled for the right word.

"Superhuman," Cici supplied for him.

"Yeah, something like that. We can beat them with the right tools."

"Thank you, Dax," she said.

He was puzzled. "For what?"

"Not giving up a third time."

His cheeks burned. "Yeah, well, let's see if we can do something to make this day last longer."

The corridor dumped back into one they had marked previously. They met Romeo and Plia. "Any luck?" he asked.

He could tell by Romeo's dour expression that he and Plia had found nothing. The floor quaked and the walls shuddered. Dust fell from the ceiling. The noise coming over their suit coms revealed the Ravers growing louder and more frantic.

"We found nothing," Plia said. "I fear the power core is growing more unstable. The Ravers sense it. The Skip explosion must have penetrated deeper into the mantle than I anticipated. The mantle may be shallower here; the reason the Lokians chose this spot for their power core."

"What are you saying?" Cici asked.

Plia stared at Cici as if explaining to a child. "The power core will fail entirely soon. The magnetic cork keeping the magma bottled will disappear, releasing the molten magma. It will explode up the shaft under tremendous pressure like a super volcano. It will destroy this part of the moon, perhaps the entire moon."

"Fuck me," Dax said.

"Yes, all of us," Plia agreed.

Ivers walked up and saw their dire expressions. He smiled. "I discovered another metal door at the end of a short corridor. It must protect something."

When no one said anything, he asked, "What's up? We might have located the weapons locker."

Dax nodded at Plia. "Tell him."

Dax watched Ivers' jaw drop at Plia's news. As if underlining her dark pronouncement, the corridor shuddered violently. Seconds later, the Ravers began hammering at the metal door.

"They know we're here," Dax said. "Let's check out this door and pray it's a thick one."

The sickening sound of shearing metal reverberated down the corridor. In less time than it had taken Plia to seal the door, the Ravers had broken through it. Dax grabbed his laser. "Go now," he told them. "I'll hold them off as long as I can."

"This is my job," Ivers argued.

To Dax's surprise, Plia grabbed one of the lasers and strode down the corridor toward the commotion. She did not look back, as she said, "I'm tired of running. This entire moon is going to crack like an egg soon. I do not wish to witness it. I have no ship, I have no home, but I will not die cowering."

"Don't do this, Plia," Dax begged.

The sound of claws scrambling on stone reached them. Plia stood at a turn of the corridor. "It's done, Captain." She fired her laser. One of the Ravers screamed.

Dax stood numbly and watched until Ivers slapped him on the shoulder. "She's giving us a chance to live. Don't waste it."

They raced down the corridor to the door Ivers had found. It was a manually operated door with a series of sliding handles along the sides. The sound of Plia's laser continued. The dead Ravers in the narrow corridor blocked the progress of the others. Eventually, they would find another way around, but she bought them time.

Ivers slid the bars and the door opened as smoothly as if oiled a few hours earlier instead of 2,000 years ago. The room beyond was in darkness. As he stepped inside, his boots echoed. His light did not reveal the true size of the space. Dax followed him inside and shone his lights along the wall, and then up the wall as far as his light would reach.

"It's not a room," he said. "It's another damn shaft."

"I think it's some type of exit," Ivers replied. "It goes up for hundreds of meters, maybe right to the top of the cliff." He pointed to a structure in the middle of the circular room. "That's some kind of lift."

Dax walked over to the platform that dominated most of the space. It was ancient and rusty. Flakes of metal came away when he brushed it with his gloved hand. "This thing is about to fall apart under its own weight."

Ivers moved his lights to illuminate two metal beams from the platform connecting with channels embedded in the opposite walls of the chamber. He touched a lever attached to a box on the handrail. It lit up. "It works." He jumped up and down on the surface of the platform. "It should hold."

Plia's voice came over the com unit. "They're breaking through, Dax. Good luck."

"Plia!" he yelled, but she had cut off communications.

"Make up your mind, Dax," Ivers urged. "She bought us a few minutes. Do you want to stay, fight, and die, or help me get these people out of here?"

Dax's head rang from being pulled in so many directions. He couldn't help Plia, but leaving her to die alone ripped chunks from his heart. Romeo was his only crewmember left. He would not let him die. He turned to Romeo. "Seal that door. We're going up."

Romeo glanced nervously up the shaft as he slammed home the bars on the door. "If you say so, Captain."

"I say so," he snapped, angry that things had come down to this. Either he trusted an ancient elevator that led to God knows where, or he faced the Ravers. "You're going home."

As Cici passed him, she reached out and touched his arm. "She was a brave woman, Dax."

He nodded. "Get going."

Once all four were on the platform, Ivers lifted the lever. Dax held his breath. If the 2,000-year-old machinery failed, they would die. If the power died on the way up, they would be trapped. The platform shuddered and groaned in protest at awakening from its long sleep, but to his great relief, it began to rise. They were getting a reprieve. The support beams sliding in the channels in the walls needed lubricating. They screeched and squealed every meter of their upward journey, but they did not falter. *Plia would have liked to see this.* He shook thoughts of her from his head, as well as Tish, Nate, and Andy. He had failed them, but he could not fail Romeo. He took a step backwards and almost fell through a hole in the platform. He hoped it held together until they reached the top.

Above the din of the lift, they heard the Ravers pounding on the metal door below. It withstood their attack for less than five minutes before Dax heard it hit the floor wrenched from its hinges.

"Here they come," he said.

He had assumed they could climb with those long claws and powerful muscles. He did not expect them to be part monkey. They scurried up the sides of the shaft as if it were a ladder. Ivers leaned over and fired a couple of shots at the Ravers with the laser rifle, but he only angered them. The lift reverberated and shook, as the creatures scrambled up the metal channels. Watching them climb, he knew the lift would never outpace them.

A group of them tried a new tactic. They passed the platform and attacked the beam where it attached to the channel, ripping at the metal around it in a frenzied effort to stop the platform. Dax knew they could succeed. If the beam slipped from the channel, they would plunge a thousand meters to the bottom.

"Do you still have that bomb?" he asked Ivers.

"Yes."

"Can you hit it with the laser if I throw it?"

Ivers was silent for a moment as he digested Dax's plan. "Yes."

"Okay."

Ivers handed him the thermos. Dax could not trust the fuse. If the bomb exploded too soon, it would kill them; too late, and it would do no good. "Here goes. Everyone should hug the floor." He waited until the platform was just below the Ravers tearing at the channel; then, lobbed the bomb toward the wall. He watched it tumble end over end, hoping his aim was true. It struck the wall just above the group of Ravers. Ivers fired.

The bomb exploded in a burst of flame and light. Ball bearings he had used as shrapnel pinged all around him, punching holes through the rusty platform. One piece struck his suit. He felt a sharp pain as it penetrated his leg. The platform jolted, throwing him down onto its surface. He watched five Ravers, some dead, some alive, fall past them into the dark depths below. Ivers picked off a few others with the laser rifle.

The explosion slowed the assault. The Ravers did not leave, but they dropped back, content now to follow the platform to the surface. Dax worried about that part as well. What would they do once they reached the surface? They couldn't run far. The way his leg felt, he might not be able to run at all. He looked upward, hoping to see an opening of some kind. He saw only darkness.

He stumbled when the platform stopped; then jerked upward again twice.

"I think the power core is failing," Ivers said.

"Great! That will leave us in a pretty fix."

"I think I see something above us," Romeo said.

Dax shined his light upward and saw rock. He hoped the platform stopped before crushing them. As the ceiling drew closer, he noticed an inset balcony around the shaft. The platform shuddered as the entire shaft trembled from a quake. Rocks showered down on them. The platform struggled the last few meters, and then stopped. Without the constant screeching of the lift arms, he heard the Ravers' claws digging into the rock.

Ivers spotted a tunnel leading from the balcony. "That way!" he shouted, as he fired down at the Ravers.

Dax risked a look over the side and saw scores of Ravers scrambling toward them. He led the way into the tunnel. The tunnel sloped upward for sixty meters before ending ended at a metal door. He hoped it did not have a magnetic lock. He didn't have Plia's skills. As he studied the door, he heard Ivers coming up the tunnel, still firing at the Ravers. They were running out of time.

The door looked like a simple hinged bulkhead door secured by thick metal rods controlled by a pressure plate mechanism. He pressed hard on the center of the door, and with a snap, the six metal rods retracted. The door creaked open a few centimeters. It resisted his efforts, but he managed to pull it open only to find a small room with a second door on the opposite wall. The small cubicle resembled an airlock. He repeated the identical operation on the second door. This door opened outward. Partially blocked by sand, it opened more slowly. He and Romeo got down on hands and knees and pushed the sand away from the door bottom of the door; then, put their combined weight into it to force it open. Sunshine spilled into the small airlock.

Ivers stood right behind them as they frantically worked on the door firing at the Ravers. Dax pulled Cici into the airlock.

"Come inside and close the inner door," Dax told Ivers.

He didn't know how long the door would deter them, but every second counted. The airlock's size allowed only one Raver at a time to enter. If they could kill the first few, it would hinder their exit.

Outside in the open, he secured the outer door and looked around. They were on top of the cliff overlooking the canyon where they had entered the ruins. There was nothing on the flat plain they could use as a shield or a place to hide. The only outcropping for hundreds of meters in any direction was the one in which the airlock was located.

As he stood there trying to figure out their next move, the ground trembled violently. He staggered trying to remain on his feet. He caught Cici as she fell and held her until the quaking stopped.

"The planet's tearing itself apart," he said. "The power core is getting ready to explode."

"Is there anything we can do?" she asked. He looked at her. She read his answer on his face. "It seems so senseless to die now after all we've been through. I don't want to die."

"We're not dead yet," he replied. It sounded trite, even to him, but it was the best he could do.

The Ravers pounded on the door. Ivers stood facing it with his laser rifle. Dax doubted the rifle had enough charge left for more than two or three shots. After that … well, he preferred not to dwell on it.

Another, stronger quake struck. It knocked all of them to the ground. Several meters of the cliff broke away and crashed into the canyon.

"If we just stand here, we'll soon right back where we started, down in the canyon."

Ivers glanced at him. "We can run, but it won't do much good. If they break out, they'll swarm us." He paused. "I'm hoping the damn planet explodes and gets rid of these hell spawn."

The ground trembled in waves, each lasting several seconds, but growing successively stronger. It looked as if Ivers was getting his wish.

"This is the UNN cruiser *Diligent*," burst over his suit com so loud it hurt his ears.

"Yes!" Ivers shouted. He hit his com link. "This is Sergeant Charles Jackson Ivers of the *Abraxas*. Where are you, *Diligent*?"

Dax felt like breaking down in tears at hearing the *Diligent*. They might still die, but the odds were turning in their favor again.

"Currently in orbit around Loki. We are responding to your message. What is your situation, Sergeant?"

"Critical. We are under attack and a power core is about to explode. It may destroy the moon."

"Read you, Sergeant. A shuttle should be at your location within minutes."

He looked at the others. "Tell them to hurry. We might not have minutes."

"I don't think they're going to make it in time," Cici said.

She clung to Dax to keep from falling. The tremors were now almost continuous. A few hundred meters away, a geyser of dust propelled by hot air erupted from a crack in the dirt. A constant low rumble presaged a major tremor.

"There it is!" Romeo shouted.

Dax followed Romeo's pointing arm and saw a shuttle two clicks away heading toward them. He did not allow himself to relax. Even if they boarded the shuttle before the Ravers escaped, the entire moon could explode beneath them. In that case, being in the shuttle offered little protection. Even the *Diligent* could be destroyed.

"How did you get here so fast?" Ivers asked the *Diligent's* commander.

"We received your message and broke a few Skip records getting here. We might have gotten here too late. If we detect a planetary-size explosion, I'll have to break orbit."

"Roger, *Diligent*. Understood."

"Do try though," Dax added.

The outer airlock door shuddered and bent outward. The Ravers were coming. Dax shoved Cici behind him. When the door flew open, Ivers fired. The Raver fell dead in the doorway blocking it, but the creatures behind it began ripping it to shreds to clear the way. Another head appeared. Ivers killed that creature as well, but his laser was running out of power. He glanced back and saw the shuttle landing twenty meters away.

"Run for it!" he shouted. He fired one last shot and flung down the useless laser.

The four of them ran toward the shuttle. Dax's injured leg slowed him down. Ivers came up behind him, grabbed him, and threw him over his back. Dax had a good view of two Ravers shooting through the doorway in pursuit. Dax knew they would never make it.

"Put me down, fool," he shouted at Ivers. "You'll kill both of us."

"Shut up," Ivers yelled back.

Dax felt the heat of laser fire from the shuttle. The powerful laser battery struck both Ravers. They screamed in pain but did not slow their pursuit. Dax turned his head toward the shuttle and saw Cici and Romeo leap inside the open door. A Marine stood just inside the door manning the laser battery. The Marine aimed directly at them. His heart climbed his throat until Ivers jogged to the side. The laser bolt passed them and struck the closest Raver, killing it.

Dust spilled around the shuttle as it began lifting. When they reached the door, Ivers tossed him inside and scrambled aboard after him. Dax hit with a thud that rang his head. The Marine gunner took out the second Raver from ten meters.

"Good shot, Marine," Ivers said.

As the shuttle lifted, Dax watched more Ravers exit the airlock. They raced around the mesa top searching for their vanished prey. The ground around them cracked and splintered. The planet was shaking itself apart.

"Can't this thing go any faster?" Dax asked the pilot, a young female Marine.

She grinned and shoved the throttle forward. The shuttle stood on its tail and leaped skyward, throwing Dax against the rear wall. As the hatch closed, he watched the area around the elevator crumble and collapse down the shaft. All but a couple of the

Ravers went with it. The two sensed what was happening and raced away from the canyon, quickly disappearing into the dust haze.

Cici reached over and grasped his hand. "We made it," she whispered.

He nodded. They were safe, but he felt no joy at surviving. Too many people, too many of his friends were still down there on Loki. They and *Fortune's Luck* had made their last voyage.

# 18

Dax lay back on the hospital bed, listening to a blues song. One of the crew was also an aficionado and loaned his player. His leg was elevated and swathed in bandages from where the medic had removed the shrapnel. His face and hands, most of his body, was covered with a thick layer of burn gel. His swollen, slick fingers had a difficult time changing tracks on the player. Until recently, Ivers had been his roommate covered with his own gel, but the indomitable sergeant had sneaked out of sickbay to join his comrades.

He had not been able to watch the power core explode, but Cici had described it to him.

"The ground in a ten-kilometer diameter circle exploded like a nuclear blast. Magma and ash shot skyward for forty kilometers. The shock wave disintegrated KB seconds later and blasted the sandstorm out like a snuffed candle. Lightning danced in the ash cloud for hours. It still hasn't dissipated. Beneath it, a lake of molten lava is sitting on the surface, glowing like a giant's red-orange eye.

"The Lokian temple, or whatever it was, is gone with all traces of their technology. The scientists on board are hoping to find another treasure trove, but I made them aware of the Ravers. As long as there is a chance some of them survived, the U.N. General Council is placing Loki under quarantine."

Dax was fine with that. In the end, the Lokians had won their won by losing it. Cici would return to Earth, the Navy would reassign Ivers. Romeo asked about shipping out with Dax, but Dax had no answer for him. *Fortune's Luck* was gone. He had neither ship nor prospects of getting a new one. He was too old to start over. Maybe he would sign on a research vessel as a mate, a ship searching for the original home of the *Huresh*. Humanity had encountered two alien races, both too late. If more aliens were out there, he would like to be among those that found them.

He had a couple of questions he would like to ask them, like why they had wiped out the Lokians and then abandoned their colony. Who knows? With luck, he might single-handedly start an interplanetary war. Wouldn't Ivers love that?

He lay back with his eyes closed listening to a Twentieth Century bluesman named B.B. King sing a tune called *The Thrill is Gone*.

*Not yet, it isn't*, B.B., he thought. He dared someone to come in and disturb him while he was in his zone.

# THE END

# CHECK OUT OTHER GREAT SCIENCE FICTION BOOKS

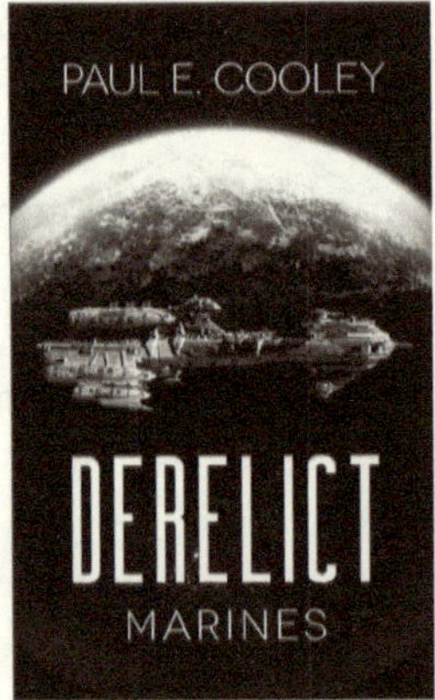


## DERELICT: MARINES
by Paul E. Cooley

Fifty years ago, Mira, humanity's last hope to find new resources, exited the solar system bound for Proxima Centauri b. Seven years into her mission, all transmissions ceased without warning. Mira and her crew were presumed lost. Humanity, unified during her construction, splintered into insurgency and rebellion.

Now, an outpost orbiting Pluto has detected a distress call from an unpowered object entering Sol space: Mira has returned. When all attempts at communications fail, S&R Black, a Sol Federation Marine Corps search and rescue vessel, is dispatched from Trident Station to intercept, investigate, and tow the beleaguered Mira to Neptune.

As the marines prepare for the journey, uncertainty and conspiracy fomented by Trident Station's governing AIs, begin to take their toll. Upon reaching Mira, they discover they've been sent on a mission that will almost certainly end in catastrophe.

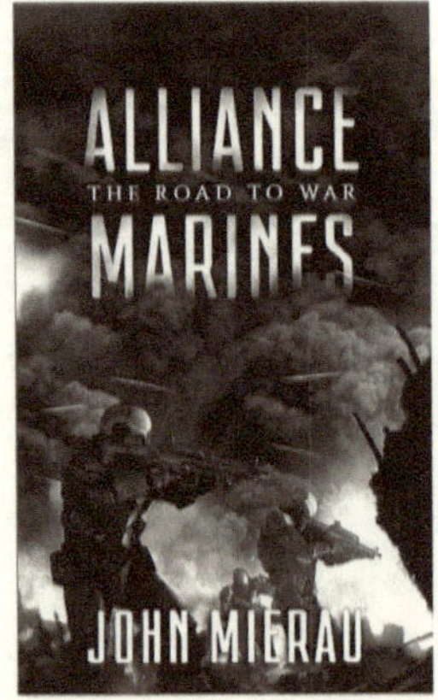


## ALLIANCE MARINES
by John Mierau

One by one, all of Earth's colonies have gone dark and silent. Reach, the last colony, teeters on the verge of civil war against its Earth-loyal overlords...and Reach-born rebel Lee Zhang has sworn to push the planet over the edge.

As the colony descends into total war, a convoy from Earth races across the galaxy, carrying news of a threat unlike anything mankind has faced before. The colonies have all been destroyed by a vast alien horde, and now Earth has fallen, too. Time is running out for sworn enemies to learn to trust and unite, or the human race is extinct. The Takers are coming to destroy mankind. If we don't do the job for them first.

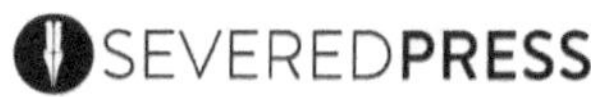


facebook.com/severedpress
twitter.com/severedpress

# CHECK OUT OTHER GREAT SCIENCE FICTION BOOKS

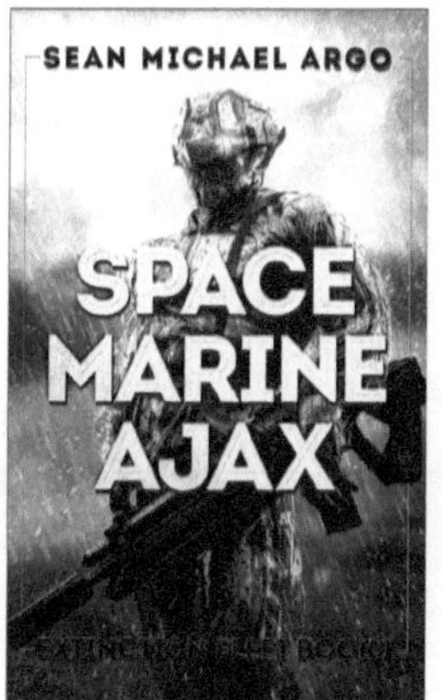


## SPACE MARINE AJAX
by Sean-Michael Argo

Ajax answers the call of duty and becomes an Einherjar space marine, charged with defending humanity against hideous alien monsters in furious combat across the galaxy.

The Garm, as they came to be called, emerged from the deepest parts of uncharted space, devouring all that lay before them, a great swarm that scoured entire star systems of all organic life. This space borne hive, this extinction fleet, made no attempts to communicate and offered no mercy.

Humanity has always been a deadly organism, and we would not so easily be made the prey. Unified against a common enemy, we fought back, meeting the swarm with soldiers upon every front.

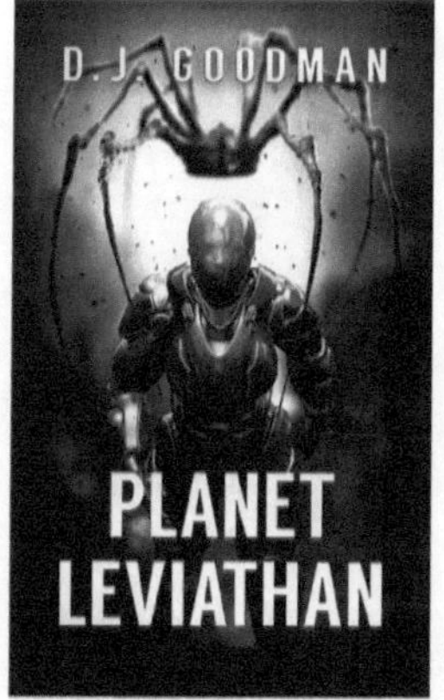


## PLANET LEVIATHAN
by D.J. Goodman

The cyborg commandos of the Galactic Marines are the greatest warriors in the galaxy, but sometimes one will go bad. Too unstable to be let back into the general population and too powerful for a normal prison to hold them, there is only one place they can be sent: Planet Leviathan.

# CHECK OUT OTHER GREAT SCIENCE FICTION BOOKS

## SALVAGE MERC ONE
by Jake Bible

Joseph Laribeau was born to be a Marine in the Galactic Fleet. He was born to fight the alien enemies known as the Skrang Alliance and travel the galaxy doing his duty as a Marine Sergeant. But when the War ended and Joe found himself medically discharged, the best job ever was over and he never thought he'd find his way again.

Then a beautiful alien walked into his life and offered him a chance at something even greater than the Fleet, a chance to serve with the Salvage Merc Corp.

Now known as Salvage Merc One Eighty-Four, Joe Laribeau is given the ultimate assignment by the SMC bosses. To his surprise it is neither a military nor a corporate salvage. Rather, Joe has to risk his life for one of his own. He has to find and bring back the legend that started the Corp.

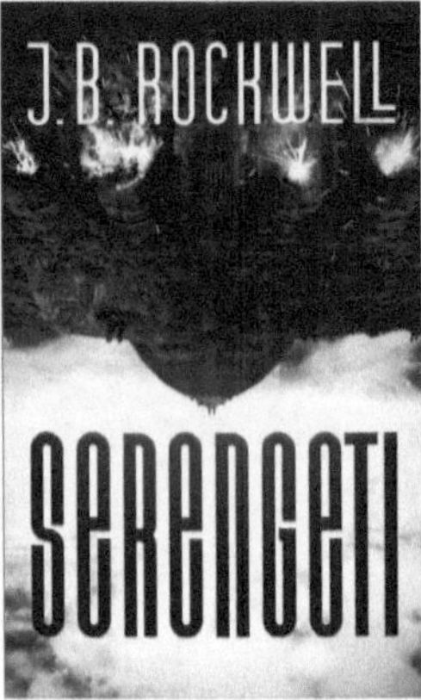


## SERENGETI
by J.B. Rockwell

It was supposed to be an easy job: find the Dark Star Revolution Starships, destroy them, and go home. But a booby-trapped vessel decimates the Meridian Alliance fleet, leaving Serengeti—a Valkyrie class warship with a sentient AI brain—on her own; wrecked and abandoned in an empty expanse of space. On the edge of total failure, Serengeti thinks only of her crew. She herds the survivors into a lifeboat, intending to sling them into space. But the escape pod sticks in her belly, locking the cryogenically frozen crew inside.

Then a scavenger ship arrives to pick Serengeti's bones clean. Her engines dead, her guns long silenced, Serengeti and her last two robots must find a way to fight the scavengers off and save the crew trapped inside her.

www.ingramcontent.com/pod-product-compliance
Lightning Source LLC
Chambersburg PA
CBHW032004170626
46807CB00006B/2640

* 9 7 8 1 9 2 5 5 9 7 5 5 4 *